Praise For

"A delightful protagonist and a clever premise combine to make this one of the most entertaining books I've read in months. Lucy is someone whose adventures you'll want to follow again and again."
—Charlaine Harris, *New York Times* bestselling author of the Sookie Stackhouse novels (basis for the HBO series *True Blood*)

"*Truly, Madly* is a fast-moving and funny love story full of sweet surprises." —Susan Donovan, *New York Times* bestselling author of *The Girl Most Likely To…*

"With characters that sparkle like diamonds on the page, this is my new favorite Valentine! Heather Webber has created a bright new world, populated by quirky characters and brim— action—I'm a fan!" —Beth H bestselling author of *S*

DUE
APR 1 7 2012
ell 6/18/12
JUL 1 0 2012
MAR 0 2 2015
ell 7/20/15
DEC 16 2015
NOV 3 0 2017

"Snappy and fresh—a delight humor!"
Mrs. Pe

"Lucy Valentine is as com name implies, not to ment smart. She has an otherwo lost objects, and will undo Heather Webber, many new—
—Harley Jane Kozak, Ag award winning author

TRULY,
MADLY,

Heather Webber

St. Martin's Paperbacks

This is a work of fiction. All of the characters, organizations, and events portrayed in this novel are either products of the author's imagination or are used fictitiously.

TRULY, MADLY

Copyright © 2010 by Heather Webber.
Excerpt from *Deeply, Desperately* copyright © 2010 by Heather Webber.

For information address St. Martin's Press, 175 Fifth Avenue, New York, NY 10010.

ISBN: 978-0-312-94613-5

Printed in the United States of America

St. Martin's Paperbacks edition / February 2010

St. Martin's Paperbacks are published by St. Martin's Press, 175 Fifth Avenue, New York, NY 10010.

10 9 8 7 6 5 4 3 2 1

ONE

There comes a time in every girl's life when she realizes her father isn't perfect.

For me that discovery had come many years ago and recurred with shocking regularity.

Most recently the realization struck again after my father had a near-fatal heart attack while partaking in the horizontal tango on a Marblehead beach with a woman other than my mother.

He being with someone else wasn't the shocker.

It was the fact that he'd been on a beach. My father detested sand.

Luckily, his current flame must have had experience with the occasional cardiac arrest, because she had seen to it that my father was in an ambulance and on his way to Mass General before any permanent damage to his ticker had taken place.

That had been two weeks ago.

Currently I watched him pace his spacious designer bedroom, trekking back and forth from his walk-in closet to the bed, where two T. Anthony leather suitcases sat open atop the rumpled duvet.

Sunlight filled the room from a bank of floor-to-ceiling windows overlooking Boston Harbor, making the room seem bright and cheerful when the atmosphere was anything but.

My father, Oscar Valentine, was handsome in a distinguished old-fashioned movie star kind of way. He'd turned fifty-five in August but could pass for late forties easily. Standing six feet tall, he had a slim, trim build thanks to his regular workouts at his exclusive condominium gym and his health-nut lifestyle. The heart attack had come as quite a surprise.

"Stop it, Lucy," he ordered me. He ran a hand through his silver-streaked dark hair and looked around the bedroom for anything he may have forgotten.

I tried not to notice how pale he appeared against the chocolate brown walls. "Stop what?"

"Staring at the bed that way."

I *had* been staring. As much as I tried, I couldn't stop thinking about how many women had been in it with him. And why he'd risk his stellar reputation by getting caught with a bimbo on the beach.

After twenty-eight years of having him as a father, I should be used to his behavior by now. I wasn't. I'd always known my father had women on the side, but I'd never seen one, never heard him speak of one, and honestly, I wished I was still living in denial.

"And you," he said to my mother, "you can stop smirking, Judith."

My mother, Judie, fanned her face with an *Architectural Digest* magazine. At fifty, she was

smack-dab in the middle of menopause and losing the battle with hot flashes. "A beach, Oscar?
You couldn't have ponied up for a decent hotel?"

"You do have more than enough money," I
piped in. As he was one of the country's wealthiest men, money was the least of his worries.
"Fifteen Beacon is a nice place. Or the Charles."

The pages of the magazine flapped, creating a
cool breeze. "I've always been partial to the Ritz-
Carlton. Ooh, or the Boston Harbor Hotel. All
are discreet. Much more so than a public beach."

My father stopped mid-pace and took a good
long hard look at us, shook his head as though
he were a man long-suffering, and resumed
packing. He folded an Armani shirt into a neat
square and placed it on top of the other six he'd
already packed in the suitcase. "You two are not
amusing."

"Oh, we are, too," my mother countered. Her
elbow poked my rib cage. "Aren't we?"

I agreed. "We're nothing if not amusing."

I think my father mumbled something about
thanking God he was getting away.

Running away was more like it.

Because in the eyes of the public, Oscar Valentine, the country's premier matchmaker, had
blatantly forsaken monogamy. He'd been caught,
quite literally, with his pants down. And if *he*
couldn't find everlasting love, then how could
his clients? There was nothing like a scandal to
obliterate his nearly perfect matchmaking track
record.

The papers, especially the *Herald*, were having a field day. Reporters were still calling, trying

to garner an exclusive interview with the King of Love himself.

His mistress-of-the-week had already sold out. Her interview hit newsstands last Thursday. It didn't take long for my father to suddenly decide he needed a little R & R.

In St. Lucia.

What the public didn't know was that my parents had been happily leading separate lives for close to twenty-five years now. Sure, they were married, but in name only, both agreeing that a renowned matchmaker seeking a divorce would be bad for the family business and, therefore, their bank accounts.

So my mother, Judie, had claimed the manor house in Cohasset, and my father, Oscar, had kept his penthouse condo in Boston's exclusive Waterfront district. They'd remained close friends, sometimes lovers, and constant companions.

They were great parents, if a bit odd.

No wonder I turned out as I did.

What the public also didn't know was that although the Valentines had been able to successfully matchmake for generations, they were hopeless at matching themselves. Every single Valentine marriage had failed. It was the family's best-kept secret.

Well, almost.

My father zipped one suitcase, set to work on the other. He snapped his fingers. "Forgot my bathing suit."

"Lord, I hope it's not the thong," my mother whispered, shuddering. "No man over fifty should own one, let alone wear one. Someone should tell him."

"Don't look at me," I said.

My father popped his head out of his huge walk-in closet, stared at us. He raised a silver-streaked eyebrow in question and then he disappeared again. However, not five seconds had gone by before he said, "Now listen, Lucy." His voice rumbled. "I've left a detailed list with Suzannah. She'll get you settled."

I straightened. "Settled?"

Out popped his head again, like a mole in an arcade game. "Yes. Settled. At the office."

"Office?"

He sighed, heavy and deep. I'd heard that sigh many times in my life, starting with when I wanted to dye my blonde hair magenta all the way to when I told him I wanted to make it on my own, without the trust fund he'd set up for me. But mostly when I decided to forsake the family business and go into hotel management.

The magenta hair had been spectacular. Turned out, he was right about the hotel thing. It wasn't for me. Neither was my stint, among other things, as a dental hygienist, barista at Starbucks, personal assistant, or, more recently, day-care worker.

And sometimes I missed the money. Like when my rent was overdue. Like now.

"Are you listening, Lucy?"

I realized he'd been chattering away. "No."

He sighed again. Twice in one day. This was a personal record.

Pulling the strap down over my heel, I slipped off my shoes. "It's silly for me to take over the business. You know I can't—"

"You'll start," he glanced at his Cartier

Roadster watch, "in an hour. Suzannah is expecting you. You have meetings with clients all afternoon."

Sure, I was currently between jobs, but I knew the family business would be better off without me. He had to know it, too. "What do you mean?"

"You," he said slowly, losing patience. "Meetings. What don't you understand, Lucy?"

"Me," I said slowly, echoing him. "Taking *your* meetings. That's what I don't understand. Haven't you been listening to me?"

He adopted his stern voice, one saved for my most egregious errors. "You, Lucy Juliet Valentine, have an obligation to this family."

"Now, Oscar." My mother fanned furiously, her cheeks fire engine red.

He held up a hand. "You know as well as I, Judie, that a Valentine must be at the helm of the business. Otherwise it will sink. Think of all the love lives out there that will flounder without our help leading them in the right direction. I've already missed too much work as is, with the attack and all. Someone needs to take over while I'm gone. And that someone is you, Lucy."

I rose and strode to the windows, the thick carpet squishing between my bare toes. Outside, the sun was losing its battle with a thick layer of clouds. Snowflakes whirled in a mesmerizing pattern, floating downward, disappearing into the dark choppy water of the harbor. Soon it would be Thanksgiving and then Christmas.

People hated to spend holidays alone. Business would be booming, all those lonely hearts looking for love.

Coming to *me* for help.

The thought turned my stomach. "How? You know perfectly well I don't have—"

He cut me off. "Fake it."

"Don't you think that will lose clients faster than someone else running the company?"

"The key to our success is in our genes. Our DNA. It has to be a Valentine running the company. You're it, Lucy. The last in a long line of Valentines—until you have children of your own."

For a second there, I thought he was going to lecture me about having babies. I heard enough of that from my grandmother, Dovie, every chance she got.

It *was* true every Valentine had the ability to matchmake. We'd been blessed with the ability to pair lovers for centuries. Rumor in the family was that the gift had been bestowed on an ancestor by Cupid himself.

But my dad left out one small detail.

Every blood Valentine possessed this gift except me.

Mine had been zapped right out of me by an electrical surge when I was fourteen, only to be replaced with an extrasensory talent of a completely different sort.

My mother set down the magazine, looked at me. "You don't have to do it."

"I heard that!" my father shouted.

"Glad your hearing wasn't affected by the infarction," she snapped playfully.

I loved the way they bantered with each other. Actually, if they weren't so busy pretending their marriage was a sham, they could probably make a decent go of it.

The mistresses notwithstanding, of course.

"Dammit! I can't find my swimsuit. Lucy?" He appeared, blinking dark brown eyes at me.

My mother shook her head, pleading with me not to do it.

I looked between the two of them, seeing my own eyes in theirs. I had my mother's slightly downward shape and a blend of their colors—a golden brown. I could see a little of myself in each of them, some traits I liked, some I didn't. But I knew one thing for sure. In a battle of begging, my father would win hands-down every time. It was the big, brown-eyed puppy-dog look that did me in.

"Oh, all right," I said to him.

He held out his hand, and I took it between both my own. In a flash, I saw the suit. "Third drawer on the right, smushed behind the stack of *Playboy* magazines."

His cheeks colored.

"Traitor," my mother murmured as he went in search.

Fighting the wave of dizziness that hit whenever I had a vision, I sank next to her on the down love seat. "Sorry. Are you all packed?"

"My bags are downstairs. We'll take the water taxi over to Logan."

"You don't have to do it," I said, echoing her words to me.

She tucked a strand of hair that had escaped my ponytail behind my ear. Tucking my hair had been a habit of hers since I could remember. "Who can turn down a trip to St. Lucia this time of year? I'd be a fool to say no. Plus, there's all that sand. I can't resist the temptation to tease your father."

"All right, but don't do anything I wouldn't do. And maybe you should have Dad take a blood test when you get to the island." I looked at the bed. "Maybe two."

She eyed me suspiciously, the golden flecks in her hazel eyes sparkling. "Is there anything you *would* do? You haven't had a date in three years."

"I've had plenty of dates."

"Just the ones Dovie's set you up on. Those don't count."

They really didn't.

"Maybe it's time to find someone for you, LucyD," she said, using her pet nickname for me.

"Why bother?" There hadn't been a single Valentine marriage that had escaped without divorce or separation. In our family the inability to stay happily wed had become depressingly known as Cupid's Curse. It was truly a painful irony—to have the ability to match . . . everyone else.

My mother's nose twitched. It did that when she knew I was right but didn't want to admit it. She dropped her head onto my shoulder, cuddling. The gelled spikes of her edgy pixie-styled blonde hair pricked my cheek. "Better to love and lose than never love at all?"

"Good try, Mum."

"Aha!" Dad shouted, thong bikini in hand.

My mother straightened. "Had you, of all people, doubted her?"

"Not at all. But it still amazes me."

"It" being my ability to find lost objects.

My family liked to play up the Cupid part of our history, but the truth was that every single Valentine had been blessed with the psychic ability to read auras. A gift, generations ago, my family capitalized on by professionally matching lovers based on their colorful auras.

The ability has always been kept secret. No one within the family wanted to battle public perception. We knew of other psychics labeled charlatans and frauds, and great pains went into keeping the family name above reproach. Inquiries as to our success rate were simply brushed off as being too pedantic to answer. In turn, most thought my family snobby. Simply not true, but a notion that was fostered to keep curiosity at bay.

When the electrical surge transformed my aura-reading abilities into the gift of finding lost objects, a type of ESP, it was also kept quiet because one revelation might lead to another. Only a few within the family knew my secret. And only a few trusted outsiders knew about the auras.

My dad held out his hand again and said, "Passport?"

I took his outstretched palm, held it. Dizzying images flashed. "In your library. Top desk drawer, right side."

"Thanks, Lucy. Are you sure you're okay about taking over? I know I can be pushy—"

"Manipulative," my mother corrected.

He ignored her. "But the pay is good, plus you'll be doing your old man a favor."

"Lordy, not the guilt, too." Three thin gold

bangle bracelets on her arms clanged as she shook her finger at him.

He shot her a look, then softened his gaze as he met mine. "Lucy?"

My rent was due. I had bills to pay. And besides, how long would it be for, anyway? How many love lives could I screw up in the span of a week or two? And maybe, just maybe, I could use this time to figure out what I really wanted to do with my life.

"Okay."

He pulled me into a hug, squeezed tight. "That's my girl. Everything will be okay. Just go with your instincts."

My instincts stunk, but I kept that tidbit to myself.

"You're welcome to stay here, as well. Closer to the office."

I thought about it for a split second before declining. I loved my cottage, despite the fact that I rented it from Dovie. Besides, if I lived here, I wouldn't be able to bring Grendel with me, since Dad was allergic to cats. "Have you spoken with Dovie yet?"

My grandmother had been vying to try her hand at matchmaking for thirty years but had been denied since she had married into the family and didn't share the Valentine gift. She wasn't going to take well to my being in charge of the business, since she knew full well I lacked any ability as well.

"I'll handle Dovie," my mother said, standing. Tall and pleasantly plump, she wore a flattering tunic top and dark denim jeans. She slipped her feet into gold ballet slippers and fastened her beautiful cream-colored cashmere wrap with a chunky gold broach.

My father zipped his last suitcase. I gave them both hugs, elicited promises to send postcards, and made a snarky comment about staying off the beaches.

"Don't look so grim, Lucy," Dad said, ignoring my jibe. "You're dealing with matters of the heart. It's not like it's life or death."

"I suppose you're right." But I couldn't help but feel that he was wrong.

Dead wrong.

TWO

Valentine, Inc., was located near the intersection of Beacon and Charles just on the outskirts of swanky Beacon Hill. Autumn leaves whirled down the street, bright wisps dancing in and out of traffic.

"There's nothing but brake lights ahead," I said.

"Lunchtime."

"Right. Lunch." My stomach churned like rusty gears at the thought of food. I shifted on the leather seat, adjusted my lap belt. My father had loaned me his Mercedes, and the services of Raphael, his driver, valet, houseman, and all around go-to guy, for the time he'd be gone. At first I balked at the extravagance, but I figured if I had to come into town every day from Cohasset on the South Shore, Raphael would make my life just that much easier.

"Nervous?" he asked me.

I'd known him since I was three years old. In some ways I thought he knew me better than my parents did. After all, he'd been the one playing marathon games of Monopoly with me while my father was off at the symphony or various other events.

True colors are often shown during high-stakes games of Monopoly.

"Yes."

"It will be all right, Uva."

He'd been calling me Uva, Spanish for "grape," since the day, at five years old, I'd thrown a temper tantrum of epic proportions on the deck of the *Mayflower II* and turned myself as purple as a Concord grape.

It was okay. I had my own pet name for him.

"I know you wouldn't lie to me, Pasa."

Translated, Pasa was a raisin. Because when he yelled at me on the deck of the ship, his face all squished up, he looked like a raisin, dark and crinkly. And really, where else would a young grape worth her salt learn her ways?

His black eyes danced with mischief. "Never."

The streets were busy. Mixed among the tourists in search of Cheers (where everybody knew your name) or the swan boats (which had long since been docked for the winter) most everyone else was seeking food.

The car inched along. My palms moistened.

4 plus 4 is 8.

102 times 3 is 306.

In times of high stress I found solving simple math problems in my head helped center my thoughts. It had become a habit over the years, one I've tried breaking, but it tended to be the only thing that worked to keep me calm.

Raphael searched the radio for a decent song,

finally landing on "Rock the Casbah." He was the biggest eighties music fan I knew.

"Perhaps I will become your first client," he said, shocking me.

Raphael's wife had died shortly after they married, years before I was born. As far as I knew, he'd never dated.

"Really?"

"It's time, don't you think?"

"Past time," I agreed.

At sixty, he was a catch. Engaging smile, bright eyes, and possibly the most decent man I knew. I for one didn't want to screw up his potential love life. "I think you should wait for Dad to come back."

He laughed. "Believe in yourself, Uva, and others will believe also."

"Don't go sounding like Yoda on me."

Undeterred, he continued. "Believe in what you're saying and others will believe in it also."

"So, basically you're telling me to make my lies believable."

"Now you're learning." Pulling to the curb, he parked the car. "See you at five, I will."

Laughing, I kissed his smooth cheek and said good-bye, glad he hadn't pursued me finding a match for him. On the sidewalk a stiff breeze stung my eyes and loosened my ponytail, blowing wavy strands of blonde into my face.

There were no media vans that I could see. That was good news—they'd been camped out front for nearly a week. I spotted a reporter lurking near the nondescript doorway leading to the upper floors and hoped she wouldn't cause trouble.

My father owned the historic three-story building where the Valentine, Inc., offices were housed. The first floor held the Porcupine, a quaint restaurant, leased by Magdalena "Maggie" Constantine. The third floor belonged to SD Investigations, run by Sam Donahue, who had worked out a deal with my father to do background checks and investigative tasks for him for a break on the rent.

On the second level, with amazing views of the Public Garden, was Valentine, Inc. The building had been owned by my family for close to a hundred and fifty years. It currently was owned by my father and would someday belong to me.

What I would do with it was anyone's guess.

I waved to Maggie inside the Porcupine. From the look of the crowd gathered, business was good.

As I neared the door discreetly nestled between storefronts, card key in hand, the reporter jumped forward. "Going up to Valentine?" she asked.

"Nope." I pushed past her, relieved she had no idea who I was. It was only a matter of time before word leaked out about my taking over the family business while my dad was away, but I hoped by then the storm would have passed.

As I climbed the creaking cherrywood stairs to the second floor, nerves took over. Leaning against the crumbly brick wall, I took a moment to gather myself together.

"Fake it," my father had said.

Easy for him to say. He wasn't going to disappoint potential clients. Or his parents. Or his grandmother. Or the legacy of his ancestors.

It was me.

At the landing, the wood floor gleamed under my feet. I looked up the next flight of stairs and noticed Sam's office door open. I wanted to go up and say hello, see how his wife and twin girls were doing. You know, hang out a little while.

Like a week or so.

Pulling in a deep breath, I gave myself a silent pep talk. Okay, so maybe I wasn't inherently a matchmaker. But I was a Valentine, and I was bound and determined not to let anyone down—one way or another. It was time to get on with it.

Light spilled through the tempered patterned glass inset into the thick mahogany door. I couldn't tell whether any clients were inside waiting for me or I'd have a few minutes to settle in before my first victim arrived.

The latch tended to stick, so I gave the door a good shove. After a slight hitch, it flew open, nearly banging the wall. Suzannah looked up from the TV in the corner of the room and beamed at me. No one else was there.

A reprieve, thank heavens.

"Lucy! It's so good to see you." Suzannah Ruggieri rushed over, gave me a big hug. A hug I found I'd desperately needed. She was a good two inches taller than my five-eight and was on the overweight side of chubby. She could easily work as a plus-sized model anywhere in the city if my father would let her go.

He wouldn't. He adored her.

Taking one look at my face, she immediately

said, "Don't be nervous. We'll get through this together. Except for three of your appointments today, the rest are follow-ups with people who've already been dating for a while. Oscar likes to gloat. I keep telling him it's not attractive, especially since the clients have no idea about the auras and all, but he doesn't listen to a word I say." She took a breath. "You look great."

I couldn't help but smile at her exuberance. "Thanks, Suz. You, too."

Suz was one of the trusted few who knew about my family's aura-reading abilities. Over the years she'd become like family. My father paid her quite well, not only to keep our secrets but also because she was invaluable to the office.

"How's Teddy?" I asked.

Her smooth alabaster complexion looked to be lit from within. "He's all right." Blue eyes twinkled. She playfully nudged me. "Unlike your father, I don't like to gloat. Well, at least not in front of him since he's the one who matched us. Someone has to keep his ego in check."

"Is that possible?"

"I'm working on it."

The office felt more like a home than a business. A fire crackled in the gas fireplace, its rustic mahogany mantel nearly an identical match to the carved door. Two suede russet-colored love seats had been angled to take advantage of both the fire and the view of the Public Garden. A beautifully detailed Kashan rug covered part of the floor. Suzannah sat at a small desk in the corner of the room. Bookcases stood proudly behind her featuring some of my father's favorite art pieces—mostly stuff I'd made as a kid. A lot of primary-colored pinch pots and lopsided ceramics. A plasma TV hung on the wall in the far corner of the room, and though the sound had been muted, it captured my attention with the BREAKING NEWS banner at the top of the screen.

"What's going on?" I motioned toward the News 5 coverage.

"Horrible story. A little boy, four years old, and his dad went fishing at Wompatuck State Park. They'd been picnicking on the shore when the dad had a seizure and passed out—when he woke up, the little boy was gone. They're searching now."

This was one of those times I questioned the gift I had. Why be blessed with an ability that offered little help to those truly in need?

Over the years I'd been able to figure out how my gift worked. There were two basic rules. The first was that the person who owned the lost object was the only one I could get a reading from. The other was that the object couldn't be human or animal. I couldn't find lost dogs. And I couldn't find lost people.

Just things. Useless, inanimate things.

Not precious little boys.

Suzannah swiped her eyes. "Just awful."

It was. Sure, the sun had won the war, emerging from the clouds, but it was still chilly, in the mid-thirties. Come nightfall, temperatures would dip into the twenties. How long could a little boy survive the cold?

Anger simmered inside me because I couldn't help. I fought to push it away. Being mad wouldn't help the little boy, and it wouldn't help me.

It was just so hard not to question my place here, to question the reason I'd been given this particular gift. Matching lovers benefited many, changed lives for the better. Finding my father's thong bathing suit didn't.

"We have a lot to do." Suzannah sprinted to her desk. She rarely moved at any pace other than fast-forward. "There's paperwork to fill out for the accountant—new-hire stuff—and you should look at these portfolios before your first clients arrive." She strode through the arch leading to the rear offices.

I followed.

"Your father suggested you use his office, but I didn't think that was a good idea. So manly in there, all those dark greens and heavy blues. I suggested you set up space in the smaller conference room." She paused at the door. "There's a desk, filing cabinets, computer, a phone— everything you should need. Feel free to make yourself at home. You know where the kitchen is and the copier." As she tapped her chin I could almost see her mental wheels turning. "That should be about all. I'll be out front if you need me. There's the buzzer now. I hope that reporter's not bothering our clients. I've tried getting rid of her, but she keeps turning up. I'd better go rescue Ms. Fellows. I'll give you about five minutes . . . will that be enough time?"

I clutched the portfolios to my chest. "When do you breathe?"

She laughed. It echoed off the soft gray-green

walls of the conference room—my new office—
and filled the space with happiness. "Every now
and again."

"Five minutes will be plenty."

I figured since I had no idea what I was doing,
it didn't matter whether I had thirty seconds or
two hours.

For the first time I wondered if what I wore
was appropriate, but Suzannah had already torn
out of the room and it felt silly to call her back
for a wardrobe check. The dark jeans, cream-
colored tank top, and emerald green blazer would
have to do.

5 times 5 is 25.

88 minus 11 is 77.

I settled behind the desk, took out the portfolio for Lola Fellows. My father required his clients to fill out long surveys of likes and dislikes,
plus an additional personality test.

He never even glanced at them.

Stapled inside Lola's folder, I found a small
square of fabric in shimmery blue. It was my father's method of filing. When he looked at Lola,
he saw a shimmery blue aura surrounding her. In
the past, Dad had used colored pencils to doodle
on his clients' files, and it had been Suz who had
introduced him to the world of swatches. He'd
been enthralled.

Lola's first meeting with Dad had been right
before his heart attack, so he probably wouldn't
have had time to go through his extensive files
to find a match for her.

I heard Suzannah greet Lola. I dashed into my
father's office. From Dad's filing cabinet I pulled
portfolios, starting with the As. It amazed me,

the variety of people looking for love. Rich, poor, old, young. My father didn't charge a flat fee but rather adjusted his rates based on a person's income. He felt that money should never stand in the way of true love but didn't mind charging an outrageous fee to those who could afford it.

Ten minutes and almost two hundred files later, I found a match in Adam Atkinson—the identical shimmery blue swatch stapled to the inside of his file.

Breathing deep, I tried to catch a second wind as I headed for the door and called Lola Fellows back to my new office.

As she approached, she held out her hand.

This presented a new dilemma. I didn't like shaking people's hands. Hugs were okay, kisses fine. But my particular ability manifested itself through people's palms. If someone was preoccupied with a belonging they'd lost and then touched my hand, then I'd see the object in an instant.

Hoping the lovely Lola hadn't lost anything recently, I gave her hand a quick shake.

Nothing.

Thank goodness. It would have been hard to explain how I knew where her favorite pair of earrings had wandered off to.

As we sat, I glanced at Lola's file. She was young, thirty-two, a financial planner who worked in the John Hancock building. Successful, smart, outgoing if her personality test was any indication.

On paper, it looked as though she had it all.

Except for love.

Sorting through all the frogs in the world to

find that one prince was next to impossible. If only everyone could read auras.

Luckily, I had the name of her prince and was ready to pass that information along.

"I was sorry to hear about your father," Lola said, crossing her legs. "I don't for a second believe what the papers are saying. Oscar is a good man."

I decided the truth would only hurt, so I kept mum on the fact that my dad was guilty as charged in the pages of the *Boston Herald*. "Thank you. He's doing much better now."

"Will he be back soon?"

"I'm not sure."

"Let me be frank, Ms. Valentine. What qualifies you to find a man for me? Where did you go to school?"

I thought about being sassy and answering, "Pequot Elementary," but decided that wouldn't make a good first impression. "I graduated from Bridgewater State."

She pursed her lips in distaste. Sure, it wasn't Harvard, but it was a great school—one that I'd worked two jobs to put myself through.

"With a degree in?"

"Business. A minor in English." I left out my stints as a barista, day-care worker, and dog walker. They probably wouldn't garner any confidence. Though I had to admit if I could handle walking ten dogs at once, then I could handle just about anything.

This reminded me that I hadn't been able to handle ten dogs. My dog-walking career had been short-lived.

Lola Fellows had reason to worry.

Her dark eyebrows dipped and unattractive creases formed at the corners of her mouth. "How is that going to help me?"

Perhaps if she wasn't so bitchy she'd have found a man by now. I almost felt guilty siccing her on poor Adam.

I straightened in my chair. "My qualifications for this job are my genes. Plain and simple. I'm a Valentine. Matching lovers is what we do."

Raphael would have been proud of me. I almost believed myself.

She drew her crimson bottom lip into her mouth, released it. "All right then. What have you found?"

I spent the next thirty minutes with Lola and the next two hours with various other clients looking for love. The tough ones were the new clients, who didn't have swatches. I tucked their portfolios away to be studied at home.

I wondered if I earned overtime for homework.

By the time Michael Lafferty sat down across from me, I was starting to believe I could be a decent matchmaker.

He had a swatch and everything. A bold orange color highlighted with shades of red. I hadn't been able to find a similar swatch in the quick search of my father's cabinet, which meant I'd need to have him come back. Until then: Stall.

I asked the prerequisite questions about background (Michael and two older sisters were raised by single mom), his age (twenty-nine), his job (a mechanic), where he lived (in the blue-collar community of North Weymouth), and his religion (Catholic). He was tall, nearly six-two, and on the skinny side of healthy. He had bright blue eyes, dark hair, fair skin.

The type of guy girls tripped over themselves for.

Yet here he was.

"Have you been married before?" I asked.

"Nah. Engaged once."

"How long ago?"

"Almost six years ago, and I'm going to be up front, Ms. Valentine. I still love her—the girl I was engaged to."

"Ah. Might make matching you a challenge."

"I certainly haven't had any luck on my own, getting over her. That's why I'm here."

Curious, I set his portfolio down. His tone tugged at my sappy heartstrings. To still be in love with someone so many years later. "What happened?" My melodramatic mind was already playing "Love Story" in my head.

"Long, sad story."

I could practically see Ryan O'Neal and Ali MacGraw.

Knowing wouldn't help me find him a match— all I needed for that was more time in my father's files. But I couldn't help myself. "I've got time. It might help in the whole matching process," I bluffed.

He shrugged. "Her name is Jennifer Thompson."

The way he spoke, full of longing, made me wonder if another woman stood a chance against such strong memories. Would finding him a match be ethical on my part?

"Jennifer and me, well, we fell in love early

on. We were high school sweethearts. Dated since tenth grade."

"Wow. That's really young."

"Sometimes love is just right. You know?"

Nope. Not a clue. Thanks to Cupid's Curse.

"We'd been together seven years. I proposed to her when we graduated high school—my mom gave me a family ring to give to her. It was an heirloom, passed down in my family for generations. We were planning to get married as soon as she finished college. You know how it goes."

I nodded.

"Then one night Jennifer was home from school for a weekend and me and her had a fight." His eyes took on a faraway look, the blue turning stormy. "Stupid one, too. About her living in town, closer to BU, and not with me. I walked out. Went to the pub. Had a few too many."

I cringed, having a feeling where this was going.

"Woke up in bed with an old classmate, girl named Elena Hart."

Deep anger lines creased his forehead. "I had to have been really lit. No way would I sleep with Elena otherwise. Not only 'cause of Jennifer, but because Elena . . ." He shook his head.

"What?"

"Well, she followed me around a lot. Her and Rachel Yurio, a friend of hers. It was creepy. And I know they gave Jennifer grief, too. Lots of hang-ups, slashing her tires. Nothing we could ever prove. But Elena had been trying to break us up for years, holding a delusion that I'd actually want to get with her if Jenny wasn't in the picture."

Suddenly this felt more like *Fatal Attraction* than *Love Story*. "Did you tell Jennifer what happened that night with Elena?"

"Elena got to her first, showed her some pictures she'd taken. Jennifer called and broke it off with me, said she put my ring in the mail. It never did show up. You know, my mother still gives me grief over that ring. And it's not like I can get in touch with Jenny to find out where it is. She stopped taking my calls after we broke up. I never saw her again."

"I'm sorry."

He clasped his hands together, twiddled his thumbs. "No one to blame but myself."

"What happened with Elena?"

"Rachel, Elena's friend? She was a real sweet girl—never sure why she hung with Elena. Anyway, one day she calls out of the blue, said she had something to tell me. Guess she had a guilty conscience. She told me that Elena had staged our whole night together. That we never slept together. I tried to call Jennifer, but at that point I couldn't track her down at all. It's like she completely disappeared. Her parents used to live in Weymouth Landing and wouldn't even answer the door when I knocked. Eventually, I stopped trying and they moved away."

"Did you ever see Elena again?" I asked.

"Elena found out that Rach had told me about the pictures and had a huge fight with her. Then Elena, she showed up at my house, just plain out of her mind. I told her to leave me alone for good. That there was never going to be anything between us. I never saw either again. Heard through the grapevine they left town." He shivered. "Look, it's taken a long time to get over all of it, but I'm finally ready to move on. I want a family. A wife. Kids. I'd even take a little house with a picket fence."

Sounded pretty good to me, too.

"You think you can help me, Ms. Valentine?"

I fingered the swatch in his file. "I'm sure I can find you a match, Michael, but I don't know if that person can ever replace Jennifer." I thought about the files in my father's office, and the sappy romantic in me bypassed them. Could I find Jennifer? See if she was willing to give Michael another chance, especially since he'd never cheated on her? Was it foolish to even think there was a possibility?

Probably. But I couldn't turn my back on how he felt for Jennifer. To still love her after all this time . . . It was worth a shot. But first I needed to find her. See if she was married. Nothing like a wedding band to put a kink in my plans.

"There's no replacing Jenny, Ms. Valentine. But she doesn't want me, and I need to move on."

I took a leap of faith. "How would you feel if I contacted Jennifer, maybe explain what really happened all those years ago, see if she had any interest in meeting with you?"

His eyebrows dipped. "I can't imagine she'd say yes."

"But?"

Hopeful, he said, "But it might be the closure I need to move on."

I agreed. Whether the idea panned out or not, a meeting might heal some old wounds for both of them. I collected some information from Michael to help find Jennifer and told him I'd call him as soon as I learned anything.

He stood, held out his hand. "Thanks."

I shook it, froze.

Images flashed through my head, like an old-fashioned movie with its reel spinning out of control. Dizzy, I swayed.

"Ms. Valentine? You okay?"

I tugged my hand from his, held it to my chest. Shakily, I said, "I'm all right."

"You went white as a ghost."

I led him toward the door and hoped I wasn't being rude. I was shaken and knew it must have shown. "I'm all right. Really. I'll call you."

As I watched him walk down the hall, I felt sick to my stomach. I'd seen a vision of an engagement ring when my palm touched his. An old-fashioned band of platinum with delicate filigree and a two-carat square-cut diamond. An heirloom type of ring.

It had been on the finger of a skeleton.

THREE

I stumbled back to my office, closed the door, sat in my chair, and put my head between my knees.

There weren't enough math problems in the world to settle my current nerves.

I'd found dozens of things over the years. My dad's cuff links, my mother's wallet, my grandmother's prized WWF pin. I'd even found things for my best friends, Marisol and Em, on occasion, without their knowing how.

Never had I found a dead body.

One that I was fairly sure had been murdered. Why else would it be buried in a shallow grave with no coffin, in a public park?

Slowly, I lifted my head. The room spun. Vertigo at its worst. I tilted my head back, sucked in a deep breath as I focused on the thin apple green and aubergine striping on the white roman shades.

The room slowly stopped spinning.

Rooting through my cavernous satchel, I came up with a bottle of water and twisted off the cap. I poured a few drops onto my fingers, spritzed my face.

To every rule there's an exception.

With my particular psychic ability, gift-giving throws my perceptions out of whack. It's the only time I'm aware of when I can get a reading from two people, where an object has two owners— the person who gave the gift . . . and the person who received it.

Which was why I'd been able to pick up on the ring's energy from Michael, even though the ring technically belonged to Jennifer.

I was at a loss.

The ring I'd seen had been on a corpse buried in a shallow grave in North Weymouth—the town where Michael lived. Coincidence? I hardly thought so.

But what did I do about it?

Call the police? It didn't take any kind of psychic ability to see where that conversation would go.

Try to find the body on my own? It was a thought. But then what?

Another option was to do absolutely nothing.

I ruled that thought out as soon as it popped into my head. I wasn't a do-nothing kind of girl.

I found Suzannah sitting at her desk, her teary eyes focused on the TV and the continuing coverage of the story TV stations had now called "Little Boy Lost," a label that flashed across the screen in bold yellow script.

"You don't look well," she said.

"I was about to say the same about you."

She motioned to the TV with her head as she opened the bottom drawer of her desk, plucked a Puffs. "My nephew is that age. The story is hitting a little too close to home."

Scanning the latest headlines, I frowned. "They took the father in for questioning?"

"Don't you remember the case where that woman drowned her little boys in the lake, then told everyone they'd been carjacked?"

"Unfortunately," I mumbled.

"The police are questioning whether the father really had a seizure or not. There weren't any witnesses. Divers are scouring the Aaron River Reservoir."

"Maybe you shouldn't watch." I knew the coverage was making me feel worse. To think a father might have taken his own child's life . . .

"You're right." She clicked off the set, jumped up, then sat back down. "I feel so useless."

"Why don't you go down and help search the woods? I'm sure they're forming search parties."

She jumped up again. "I should. I will!" Dashing to the closet, she grabbed her Burberry trench coat and her handbag. Dusk had fallen, casting shadows. I walked over, pulled the drapes, and turned on a floor lamp.

Rushing to the door, Suzannah stopped abruptly. "What about you?"

"I'll be all right. I'm going to see to the fire, lock up and head upstairs to see Sam for a few minutes, then go home." I needed a dose of familiarity after the day I'd had.

"How are Em and Marisol these days?"

"I hardly ever see them. Marisol is so wrapped up with her internship at the vet clinic, and Em's slowly going out of her mind between her pediatric internship and the wedding."

Suz belted her coat and nodded. "Wedding planning will do that to you."

"Especially when her mother has completely taken over the planning and is two hundred thousand over a quarter-million-dollar budget, one of her flower girls decided she wanted to be the ring bearer, and Em's gained ten pounds and doesn't fit into her dress anymore."

Suzannah whistled. "That's some budget."

"Always the best for a Baumbach," I said, repeating Em's family mantra.

"When's the wedding?"

"Valentine's Day."

"Aww, how romantic. I'm sure it will all work out," she said. "You should have seen me two months before my wedding."

I smiled. "I did."

"Oh. That's right." Color surged into her cheeks.

"Don't worry; I don't hold it against you."

She ran over, pecked my cheek. "Get some rest—you really don't look well."

"I will. Just need to check with Sam on something."

Heaving open the door, Suzannah stopped short. "Wait. Sam's on Maui with his family."

"He is? I saw his door open when I came in."

"Sean's up there."

"Sean?"

"Sam's brother. Used to be a firefighter until some sort of injury sidelined him. Sam made him a partner in the company about nine months ago."

Odd that I hadn't heard about it until now. "When does Sam get back?"

"Sunday."

It was only Wednesday. Could I wait that long?

Suzannah must have seen my hesitation. "Sean's good. You can trust him."

"You sure?"

"I'm never wrong, Lucy." She beamed, her eyes flicking to the stairs.

"What are you smiling about?"

"Oh, nothing. Nothing at all," she said as she walked out.

I didn't believe her for a second.

Peeking through the drapes, I watched as she ignored the reporter lurking on the sidewalk and hurried down the street toward the T station. Back in my office, I gathered up the files I wanted to take home and placed Michael Lafferty's on top. I locked the door behind me and hesitantly climbed the stairs to SD Investigations. The door was still open.

I stuck my head in but didn't see anyone. "Hello? Sean?" I took a step in. "Mr. Donahue?" Another step. "Sean? Hello?"

This office was the same size and layout as my father's, and it was obvious that they'd used the same interior designer. Gleaming hardwoods, thick area rugs, and oversized comfy furniture welcomed me in.

Overhead pot lights shone on the burnt orange walls, creating a soft glow throughout the room. There was a hint of freshly ground coffee in the air, along with strongly scented cinnamon.

"Hellooo," I called out a bit louder as I walked through the archway leading to the back offices.

On a console table in the hallway I found the

source of the cinnamon—a Yankee candle flickering in the dim light. I could hear the faint sound of a male voice coming from down the hallway— the office directly above mine.

As I neared, the voice became clearer. Sean Donahue was on the phone.

"Yes, I've got it. . . . No, I don't mind. . . . Yes, I'm sure. Raspberry yogurt, Swiss cheese, turkey breast, and toilet paper." There was a stretch of silence before he said, "I won't forget. I didn't lose my mind, Cara."

I heard the annoyance in his tone and wondered if I should come back in the morning. Then I flashed to the vision of the diamond ring. My stomach turned and my head swirled. I took a deep breath to keep from passing out. What a first impression that would make.

For a second I thought about heading back to the reception area, waiting for Sean Donahue to finish his call, but a quick check of my watch spurred me to interrupt his conversation. Raphael would be here in fifteen minutes.

I stepped into the doorway and raised my hand to knock on the jamb when Sean said, "I don't know. Late. I have a stack of files on my desk that needs to be taken care of."

My knock hit the wood just as his desk chair spun away from the window. His body tensed as his gaze jumped to mine.

Whoa.

I leaned against the door frame so I wouldn't fall over.

"Cara, I've got to go; someone's at the door." His lips tensed. "I'll call you before I leave here. Bye."

He snapped his cell phone closed, rose to his feet.

I didn't think mine would hold my full weight, so I didn't budge.

He wasn't handsome in the classical sense. His face was too angular, his dark hair too short, his neck too thick, and his nose had been broken once, maybe more, and he had a jaw straight from the pages of a superhero comic book. But there was something about him that sucked the breath from my lungs and made my legs jiggle like pudding. Something . . . dare I say it?

Sensual. Alluring.

Now I knew why Suzannah had been smiling.

I'd never had a reaction like this to a man, and I wasn't sure what to make of it. At this point, I wasn't liking it—I'm sure I looked like a perfect fool.

His gaze held mine—he didn't blink or look away. In all my twenty-eight years I'd never seen eyes so gray. A milky gray that glimmered like pearls. They were mesmerizing, his eyes. And I was mesmerized. It took me a good thirty seconds to get a grip.

Clearing my throat, I said, "Hi."

"You *can* talk. I was beginning to have my doubts."

Heat surged up my throat. Obviously, my appearance hadn't created that same dumbfounded feeling within him.

"I knocked and called out. You didn't hear me." I tested my legs. They held. I walked into the room. "I'm Lucy Valentine. Oscar's daughter."

His expression changed from guarded to . . . pleased? It took a second before I realized he'd had no clue who I was—I could have been any crazy off the street, suddenly standing here in his office.

"Sorry I didn't hear you." He held out his hand to shake mine. "Sean Donahue."

I stared at it. Oh no.

"I don't have cooties, Ms. Valentine."

I tucked the files I'd carried into the crook of my left arm. Bracing myself, I said, "Of course not, and call me Lucy." Reaching across his desk, I shook his hand quickly. The room whirled, spinning. It wasn't that same movie-reel-out-of-control feeling I was used to. It was more of a slow-motion flip-book feeling. Images coming lazily, page after page. However, I couldn't make any sense of what I saw. The pictures were blurred, out of focus . . .

Except for one. I yanked my hand away.

He stared at his own hand long enough to make me wonder if he'd felt something, seen something, too. But no, that was impossible.

I didn't know what to make of the whole slow-motion feeling. It was new. And I certainly didn't know what to make of the one clear image in my vision. There certainly hadn't been any lost objects to be seen.

Deciding I would try to pick it apart later, I sat in the chair across from him. We looked at each other for a good ten seconds. And funny enough, it wasn't awkward. It was kind of like . . . meeting an old friend. Which made no sense, since I'd never met him before. No way would I forget eyes like those.

I tried to shake off the feeling. I hated keeping Raphael waiting, and if I kept making goo-goo eyes at Sean Donahue, then I'd never get out of here.

"I, um, need your help."

"All right."

"With a client."

He leaned back in his chair. "Go on."

"I need to find a girl." I settled my files in my lap. My desire to find Jennifer Thompson was twofold. First and foremost, I had to figure out if she was the body in the grave. The skeleton, after all, had been wearing Michael's engagement ring. She was the last to have it.

Second, if Jennifer wasn't mysteriously missing I had to implement my plan to reunite the two, skeleton or not. But I hoped she'd be able to shed some light on who might have possession of Michael's family heirloom.

"Her name?"

"Jennifer Thompson."

Sean jotted a note on a pad of paper he pulled from his desk drawer. "Social Security?"

I shrugged.

"Why do you want to find her?"

"For a client," I evaded. "You'll be able to find out if she's married . . . or dead, right?"

"Dead?"

"Theoretically."

"That's some theory."

I didn't comment. No need to tell him about the skeleton.

"Okay," he said. "A girl named Jennifer Thompson. Piece of cake. There's probably only a couple thousand Jennifer Thompsons around."

I shifted in my seat. "You don't need to mock."

The corner of his mouth rose up in a little

grin. "It's what I do best. Do you have any other info on her?"

"She went to BU, probably graduated six or seven years ago. Her family used to live in Weymouth Landing; her birthday is May eleventh."

He scribbled on a notepad. "That helps."

My cell phone rang, a jazzy rendition of "Jingle Bells." I fished the phone from my satchel, checked the ID, and groaned. Dovie. I silenced the call, dropped the phone back into the depths from which it came.

"Sorry," I said.

"'Jingle Bells'? It's barely November."

"It's never too early for Christmas."

He smiled, and it sent my heart pounding crazily in my chest. For a second there, I thought maybe I'd be taking the same trip to Mass General my father had.

"I'll do a search, see what turns up. I'll have news for you as soon as possible."

"I know you're busy," I said, recalling what he'd said on the phone about needing to work through the files stacked on his desk.

Only . . . his desk was perfectly clear, except for a pad of paper, a pen, a phone, and a picture of two adorable little girls—Sam's daughters, Sean's nieces.

Obviously Sean hadn't wanted to go home and had lied to his—I checked for a wedding band—his girlfriend?

His look dared me to question him.

Nope. No way.

For some reason, I thought it best to keep my distance from Sean. I stood, grasped my file folders. "Thanks for your help."

"Don't thank me yet."

"I'll just," I motioned toward the door, "see myself out."

He nodded.

I took the stairs slowly. My heart was still acting funny, feeling as though it had skipped beats, in addition to the palpitations I felt earlier.

Outside, the reporter had finally gone. Darkness had fallen, and the street lamps flooded the area with light. I waited for Raphael, who was probably circling since all the spots along Beacon were taken.

I pulled out my phone, saw that Dovie had left a message. I dialed into my voice mail.

"LucyD, have I got the man for you! Met him today at the Hingham market. He's a meat cutter there. A doll. A genuine doll. You have a date for tomorrow night. Oh, his name is Butch. Butch is a butcher. How's that for coincidence? He's perfect for you! Gotta run. Ciao!"

"No, no, no, no," I mumbled.

Raphael honked.

I opened the door, climbed in, and fairly collapsed against the seat.

He took one look at me and said, "Do you want me to drive you home?"

"Thanks, but no. The commuter boat is fine." I'd use the thirty-five-minute ride to clear my head.

"Bad day, Uva?" he asked.

Let's see. My parents skipped town, leaving me behind to run a company I had no business being in charge of; there was a little boy possibly lost in the woods I could do nothing to find; I saw a vision of a ring on a skeleton of someone who'd probably been murdered; I made a fool out of myself in front of Sean Donahue; and my grandmother had set me up with a meat cutter named Butch.

Worst of all, I conjured that one clear image I'd seen while I shook Sean's hand. . . . It had been of the two of us.

In bed. Naked.

"Maybe tomorrow will be better."

But I had the uneasy feeling it wouldn't be.

FOUR

Raphael dropped me in front of the Long Wharf Marriott. From there it was a short walk to the commuter boat dock, located at Rowes Wharf, between the hotel and the New England Aquarium. The temperature had dropped with the setting sun.

I promised to call him if I needed anything.

"Think about what I said, Uva."

"About?"

"Finding someone for me. It's time."

The heartbreaking loneliness in his voice tore at me, weakening any resolve I had to stay out of his love life. Even if I didn't have any matchmaking abilities, perhaps a few blind dates to test the waters wouldn't be so bad.

"All right," I said, kissing his cheek.

He smiled. "Go, there's the boat now."

I hurried toward the dock, dodging vendors and lingering tourists, and boarded. Instead of heading inside the warm cabin, I walked along the deck, drawing my trench coat tighter.

My many thoughts swam, nearly drowning each other out.

Seagulls circled overhead as the boat turned toward the Hingham Shipyard, crowded with the early-evening rush. The bow cut through the harbor water, leaving behind a mesmerizing wake.

My thoughts circled around Sean Donahue and what I'd seen when we touched.

The two of us. In bed. Together. Naked.

Had it been an actual vision? Or simply wishful thinking?

True, he was an attractive man. And I'd definitely been attracted.

But the vision had been so clear. So real.

I grasped onto the railing, the cold biting into my fingers.

If it had been a true vision I couldn't explain it, I didn't understand it, and I simply couldn't wrap my head around it. My grip tightened.

My type of ESP related only to lost objects, and that certainly didn't pertain to what I'd seen in the images of me with Sean. Not even close.

Frustrated, I fished my cell phone out of my bag and did the only thing I could think of.

I called my mother.

Overhead, a crescent moon peekabooed with fluffy dark clouds. Slivers of moonbeams danced along the water. Usually I found the image peaceful. Today I was in a state that refused to be pacified, despite the beauty stretching out in front of me.

Mum answered on the third ring. She and Dad were in Miami, waiting for their connection to St. Lucia.

"Is something wrong, LucyD?"

The nickname made me smile. My mother and Dovie had been calling me LucyD for as long as I could remember. Short for "Lucy in the Sky with Diamonds," the Beatle song I was named after.

"Kind of," I said. "I had a vision."

"Did someone lose something?"

I flashed to the diamond ring and the skeleton it had been with. I shivered—and not from the cold.

That problem, however, would have to wait.

"No," I said, turning so the wind wouldn't cause static. "I had a vision of . . . the future."

"Are you sure?"

"Fairly."

"How fabulous."

Leave it to my mom to be unfazed. The boat slid through the water. Lights from the shore twinkled prettily. "Is it? Do you think it's really possible? Could I have been hallucinating?"

Her laugh didn't cheer me. "To my knowledge, you've never once hallucinated. You're the sanest person I know. Quite a miracle, considering your bloodlines."

I wasn't sure if she was referring to her side of the family or my father's.

It was a toss-up, either way.

She went on. "You know yourself better than I do, Lucy."

I wished it were true. When it came to my abilities, the truth was I knew very little. After the electrical surge, I thought my psychic abilities were gone forever. The colorful auras I used to see around people had disappeared in, well, a flash. It wasn't until a chance encounter with Raphael when he lost his wallet that I realized

I could find lost objects. My family's insistence on secrecy limited any scientific testing. The truth was, I didn't know of what I was capable.

I wanted to vent, but there was really no one I could talk to about how I was feeling. Only Mum, Dad, Dovie, and Raphael knew about my gift. And look where talking to my mother had gotten me so far. I was still as lost as I had been when I left the office.

It was times like these when I wished more people knew what I could do. My friends. Suz. Anyone who could help me sort out my confusing life.

"But do you think it's possible?" I realized my teeth were chattering and started for the door leading into the boat's cabin. "Probable?"

"Lucy, I've come to expect anything is possible."

"But what do I do about it?"

There was a long stretch of silence, and I thought I'd lost the connection. "Mum?"

"I'm here. I think that only you can answer that question."

I was scared she might be right.

"We're boarding, Lucy. I don't know what kind of service I'll have on the island, so I might not be able to check in for a while. As soon as I can, I will."

I hung up, dissatisfied. With the odd vision. With my parents.

Stressed, I ducked into the cabin and decided that not thinking about anything to do with visions might be my best option at this point. Which was easier said than done.

By the time I'd found my car parked in the lot

at the Hingham Shipyard and blasted the heater, I decided to try to forget I'd ever had the vision of Sean and me together.

I'd just pretend it never happened and be done with it. Otherwise, I was going to drive myself crazy with what-ifs and hows.

Instead of turning left on 3A toward home, I went right. If I was going to pretend that the vision I'd had of me and Sean wasn't real, then I needed something else to occupy my thoughts.

That something else was Michael Lafferty and the missing diamond ring.

A few miles north, I pulled into a Dunkin' Donuts lot and parked. I fought the urge to run in and get a pumpkin spice latte and a French cruller to go.

I switched off the radio, tilted my seat back. The heater warmed my hands, my feet, my face.

Closing my eyes, I took a deep breath, let it out. I allowed myself to relax enough to see the vision of the ring again, trying to slow the images down. I knew from the first time around that the ring wasn't too far from where I was parked now. I just needed clearer directions from this point.

Vertigo washed over me, spinning my thoughts. Round and round, I fought the dizziness while trying to sort out street names, landmarks. Left at the intersection, left a side road, through a gated parking lot, up a paved trail, up a stone staircase, through a thick copse of trees . . .

Finally, I couldn't stand it anymore and sat up, my head still spinning. My stomach bobbed, and I switched off the heater and powered down my window. Cold blasted in. I took deep breaths.

The vision hadn't changed the second time around.

My cell phone rang, startling me. I glanced at the readout. Dovie again.

I couldn't deal with her and her matchmaking right now.

Starting the car, I followed the route my vision had mapped out. A few minutes later, my headlights slid across two metal gates that had closed off the small, dark parking lot for Great Esker Park.

I idled, staring ahead to where the trailhead began, but didn't get out. I couldn't bring myself to do it. It was too dark. Too cold. Too creepy.

My cell phone rang again, nearly scaring me out of my seat. The number that came up was unfamiliar. I didn't answer it, fearing it could be that annoying reporter or worse—Butch, the butcher.

A second later, my phone beeped. I checked my voice mail. Something primal washed over me when I heard Sean Donahue's voice.

So much for forgetting.

"Lucy, I wanted to let you know I'm still working on your request. I'm going to do a little more checking and will call you back in an hour or so."

He didn't say good-bye.

A chill seeped into the car. I fussed with the heater, still unable to bring myself to get out of the car and poke around the area.

One thought kept recurring as I sat there, trying to build courage.

Was Jennifer dead?

I stared at the woods rising up along a steep ridgeline. Who else would have access to Michael's ring? And he did say he hadn't seen her in years . . . that she'd essentially disappeared.

And for some reason I couldn't stop thinking that Michael lived near here somewhere.

How close?

Spurred on by this thought, I drove back to the Dunkin' Donuts, rounded the drive-thru, and ordered that latte. As I paid the tired-looking cashier, I asked for directions to Michael's house, using the address from his portfolio.

As I wound my way down side roads, I drove farther and farther away from the park. At least five miles.

Turning left onto a dead-end road, I coasted, looking for the right house. Michael's was the corner house on a street of only ten homes. Dark woods loomed at the end of the street, the dismal light from an ancient street lamp not nearly enough to illuminate the whole area.

I slowed in front of the small gambrel-style home, sparsely—but neatly—landscaped. No picket fence in sight.

I'd answered my question—he lived nowhere near the park.

I relaxed a little and finally admitted what I'd been afraid to even think. That Michael might be responsible for the skeleton being in the woods.

It was time to go. The last thing I wanted was to get caught out here, snooping.

As I rolled forward to make a three-point turn, like an apparition a figure came walking out of the woods at the end of the street. He was tall and had a dog prancing at his heels.

My headlights outlined his face. It was Michael.

Shit.

There was nowhere for me to go. I was caught. Slowly, I rolled down the window.

"Ms. Valentine?" he asked, squinting in the light of the street lamp. "What are you doing here?"

What *was* I doing here? "Um, I, ah, like to see where my clients live. Get a better idea of who they are. And please call me Lucy."

He nodded appreciatively. "Very thorough of you."

Thorough. Right. I could work with that.

"*Lucy*, this is Little Rabbit Foo Foo. I call her Foo for short," he added, rubbing the golden retriever's head.

"You didn't like her attitude?" I asked, watching the way the dog looked up at him with adoring eyes.

"You've read the book," Michael said, his voice deep and oddly soothing.

"I once worked in a day care."

He laughed. "She was a handful as a puppy. And this is my place." He gestured to the house. "It's not much, but it's home." His breath puffed out in small white clouds. "Do you want a tour?"

"Actually, I should be getting home. Like I said, I just wanted to see it. A drive-by if you will."

The clouds shifted, spreading moonlight across the street. At the end of the road, I could clearly see the opening, a path, and a brown sign that was too far away for me to read.

A sense of foreboding washed over me.

"This is a nice area." I pointed in the direction of the path. "What's over there?"

"Oh, that?" Michael said. "It's part of Great Esker Park. The path goes for miles."

The hair on my neck stood on end.

Michael rubbed Foo's head. "We go for lots of walks there, don't we, Foo?" His gaze held mine, chilling me to the bone as he added, "I know it like the back of my hand."

FIVE

I took 3A south toward home in Cohasset.

Wealth flowed in this small coastal town on the South Shore of Massachusetts. Old money, mostly, as this was once where Boston's elite summered. Over time, though, newcomers trickled in, building bigger and more beautiful year-round estates. As I turned off the main road, heading toward the ocean, I drove slowly though twisting roads, canopied with the spindly branches of dormant trees. Leaves scattered along the street, and my headlights cut through the creeping darkness.

My grandmother's estate was on Atlantic Avenue, one of this area's most scenic roads. From here the mansions and estates overlooking the ocean often had the street packed with sightseers on the weekends, driving slowly, gaping, dreaming.

I carefully rolled into the mailbox pull-off and gathered my bills from one of the two boxes. Gravel spit as I navigated between two stacked stone columns flanking the private driveway sloping upward toward home. "*AERIE*" had been embossed in a flowing white script on a brick red wooden sign attached to one of the columns. The estate had originally been named "White Cap," but once Dovie had divorced Grandpa Henry, the name had been immediately changed.

Tall evergreens lined the driveway near street level, giving way to maples and beech trees and finally expansive lawns and gardens already bedded down for the winter. Straight ahead, the gravel road circled in front of Dovie's house, a sprawling New England colonial—a slate-roofed, shingled masterpiece that overshadowed the charming cottage I lived in. The drive took a jog to the right, turning into a crushed-shell lane, and I followed it a quarter mile downhill to my home, which had once been an artist's studio for the original owner of the main house, built over a hundred years ago.

Both places sat high atop a bluff, overlooking the Atlantic Ocean. We had no beach access— unless one wanted to plunge fifty feet into the rocky ocean below. It was a stunning view.

Come the height of winter, I'd park my car in Dovie's three-car garage, but until the snow fell in earnest I liked to be close to my front door.

Grendel twined around my legs as soon as I walked into the house. Immediately I was glad I'd forgone the donut. The scent of something exotic and wonderful filled the air with the promise of a delicious dinner. That could only mean one thing.

Dovie was here.

Sure enough, she stood in the kitchen, her back to me. She hummed while she stirred something in a pan on the stovetop.

I set my things down on the sofa, made my way across the tiny living room.

Grendel, a three-legged Maine Coon cat given to me by Marisol, my best friend since we were five, tapped at my jeans until I picked him up. I stroked his long orange-cream and white fur until he purred happily.

Having Dovie drop in at a moment's notice was the downfall of living on her property.

It was the only negative.

I loved everything about my one-bedroom house. The tiny size, the open floor plan, the enormous windows, the view of the Atlantic, the seclusion and the serenity. Dovie had given me free rein to decorate as I wished, and I chose an English country style that complemented the architecture of the estate. Overstuffed furniture, deep colors, cushy rugs over the original plank floors. I hadn't been able to afford many quality pieces, so my place was sparsely furnished at this point, but I adored it.

It had taken a lot of stubbornness on my part to get Dovie to accept rent. When I'd cut myself off from my family's fortune, I'd meant it.

Dovie, however, reminded me often that she had been putting my rent money into a mutual fund that would someday be mine.

My mother was just as bad, mentioning that my trust fund was waiting for me when I "came to my senses."

They didn't understand. If I was completely truthful with myself, I had to admit I didn't quite understand my motivation, either. I thought it might have something to do with not feeling worthy of the money after losing my ability to read auras, but it would probably take a therapist to sort it out completely.

And as much as I needed one, therapists were out of the question. No one was to know of my gift, and if I couldn't talk about my family and our eccentricities, then I'd probably spend the whole hour talking about the weather. Not much mental health help there.

Dovie spun and nearly dropped her spatula when she saw me. "LucyD! You're home."

"Indian?" I ventured, sniffing the air.

"Good nose. Masala Bhindi."

I leaned up and kissed both her flushed cheeks. At an even six feet, she was tall and lithe. Part of her physique came from her dancer background; part of it came from liposuction.

Striking white hair cascaded down her back, stopping just shy of her shoulder blades, in stark contrast to the black turtleneck she wore. Tight jeans tucked into knee-high leather riding boots completed the outfit. Six bangles (she and my mother shared a love of bracelets) on each arm jangled as Dovie gestured. Two long jade rope necklaces looped around her graceful neck.

She'd come a long way from the slums of New York City, where she grew up. My grandfather had first spotted her when she was dancing burlesque at a little club in Manhattan.

He'd claimed it was love at first sight.

As a Valentine he should have known better.

Dovie's gorgeous peaches-and-cream complexion glowed with good health. She'd had cosmetic help through the years and was now reaping the benefits, looking much younger than her seventy-five years. Except for the snow-white hair, she could pass for my father's sister instead of his mother.

"I tried calling," she said, scratching Grendel under his chin. He purred contentedly.

"Really?"

She arched an eyebrow at me, clearly not buying my feigned confusion. "I hope you didn't have dinner plans."

"I didn't." The smells coming from the sauté pan on my cooktop had awakened my appetite. I'd lost it after my little visit to the park and Michael's.

I was at a loss, not sure what to do next or who to turn to.

As it stood right now, I needed absolute proof that there was, in fact, a body buried in Great Esker before I called the police to investigate. That meant only one thing. I was going to have to do a little digging. Literally.

And until then I would try not to jump to the conclusion that Michael had anything to do with putting the body there, though my mind had already made that leap.

The TV was on in the living room, the sound low. Images of Wompatuck State Park flashed across the screen. Dozens of volunteers searched ravines, thick forests, and marshes. Had Suzannah made it down?

"Horrible," Dovie said, motioning to the TV.

"Do they still think the father did it?"

"No word yet."

"Suzannah is helping search."

"Oh? Did you see her today?"

I set Grendel down and slid onto a wrought-iron counter stool. I adjusted the floral padded cushion so it wouldn't slip off. "Mum didn't talk to you?"

Dovie put down her wooden spoon. "Should she have?"

I was going to kill my mother.

"She left town today," I said, trying to sound casual.

Dovie's snow-white eyebrows dipped beneath blunt-cut bangs that lent a youthful air to her face. "Odd that she didn't tell me."

Dovie was my mother's closest friend. Which simply drove my father to distraction.

"Where to on such short notice?" Dovie asked.

I focused on the specks in my granite countertop.

50 times 3 is 150.

The square root of 400 is 20.

"St. Lucia," I said.

"How lovely," she said suspiciously.

"With Dad." I cringed.

"Pardon?"

"She and Dad went to St. Lucia to escape the media storm."

Dovie rolled her eyes. "It's not like Oscar to be such a coward."

"I believe it was doctor's orders."

"Hooey. His heart is just fine now. It's his pride that's stinging."

Though I thought Dad's cardiologist might not agree, I had to admit Dovie was right also. Dad's pride was hurt. As well as his reputation.

Dovie tapped her spoon against the edge of the pan. "How long will he be gone?"

"Two weeks."

"He's just recently returned after his heart attack. He's backlogged. Now is not a good time for him to shut down the business."

I couldn't look at her. "He didn't close down."

"Explain yourself, LucyD."

"Well, ah, Dad put me in charge of his clients for two weeks."

Glacial green eyes narrowed. "You?"

I fiddled with the ruffle on the seat cushion.

Dovie picked up her glass of wine and chugged.

"Something about the bloodlines," I murmured, feeling the need to explain. Wine sounded good. Really good. I poured myself a glass while Dovie stewed, absently stirring the nirvana in the pan.

"Bloodlines, my freckled behind. He does realize I was the one who set him up with your mother?"

My mother had grown up on the California coast, the daughter of tried-and-true hippies. She'd migrated east to go to school at Berklee College of Music and had met my father during an anti-busing protest. Mum had been there to picket; he'd been there to try to stop Dovie from chaining herself to something. Somehow Dovie managed to involve herself in every protest and movement she felt strongly about, and didn't care if she was arrested trying to make her point, despite the embarrassment to the family.

Being of similar minds, my mother and Dovie had hit it off right away, and it had been Dovie's matchmaking that had brought Mum and Dad together.

Which was precisely why my father wouldn't let Dovie run Valentine, Inc.

"Why choose you over me?" she asked.

I figured it was a rhetorical question and therefore didn't answer. Grendel pawed at my leg and I lifted him into my lap.

Marisol, during her third year of veterinary medicine at Tufts, had rescued him from euthanasia after he'd been hit by a car. He'd lost his back left leg but otherwise was a normal healthy cat—if you didn't count his separation anxiety.

"I can match," Dovie said. "Didn't I find Elizabeth Petersby a new husband?"

"Only because you foisted one of your many admirers onto her at your annual Christmas party last year and he latched on."

"Did they not fall in love because of it?"

I scratched Grendel behind his ears. He purred so loud it vibrated the wine in my glass.

Debating with Dovie about her merits as a matchmaker was pointless. Simply because my credentials weren't any better. But my father had made up his mind, and if there was one thing I knew from twenty-eight years' experience, it was that he rarely changed it.

"You should talk to Dad."

"Does that mean you don't want the job?"

"I didn't say that." Why was I so quick to defend? I *didn't* want the job.

Did I?

I supposed my hesitation had something to do with Michael Lafferty, that missing diamond ring, and the body in the woods.

I refused to believe it had anything at all to do with Sean Donahue and my sudden hots for him. He was apparently involved with someone else if that phone call was any indication. Completely off-limits in my book. I'd learned that lesson a few years ago, the hard way.

"I'll talk to him," Dovie said, downing another glass of Pinot Grigio. Looking at me pointedly, she added, "And did you know that Elizabeth just had her first *great*-grandchild?"

"Boy or girl?" I asked.

"Girl. Isn't it lovely to have had a *great*-grandchild so young in life?" She tittered pretentiously. "I certainly wish I'll be able to see a *great*-grandchild before I'm too old and feeble to enjoy the blessing."

"You'll never be too old. Or too feeble."

Dovie retrieved plates from an overhead cabinet. "One never knows what life has in store."

Not wanting to play her game, I turned my attention to the TV and the continuous coverage of the Little Boy Lost. Salty gusts of wind buffeted the cottage's windows. How long would the little boy last outside?

If he was even alive.

Dovie set the dishes on the dining room table, a rickety plastic folding table complete with tacky metal chairs. I'd been saving for my dream table but was still many dollars short of my goal. Until then a nice tablecloth and slipcovers did a great job camouflaging.

I did a double take.

"Four plates? Why four?"

Even if she had included Grendel in the meal, which had happened more often than I liked to admit, that would be three plates. "Who's coming?"

Dovie waved a hand in casual dismissal. "Marisol called earlier. Said she had something for you."

Oh no. Whenever Marisol brought me something, it was usually furry and needed a lot of TLC.

"Who else?" I asked.

"Don't you worry about such things."

Grendel must have sensed my agitation; he jumped off my lap with a loud *rrreow*.

"Who?" I asked again, slipping off the stool.

Ignoring me, she launched into a cheery rendition of "Lucy in the Sky with Diamonds."

Panic set in.

She couldn't have possibly . . .

I eyed her.

She would have—she absolutely would have invited Butch the butcher to my house.

My cell phone rang. I pounced on it, not even looking at the ID screen.

"Hello." Please let it be salvation calling.

"Lucy? It's Sean."

Temptation—not salvation. Close enough in my book.

My grandmother raised a thinly plucked eyebrow in my direction. Fight-or-flight had set in, and seeking to get out of my house as soon as humanly possible was foremost on my mind. I focused on the TV set, on the pictures of the little boy, and I quickly formed a plot to escape.

"Oh, hi, Suz," I said airily. "Any word on the little boy?"

"It's Sean," he corrected.

"Oh, that's so sad," I said. "They need more help? I don't think I can. My grandmother made din . . ." I paused for dramatic effect. "I know a little boy's life is at stake. . . . Okay, okay, she'll understand."

"She will not," Dovie chimed in, tapping her foot. The staccato beat of her heel echocd.

"I'll call," I said, "as soon as I get there."

Sean cleared his throat. "Do you need me to call you back?"

"That would be great." I darted for my coat and dug through my front closet for a suitable pair of shoes, a pair of mittens, and my Red Sox stocking cap. "See you then."

Dovie stared me down, hands on hips. "You cannot leave."

"Sorry, Dovie, but they need more help, looking for the little boy. Gotta run."

"You wouldn't be trying to pull one over on your grandmother, would you?"

"Tell Marisol I said hi!" I dashed out the door into the chilly night, my cell phone clutched in my hand.

I should have been feeling bad about leaving Marisol to deal with Butch. Or thinking about the little boy lost in the woods—because I really was going there to help look for him. Or even about Michael Lafferty and how finding him a match had suddenly turned my life inside out.

But all I could think about was Sean Donahue and wanting to hear his voice again.

Even though I knew better.

SIX

My cell rang ten minutes later, as I was winding my way down Route 228 toward the main gate of Wompatuck State Park in Hingham. The moon hung in the sky like something out of a children's picture book, lending little light. Scattered lampposts weren't enough to cut through the darkness. My high beams cut through the shadows. Old colonials, Cape Cods, and gambrels lined the Hingham road, most with long drives, landscaped lawns, and high price tags.

Carefully, I answered the phone one-handed.

"Do I want to know what that was all about?" Sean asked.

His voice sent confusing spirals of desire through me. I wasn't a thirteen-year-old girl who had her first crush, though I was suddenly feeling like it. I seriously needed to get a grip. I'd only met the man today, for what? Ten minutes, tops?

But the vision . . .

I shook my head. The vision was one I couldn't trust. And I really couldn't trust my attraction to him, either. I had to remember Cupid's Curse.

But a fling would be nice—

I snapped out of it. A fling would be out of the question. He had a girlfriend. Period. End of sentence. Stop acting like a love-struck fool, Lucy.

"Lucy? Are you there?" he asked.

"I'm here," I said. "Sorry. The road is dark and twisty."

"Where are you?"

"On my way to Wompatuck."

"The Little Boy Lost?" he asked.

"I'm going to do my best to help find him."

"Very charitable of you."

"Hardly. I'd wanted to escape my grandmother's romantic scheming."

"Sounds like there's a story there."

"Many stories," I said, thinking back to all the times Dovie had tried to set me up. But talking to Sean about anything romantic didn't bode well for my psychological health. I needed to change the subject. Fast. "Did you have news for me?"

I heard papers shuffling. Ahead, I spotted oncoming headlights, and I switched off my high beams. I wasn't fond of driving at night, and as a result I tended to drive much too slow, creeping along.

"I tracked her parents, Martin and Regina, to a new address in Lynn. Jennifer has an older sister named Melissa Antonelli, who also lives in Lynn. Oddly, I couldn't find anything on Jennifer specifically since she graduated college," he said. "Unfortunately, there are a lot of Jennifers out there."

"Then she's not . . . missing?"

"Not that I've found, and that would have turned up. Is there something you're not telling me?"

Too much to go into. "Not really."

There was a brief silence before he said, "Do you want me to call Jennifer's parents? See if they'll give me an address?"

"You can try. Tell them it's in regard to Michael Lafferty."

"I'll call you back."

If it were Jennifer in that grave, someone would have reported her missing. Her family, friends . . . Which left only one conclusion.

It wasn't Jennifer in the grave.

Then who was it? And why was she wearing Michael's ring?

My phone rang. It was Sean.

"Strange," he said.

"What?"

"I spoke with her mother. She wouldn't give me any information at all. And wouldn't take my information, either, to pass along. All she said was that Jennifer was happy and to leave her alone."

"Protective," I said, wondering why. Was she trying to protect Jennifer from being hurt by Michael again, still believing he had betrayed her? Or from something . . . or someone else? Like the evil Elena and her trusty sidekick, Rachel?

"I tried the sister, too. No one answered. I'll call again tomorrow."

The moon slipped behind the clouds. I focused hard on the dotted white line separating lanes.

"What's going on, Lucy? This is for a match-making client? This isn't the usual check your father runs."

"Yes, it's for a client," I said truthfully. "I'm doing things a little differently."

"You want me to keep digging?"

"That would be great."

Maybe Jennifer had pawned Michael's ring? Right. And the person who bought it coincidentally ended up murdered and buried in Michael's home town, practically in his backyard?

I approached the entrance to the park and turned in. Cars lined both sides of the road leading to the gatehouse. News crews milled about. I found a place to park and shut off my engine.

I made a snap decision. "Are you busy tomorrow? There's something I might need you for."

"Sounds intriguing."

My stomach tightened with his flirtatious tone.

"I'll be in bright and early," he said.

I didn't miss that he worked long hours and didn't seem to be in a rush to get home to his girlfriend. Was she his girlfriend? Now that I thought of it, he didn't sound all lovey-dovey on the phone. Yet he was doing her shopping. . . . "I'll come up and see you. Thanks for staying late tonight."

"You're welcome."

I said a quick good-bye before I went and did something stupid like ask him if he believed in love at first sight.

Tall trees diffused the wind, but the temps continued to fall. I pulled on my stocking hat, slipped my mittens into my coat pocket. The night air was scented with burning pine, decomposing leaves, and the sharp sting of strong coffee.

The command post had been set up in the park's visitor center. Outside the building, hundreds of people streamed around. To one side of the center, a small tent had been set up, according to a handmade sign, by the Friends of Wompatuck to serve coffee and snacks. On the other side, a line of police cars—local, state, and environmental—and two ambulances sat abandoned. There were several officers on horseback and bicycles. Several ATVs, four-wheeled all-terrain vehicles, were being ridden around the camp, others parked in a crowded parking lot across from the center.

Floodlights had been set up as well as portable heaters. Someone had started a campfire inside a ring of rocks in the center of the crowd. People hovered around the flames, warming their hands.

Blinking against the harsh artificial lighting, I didn't know where to start. I hadn't seen Suzannah, but I had the feeling she was around somewhere. Knowing her, she wasn't as lost as I felt. She'd probably barreled in and taken over the search.

Leaves crunched beneath my feet as I stopped near a tree to digest all that was going on around me.

It looked to be chaos, but as I stood there a man on a megaphone corralled volunteers onto a school bus that would drive them deep into the four-thousand-acre park to continue the search.

Every few minutes, a roving reporter would be bathed in spotlights, updating the viewing audience on the search's progress. I stood nearby one reporter as she fed her news to the evening anchor.

"Maxwell O'Brien has been missing for close to ten hours now. Tired searchers have been scouring Wompatuck State Park for any signs of the four-year-old boy, who goes by the name Max. Efforts to find the little boy are hampered by the sheer size of the park, the many trails, ponds, and marshes. Hope lies in the many places Max could seek shelter. Back in World War Two, this site was owned by the military, and many of the old ammunition bunkers still remain standing."

She went on to describe the park's topology and included a warning about falling temperatures and wild animals, including foxes, bobcats, and coyotes, before getting to the meat of the story: whether the father was guilty.

"John O'Brien, the boy's father, is still answering police questions at this hour. He has not been charged or labeled as a person of interest. Divers continue to search the reservoir and various ponds. K-nine search and rescue has been brought in by the state police. The boy's mother, Katherine O'Brien, is anxiously awaiting news of her son."

At this point, the cameraman swiveled toward a group of people standing near doors of the visitor center. Among them stood a slight woman, early thirties, whose eyes held a vacant, faraway look.

"Mrs. O'Brien stands firm in her belief that

her son is alive and well. Again, here is a picture of Max O'Brien. He's four years old, forty-five pounds, blond hair, blue eyes. He was wearing jeans, a navy blue long-sleeved T-shirt, and Nike sneakers. If anyone has any information, please call the number on the screen. Police, at this time, are not ruling out an abduction, so please be on the lookout."

Tuning out the rest of the news report, I focused on the little boy's mother. She looked to be living her worst nightmare.

I stood there a minute, watching her. The numb way she moved, the emotionless way she spoke. Fear radiated from her every breath.

I simply couldn't imagine what it would be like to lose my child. And in such a way, too. Not knowing whether the man you loved was responsible, or if a stranger took the boy, or if he'd simply wandered away.

But most of all, not knowing if you'd get him back.

My heart broke for her.

I thought about the boy's father being questioned by the authorities. Was he innocent? If so, what kind of hell was he going through right now? To have everyone in New England thinking you were a child killer? What would he see when he looked into his wife's eyes? Would there be doubt? Or would there be trust? Trust that he'd never hurt the child they'd created together?

Yet if he was guilty . . .

I shivered. Slipping on my mittens, I looked around at all the volunteers. Frustration and depression settled around me like a thick fog. With my talent, I should be able to do more than look under bushes or serve a Styrofoam cup of coffee. I should be able to touch Katherine O'Brien's hand and find her son. To bring him back to her, one way or another.

Why else have a gift like mine? I just didn't understand it.

My fingers cramped from being balled into fists, and I flexed them inside my mittens. There was no point in dwelling on what I couldn't do.

Instead of standing around being as useless as I felt, I worked my way into a crowd waiting for the next bus leading into the park. I climbed on and sat down next to the window.

Just as the bus pulled away, Katherine O'Brien looked up. She couldn't see me in the darkness, yet I felt as though she were looking into my soul. And I made the silent promise that I'd do my best to bring her little boy back to her.

I just couldn't help feeling that my best wasn't good enough.

My house was dark when I arrived home. It was well after 3:00 A.M.

Sheer exhaustion, both physical and emotional, had me dropping onto the couch soon after I closed my front door.

No sooner had I sat than Grendel pounced on my lap, pawed at the zipper on my coat. I switched on a lamp, happy to see that Dovie had cleaned up after her impromptu dinner party.

And I was very happy that Butch hadn't been invited to sleep over. I wouldn't put it past my grandmother.

Trying not to disturb a kneading Grendel, I

slipped off my coat and my shoes. Pulling my legs under me, I curled up, scratching Grendel's ears. He purred happily.

There had been no progress in the search for little Max O'Brien. No evidence, no leads. No nothing. The FBI hadn't been called in yet because there was no proof that he'd been kidnapped. It seemed as though the case was at a standstill.

Most of the local volunteers had cleared out around 1:00 A.M. I'd stayed longer, tramping through the woods with a borrowed flashlight, calling Max's name until I'd lost my voice.

When I left, I noticed that Katherine O'Brien was still wearing that faraway look in her eyes.

I rested my head against the sofa cushion. In a perfect world, I'd wake up in the morning and the TV would announce that Max had been found safe and sound and was back in the loving arms of his parents.

But I knew all too well that this wasn't a perfect world. More than likely, searchers would be out in the woods again the next day, looking for the Little Boy Lost.

A noise from my bedroom had me bolting upright. Grendel *rrreowed* in protest but clung to me. He was such a scaredy-cat.

I heard the squeaking sound again and wondered what in the world could be making such a noise. It wasn't menacing in nature—more mechanical than anything.

Rising, I tried to set Grendel down, but his claws came out and latched into the fabric of my blazer. Brief panic that perhaps Butch had stayed for a sleepover dissipated as I peeked into my bedroom. The bed was empty.

I flipped on the overhead light and looked around and blinked in surprise at what was on my dresser—a plastic cage.

Grendel retracted his claws and jumped to the floor, his tail in the air. Obviously, he wasn't a fan of Marisol's newest gift.

There was no note or instructions attached to the colorful cage. Two bags sat alongside it—food and treats. Hamster food and treats.

I made kissy noises. A tiny black and white hamster stood inside a wire wheel, his front paws in the air. One eye stared at me intently. The other had been stitched closed.

Grendel performed figure eights around my feet as I opened the cage's door and let the hamster sniff my fingers. A little bowl of food sat in the corner of the cage, and a tunnel led up to a bottle of water. A little plastic box lay nestled in pine shavings. After a second the hamster went back to running on the wheel, his little legs pumping.

I closed the door to the cage and sat on the bed. Grendel immediately hopped into my lap.

"What are we going to do with a one-eyed hamster?" I asked him.

He looked at me like he knew exactly what to do with a bothersome rodent—if he wasn't so scared of it.

Tomorrow, I'd call Marisol and get the scoop. Until then, I figured I'd better get some sleep.

In the living room, I locked the doors and was about to switch off the lamp when I saw the files I had brought home from work on the coffee table.

They looked as though they'd been riffled through.

Dovie's handiwork, no doubt.

I flipped through a few of the files, fighting back a yawn. There wasn't anything here that couldn't wait till tomorrow morning. I dropped the files back onto the table, and a swatch of bold orange caught my attention.

It was Michael Lafferty's file.

Separating it from the rest, I looked it over, analyzing it this time. All his answers seemed so normal. Just your average everyday good old boy from next door.

Unfortunately, I knew looks could be deceiving.

SEVEN

The Greenbush Line was a light-rail MBTA commuter train that ran to and from the South Shore
and Boston. I preferred the commuter boat,
though it took a bit longer—longer only because
I had to drive into Hingham. When I was in a
hurry, I took the train.

Like today.

I overslept and was dangerously close to being late for my first appointment of the day, a
follow-up with a woman named Mary Keegan. I
needed to get in town fast. So, I phoned Raphael
and had him meet me at South Station instead of
the dock.

Suzannah was highly capable of holding Valentine, Inc., steady when no one was there; she'd
been doing it for years, ever since she walked in
looking for love and left with a job. Two years
later, she was entrusted with our family secret
after questioning my father about why he had
been coloring on people's files. She'd been working for my father for nearly five years and was
practically part of my family. What's one more

person to add to the dysfunction? However, as far as I could see, Suz was the sanest of us all.

And she certainly wouldn't rat me out to my dad if I was late. Even still . . .

My father trusted me, me of the barista, dog-walking, day-care fame—to run his beloved company. Leading me to believe that he saw potential I didn't see in myself.

I didn't want to fail. The company needed to thrive under my leadership, even if it was for two weeks only. I didn't want to let my father down. Again. I'd let him down enough when I lost my ability to read auras.

Dropping my head against the seat, I wished the train would hurry up already. I was too agitated to attempt math problems, even easy ones. Instead I started a mental to-do list. Number one was getting to work on time (it would be a miracle). If my first client hadn't yet arrived, I'd call Marisol to make sure she didn't have any more injured critters for me to care for.

The hamster she dropped off last night had been asleep when I woke up, curled tightly into the little plastic box in the corner of his cage. I'd decided to name him Odysseus.

And by naming him, I was fairly certain that I'd be keeping him. I hoped he wouldn't be as needy as Grendel, and I also hoped Grendel would get over the indignation of having to share my affection with a rodent.

In my rush to eat breakfast, I also noticed three empty bottles of wine in my recycling bin. It must have been some dinner party.

Before I left home, I'd checked the news while downing my coffee, blowing dry my hair, and dabbing some mascara on my eyelashes (and also on my eyelids, but that was Grendel's fault).

Max hadn't been found, the search continued, and Katherine O'Brien's face haunted me, even now as the train finally (mercifully) slowed to a stop at the station.

I didn't know if I could return to the park to help search. The guilt at not being able to use my psychic abilities to find Max weighed heavily on my conscience.

Raphael waited for me outside the station, the car idling. White stubble scratched my mouth as I gave him a quick peck—he never shaved when my father was out of town.

Once we were seated inside the car, Raphael said, "Why in such a hurry to get to work?" He pulled his seat belt across his chest.

I buckled in, set my bag at my feet. In it were the files I'd brought home last night and a change of clothes for my date later that night. "I don't want to be late for my first appointment."

"Mmm-hmm."

I tucked my bag under my feet. Bright sun burned off morning clouds. Temps slowly rose, and the warmer weather could only be a good thing for little Max—if he was in fact lost in the vast park. "All right, out with it," I said.

"Out with what?"

"You only 'mmm-hmm' when you have a point you're trying to get across to me and I'm too dense to see it."

He smiled, bringing light into his dark eyes. "'Dense' is not a term I'd use to describe you."

"You're avoiding."

"Did you have a chance to look for a match for me?" he asked.

"Now you're really avoiding."

"Just lonely, Uva."

I had a feeling he was manipulating me, but there was a ring of truth in his tone. One I couldn't bring myself to tease about. "I'll start today."

Traffic lurched along. The sun rode low on the horizon, slowly inching its way higher and higher, above the skyscrapers, up into the deep blue sky. I lowered my visor to protect my eyes from the UV rays. The car still held its appealing "new" smell, blended with the scent of luxurious leather. My father required a new vehicle every nine months.

"What's your type?" I dreaded the task of finding Raphael a mate, yet oddly looked forward to it as well.

"You tell me." He adjusted the radio and the heater at the same time. His long fingers then curved around the steering wheel and thumped along to the music—an ancient tune from Men at Work.

I'd known Raphael nearly all my life, yet had never seen him on a date. Hadn't so much as seen him ogle a woman walking down the street. If he had enjoyed a certain type—tall, short, thin, curvy, blonde, brunette, redhead—he never let on to me.

And I told him so.

"Mmm-hmm."

"Not again!"

He laughed, a rich sound that vibrated his chest. "You know me better than anyone, Uva. You have all the information you need."

I was coming to realize matchmaking was harder than it looked.

As I gazed out the window at the crowded city sidewalks, I thought about Raphael, about his quirks, his traits, his likes, his dislikes.

We pulled to a stop at a red light, and Raphael tapped his fingers on the steering wheel, waiting patiently for *me* to tell *him* what his type was.

This was so like him.

"Okay." I ticked off fingers. "She has to have a good sense of humor; be loyal, faithful, and hardworking; be independent enough not to resent your hours . . . yet," I looked at him, "be willing to let you take care of her on occasion. She has to love food as much as you, good books, eighties music, the ocean. A passion for the Red Sox is a must. She has to be willing to travel and not mind you smoking a cigar on occasion. I'd choose someone who likes to talk, because you're too quiet. A relationship needs noise."

He smiled at that.

"Above all, she has to be your friend." I shifted in my seat as he pulled up to Valentine, Inc. "How'd I do?"

He nodded. "It's a start."

I laughed. "Now I've just got to find her."

"I have complete faith."

"At least one of us does," I murmured, though I was going to do my best to make him happy. He deserved it. I suspected the problem would lie in finding someone worthy of him.

I slid out of the car, held the door. His comment about being lonely kept playing in my head. "How about lunch today?" I'd have offered dinner, but I had a blind date with Butch the butcher.

"Sounds perfect," Raphael said with a crooked, endearing smile. "Come to the penthouse; I'll whip something up."

"Oh no! You deserve someone to cook for you once in a while."

His face blanched. "Not you. . . ."

"I won't take that personally, Pasa." A breeze loosened the knot my hair had been swept into. "We'll go out. Where to? The Oyster House?"

"Nothing fancy. You know I don't like fancy."

I looked around. The perfect choice was right in front of me. "The Porcupine? At noon?"

"I'll be here."

I closed the door and waved good-bye. As soon as I turned around, I came face-to-face with the persistent reporter.

"You're Lucy Valentine, correct?"

Somebody had been doing her homework.

"And you are?" I asked.

"Preston Bailey, reporter for the *South Shore Beacon*."

It was a small newspaper, local to where I lived. One that usually stuck to regional news and not gossipy articles about famous matchmakers who cheated on their wives. I had two options. I could blow her off and hope she'd go away, or I could act like a human and hope she'd go away.

"Nice to meet you."

She looked stunned that I'd used manners. Shaggy shoulder-length blonde hair had been pushed back behind her ears. Serious blue eyes peered at me beneath fringe bangs.

Walking with me toward the door, she said, "I'm going to be honest. I want a job with one of the bigger papers. The *Globe*, the *Herald*. If I can get a scoop from you, it may just be the stepping-stone I need to be looked at seriously. Can I ask you a few questions?"

"I'm sorry. I don't really have anything to say." I hurried to the entrance of Valentine, Inc. At five-foot-eight, I had four, maybe five, inches on Preston Bailey, roving reporter, and therefore my strides were longer. She had to jog to keep up.

"I find that hard to believe." She didn't wait for a response from me. Instead she launched into her next question. "Is it true that your father has left town, leaving the running of the company to you?"

She was good. I wasn't sure where she had gotten her information, but she had pretty much nailed it.

"My father has taken a medical leave of absence."

"In St. Lucia?"

I smiled as I swiped the card key. "Where better?"

She answered with another question. "With your mother, correct? Does this mean she's forgiven him for his little dalliance?"

"Cute shoes," I said, eyeing her boots.

She looked down at her feet. "Thanks."

While her attention had been diverted, I'd pulled open the door and stepped in before she could follow me.

"Hey! Wait!" she cried. "I've got more questions!"

"I'm sorry. I have clients waiting."

I quickly pulled the door closed, but I swore I could have heard her say, "You'd think he'd avoid the beach."

I couldn't help but smile. I'd thought the same thing.

As I stopped on the second-floor landing, I looked up the next flight of steps. On the third floor, the door to SD Investigations stood open wide. Unfortunately, I didn't have time to run up right now and chat with Sean.

And see if he truly affected me the way I thought he did.

I shoved open the door to Valentine, Inc., and stopped dead in my tracks.

"You're late," Dovie said, eyeing the antique mahogany longcase clock standing regally in the corner of the room.

"What are you doing here?"

I couldn't believe Dovie was even functioning this morning, as someone who'd probably drunk her fair share of three bottles of wine.

"Suzannah called me. She took the day off to keep searching for the little boy."

"And she didn't call me?"

"She tried. Your home line was busy, and your cell is off."

Busy? I hadn't been on the phone that morning. Then it hit me—Grendel. One of his favorite games was knocking my phone off the hook. I checked my cell. Sure enough, it was off. In addition to Suzannah's call, I'd also missed one from my mother. She'd left a quick message about changing hotels but didn't mention why.

"Suz called me after that." Dovie shuffled a

pile of papers. "I'm glad she did. This is an opportunity I'm not going to waste."

There was no doubt in my mind that Dovie *would* rat me out to my father for being late. She wanted my job, after all. For a second I pondered why she hadn't woken me up to come with her into the city. But I knew the answer—I would have put up a fuss about her taking over Suz's job. This way, Dovie got her way.

Grinning at me, she picked a piece of lint off navy blue pleated trousers that had been tailored to fit her thin frame. A crisp striped oxford, sleeves cuffed, had been left untucked, the top four buttons undone, revealing a white lace camisole beneath. Her usual assortment of bangles slid up and down her arm. Two chopsticks held her hair back in a twist. Green eyes shone with excitement, and the last thing I wanted to do was burst her bubble.

"Did you run your temp job by Dad?"

She cringed at the words "temp job," but my concerns were swatted away with a wave of her hand. "Hooey. I gave birth to your father. I hold majority in this family."

I smiled. I loved when Dovie made a stand. Even though once my father found out about her involvement in the office he might have himself another heart attack. Dovie tended to . . . complicate things.

"And you need the help. Admit it. Without Suz here, you're lost."

I had a feeling I'd be more lost with Dovie running things.

I didn't mention so. Some things were better

left unsaid. Especially when the person hurt by those words was your landlady.

"You don't have to look so worried," she said. "I'm just going to sit here behind the desk, answer the phone, talk to clients, look divine— don't you love the shirt?—and mind my own business."

I was in serious trouble when my father found out about this.

"The shirt is nice. Chanel?"

"Dior."

My budget for designer clothes was practically nonexistent, though I always bought classic pieces. They were pricey but didn't need to be replaced every year. Today I'd thrown on a pair of cream dress pants, a brown cashmere sweater, and brown kitten-heeled boots I'd found on sale at Macy's. Not bad, but certainly not on the level of Chanel or Dior. But that was the choice I'd made when I'd given up my trust fund.

I closed the door and noticed Dovie had already started the fire in the fireplace. Flames licked the ceramic logs. The pillows on the couches had been fluffed, awaiting the first clients of the day.

A flash of panic swept over me. Could I really do this? Look how my first day had gone, after all. Sure, a few of my meetings had been cut-and-dried. But then there had been Michael Lafferty and the skeleton I'd seen.

Sooner or later, I was going to have to deal with that body, and I could imagine how that would affect business and the family reputation. I needed the police to "find" the body without them knowing I was involved. And I had to come up with a plan to protect the company and myself.

I was lost in the notion of Valentine, Inc., failing under my watch when my grandmother's sharp voice snapped me out of my miserable reverie.

"LucyD, I'll have you know I was running this office years before you were born. Years before your father was born. So stop looking like that."

Actually, I hadn't been thinking of her at all, but she also didn't need to know about the skeleton in the woods. "Sorry. Just scattered in my rush to get here."

"I could have covered your first appointment."

"What happened to just answering phones?"

She smiled, much like the Cheshire cat. "I'm being hypothetical."

"Right."

The buzzer sounded on the door, and Dovie bounded to the intercom on Suz's desk.

"It's Mary Keegan." The sounds of the morning's traffic were a noisy accompaniment to the small voice.

"Come right up." Dovie released the button.

"My first appointment," I said, trying to tamp down a feeling of dread.

"Not quite." Dovie adjusted her bangles. "Lola Fellows is in your office. And she doesn't seem happy." Leaning in, Dovie whispered, "That woman scares me."

Lola? What was she doing back so soon?

"Go, go," Dovie urged. "I'll handle things out here."

That's one of the many things I was afraid of.

Taking a deep breath, I strode into my office. Lola stood, looking out the window into the narrow alley behind the building. She turned when I came in, arms folded against her chest, her eyes steeled for war.

"Good morning," I said, trying to keep my tone light.

I set my tote bag on my desk and pulled out the files I'd brought home the night before. "Would you like to sit down?"

Lola glared. "No, I do not want to sit down. What I want is my money back. You're fired, Ms. Valentine."

EIGHT

I sank into my chair. My worst fear was coming true—I was ruining the family business. I'd been in charge of the company for one day and it was already headed down the tubes.

That had to be some kind of record.

"Can I ask why?" I asked.

Lola tapped her foot furiously. "Adam Atkinson is why."

I recognized the name immediately. He was the man I'd found with an identical shimmery blue swatch as Lola's. "Why don't you sit down for a minute?"

Her red lips thinned. After a brief hesitation, she sat. Legs and arms crossed, she said, "I *knew* I should have waited for your father to handle my case. Now I want nothing to do with Valentine, Inc. What a laugh."

Worried about losing one of my father's clients, I asked, "Something wrong with Adam? All our clients are put through an extensive background check—"

"Yes, there's something wrong with him! He's,

he's a . . ." Her jaw locked. "He's a sanitation engineer," she squeezed out between clenched veneered teeth.

"A sanitation engineer?" I blinked. "You mean a trashman?"

She growled. "Yes, a trashman. How on earth could you think *I* would match with a *trashman*?"

Letting out a deep breath, I leaned back in my chair, trying to tamp down my rising anger. "I take it you spoke with him?"

"He's a *trash*man, Ms. Valentine. As soon as I learned of his profession the conversation was over. Our worlds would never blend." She jabbed a manicured finger in the air, its red tip flashing. "Something you as a matchmaker should have realized before you embarrassed me in such a way. Can you imagine him at the symphony? At a corporate dinner? Dressed in Armani?" She shuddered.

I bit my tongue.

She stood, shivering in self-righteousness. "I want an apology, I want my money back, and I will have a word with your father when he returns."

Forcing myself to unclench my hands, relax my shoulders, and sit up straight, I wondered how best to handle this. As Lola strode to the door, I casually threw out, "Do you know why my father, one of the wealthiest men in the country, one of the most dashing, debonair, sophisticated men you'll ever meet, has a *trashman* as a client?"

Slowly, she turned around. "I'm sure I don't care."

I rose from my chair and was surprised my legs didn't wobble. "Adam, like you, is a client because love, true love, knows no boundaries. Not money, societal class, race, or religion."

Where was this stuff coming from? Had some of my father's many lectures actually sunk in?

"The value of a person is found in their heart," I said, sounding like a sappy Hallmark card. "Not in their bank account or occupation. Love doesn't care if Adam is a trashman or if he's a brain surgeon."

Face flaming, she said, "Well, *I* care."

"Exactly."

"What is that supposed to mean, Ms. Valentine?"

"It means you're a snob, Ms. Fellows."

She bristled and took a step forward. "I am not a snob for wanting to date an equal."

"Really? And how's that been working for you so far?"

Her face lost all color. "You bitch."

Pointedly I said, "I was thinking along the same lines." And I hadn't needed an aura to help me reach that conclusion.

Crimson lips parted and her jaw dropped. "How dare you?"

"Look, you're thirty-two years old and have never had a meaningful relationship. You tried things your way, and they didn't work. You came here to try things our way, which you refuse to do. To my way of thinking, you have two options. One is that you walk out of here miserable and lonely."

Though I had zero confidence in my own matchmaking abilities, I fully trusted my father's gift. If Adam had a shimmery blue aura, then he was the man for Lola. Poor, poor unsuspecting guy.

"Option two is to trust us. We know what we're doing. Adam Atkinson *is* the perfect man for you. You need to stop thinking with your brain and start feeling with your heart. Give the man a chance. Give yourself a chance," I added softly, wondering whether this melodramatic side of me had always been there or it was something new.

I didn't know, but it felt like a lot of BS. Of course I'd seen that true love existed. You couldn't look at my father's track record and not be convinced. However, no one close to me had ever been in a happy relationship.

It only made sense that I was a little skeptical, but as I heard myself talking to Lola, I almost bought in to the hype and thought maybe one day I could find true love, too.

Then I remembered Cupid's Curse.

There was little hope for me.

Lola's brow furrowed; I felt her weakening and added honey to the pot. "Last year, our success rate was ninety-eight percent."

"And what, per se, happened to the two percent?"

Leave it to her to focus on the negative. "They were people, like you, who couldn't trust us, who needed to control everything around them at the cost of finding true happiness." I didn't mention the client who had gotten hit by a car and the one who'd failed the background check miserably. "It's up to you now. Do you want to fall in love? It's as simple as that."

Her face crumpled. "Why couldn't he be anything but a trashman? Do you think he smells?"

This time I bit my lip to keep from laughing. "There's only one way to tell."

Perfectly plucked eyebrows arched. "I'm not apologizing to you."

"I didn't ask you to."

Her delicate chin lifted; her shoulders stiffened. "I'll call him."

"Be nice to him."

"I'm always nice." She burst out laughing, short staccato sounds that hurt my ears.

Poor Adam.

"Okay, maybe not," she conceded. "But if he's my perfect match, then he won't mind, will he?"

I hadn't thought of it that way. Was it possible he was just as bad as Lola? "I suppose not."

"Good day, Ms. Valentine." She power-walked from my office, and I'd barely had time to take a deep breath before Dovie buzzed me on the intercom. "Mary Keegan is on her way in. Oh, and there's a Sean Donahue to see you, as well. What a cutie-pie he is. A former firefighter, and you know what they say about firefighters. They're too hot—"

I stabbed the intercom button, perfectly aware that anyone in the reception area could hear her. Especially Sean. "Thank you, Dovie," I said sharply.

Sean. My heart leapt into my throat at the thought of seeing him again.

I cursed myself for it. It was nothing short of idiocy.

Before I had time to collect myself, Mary Keegan was standing in the doorway, her beautiful brown eyes wide and blinking. She was middle-aged, soft and doughy. Her translucent skin glowed with good health and happiness.

I walked over to the door to greet her. Reluctantly, I held out my hand. The dreaded handshake. I silently pleaded that she hadn't lost anything lately. "Lucy Valentine," I said, hoping my internal cringing didn't show on my face.

Pumping my hand, she beamed at me.

Nothing. No images. Whew.

"Have a seat," I said.

"No, no."

Confused, I tipped my head in silent question.

"I came," she said, "because I was worried."

"About?" Was another client about to jump ship?

"How well my relationship was going with Barry. He's the new man in my life—your father set us up. But after hearing you speak to that other woman, I realized that I need to let go of my fear, and let my heart lead the way."

"The other woman?"

"The one who just left. Red lips, big attitude, intimidating."

That about summed up Lola Fellows. "How did you hear our conversation?" We hadn't raised our voices . . . much.

Her cheeks colored. "It did feel a bit like eavesdropping, but the lovely woman at the front desk seemed like it was perfectly normal to be listening through the intercom."

"I see." Dovie was dead meat.

"You gave that woman great advice—advice I'll be taking as well. I just wanted to come back here and tell you so. I won't take up any more of your time. Please let your father know an invitation to my wedding will be in the mail soon."

She shook my hand again (again, nothing) and left.

I listened carefully, while slowly counting in my head, until the front door closed. "Dovie!" I bellowed.

A second later Sean appeared in my doorway, a lazy smile on his face. "She hightailed it out of here as soon as Ms. Keegan enlightened you about the eavesdropping."

My heart pounded wildly at the sight of him. So much for imagining my reaction. "I'm going to kill her."

"It would mean life without the possibility of parole."

He brushed past me, his arm touching mine as he went by. Heat shot from my skin into my bloodstream. The whisper of his breath warmed my neck.

I was doomed. Plain and simple. Doomed.

"It would be worth it," I said, trying to compose myself. I could not let this go on.

He looked around, found a second intercom hiding under my desk. He disconnected it. "You might want to look around before having any more private conversations."

"Think I'd look good in prison orange?"

His gaze slid down my body and up again. "I imagine you'd look good in anything, Ms. Valentine."

Was it possible to self-combust from one look?

I decided it was.

"Call me Lucy, please."

"Only if you call me Mr. Donahue."

I did a double take. Again, that lazy smile tugged at his lips. Lips that on any other man would be boring, plain old lips. On him, they promised wicked, wicked, delicious things.

When I didn't say anything, he said, "I'm kidding."

"I know." I laughed. "I'm just—" I made a tornado motion above my head with my hand. "A little out of it. It's already been a long day and it's not even ten. I was going to come upstairs and see you as soon as I had a break."

"Before or after you called your client a bitch?"

My cheeks heated. "I didn't call her one. I implied it."

"Semantics, Lucy."

My stomach somersaulted at the sound of my name from his sexy lips. Get a grip, I told myself. It's not as though I hadn't heard my name spoken before. A million times.

"Lucy?"

Oh, not again! There was just something about the way he said it. Something . . . promising.

"You okay?" he asked. "Maybe you should sit down."

"I'm good." I pulled my shoulders back, lifted my chin.

"So I see."

Oh. My.

Inhaling deeply, I said, "I'm sorry if Dovie, you know, offended you."

"How? By saying I was cute? Or that I was too hot . . . to something." He smirked, looking like he knew exactly how hot he was. "Very offensive."

Thinking I was just digging a deeper hole for myself, I scooted around my desk and sat in my chair. I shuffled files, trying to think of something to say that wouldn't lead to any more innuendos. My heart couldn't take them.

"Am I interrupting your schedule?" he asked, smoky gray eyes turning serious.

I checked the printout of today's appointments Dovie had left on my desk. "No, actually."

"Good." He sank down into the chair across from my desk and rubbed his finger over the raised swirls of the textured fabric. "Can I ask you something?"

If he wanted to go to bed with me, the answer was yes. Which was awful, because I suspected he had a girlfriend. Here I was supposed to be a matchmaker, yet I'd jump at the chance to become a home wrecker.

I obviously had issues.

My voice wavered. "Sure."

"What's the deal with Jennifer Thompson?"

Michael Lafferty's file lay next to my tote bag. "It's complicated."

He eyed me. "I like complicated."

"Yes, well." Possible girlfriend, I silently chanted, over and over and over again. "The thing is, I'm not sure I can trust you. I barely know you."

"Now you've really got me interested."

He's talking about the case, he's talking about the case. . . .

Breathe.

I knew myself well enough not to embark alone

on this journey to find out what happened to the body buried in the woods. I needed help, and Sean was more than qualified. But if I brought him into this, he would have questions.

Ones I wasn't sure I could answer.

"What have you gotten yourself into, Lucy?" he asked.

"Nothing that's going to turn out well."

"Are you in over your head?"

"It's complicated," I repeated. "But it's not something I want to do alone."

"You can trust me," he said in a voice heavy with sincerity.

I looked deep into his eyes, fought the urge to run my finger over the bump on his nose, and said, "Even if that's true, can you trust me?"

His eyebrows dipped. "Trust *you*?"

I'd taken him by surprise. "Yes, trust me."

He studied me for a long time, his gaze never leaving my face, his eyes searching mine. "Yeah, I think I can."

"All right then. We need to go on a little field trip. Today? Around dusk?"

"What kind of field trip is this?"

"You'll see. Oh, and you'll want to bring a shovel, and is there any chance you could bring a dog with you?"

"A dog? Why?"

"For a cover, naturally."

"A shovel and a dog."

"That about sums it up. Oh, and a couple of flashlights."

"You're a woman of mystery, Lucy Valentine."

"You have no idea, Mr. Donahue."

NINE

The phone rang not long after Sean left the office. Since Dovie had yet to reappear, I was fielding phone calls.

"Hello, Valentine, Inc.," I said from my knees as I dug through my father's file cabinet. I was halfheartedly looking for matches for my few clients.

Sean and I had exchanged cell phone numbers and made plans to meet at the Hingham Shipyard at four thirty. I told myself I wasn't looking forward to seeing him again, but who was I kidding?

"This is Preston Bailey with the *South Shore Beacon*. May I speak to Ms. Valentine?"

"I'm sorry, but she's gone to lunch," I lied, trying to disguise my voice with a nasal whine.

She hummphed and hung up.

I smiled and sat back, stretching my legs and wiggling my toes. My kitten-heeled boots lay atop each other near the door.

As I searched files, I couldn't stop thinking about Michael.

In the back of my mind lurked the suspicion that he might be responsible for the skeleton. And no matter how I tried to dismiss the theory, I couldn't.

The body was buried in his hometown. His ring was on the body . . .

But wait.

His ring!

If Michael *had* been responsible for the body in the grave, he would have already known where his family ring was. Therefore he wouldn't have been thinking about the ring being lost when I shook his hand. I never would have seen the ring on the finger of the skeleton.

He hadn't known where the ring was.

He didn't know about the body.

He wasn't a killer.

That I knew for sure.

I smiled, suddenly relieved that one of Valentine, Inc.'s clients wasn't a cold-blooded murderer. Talk about bad for business. I don't think there was a vacation long enough or an island far enough to escape that kind of news.

My relief was short-lived.

Someone had been killed. And as of right now, only two people knew about the murder. The killer. And me.

How did I get into this situation? I was currently (albeit reluctantly) in the business of love, not murder.

Closing the file cabinet, I sighed. I was done for the day. There were only so many files I could look at before going cross-eyed.

However, I had pulled a few files with Raphael in mind. Relying solely on the personality quizzes, I'd found three women who might—might—be good matches for him. Oddly, I was suddenly excited by the prospect of setting him up. I just hoped I didn't let him down.

My cell phone rang, and I reached for it. It was Marisol.

"Have you seen Em?" she asked.

I'd met Marisol Valerius and Emerson Baumbach during a mom and tot yoga class when we were three years old. As our mothers liked to remind us on every possible occasion, we'd despised each other at first sight.

It wasn't until kindergarten when bad seed Johnny Campanto cut off Marisol's braids that we girls all bonded. It helped that Em and I had rubber-cemented the seat of his chair in retaliation. He'd been stuck for an hour. The good old days.

We girls have been best friends ever since.

"Seen her? Is she missing?" I asked, suddenly worried.

"I talked to her last night, but *he's* worried. He just called me looking for her. And you know if he called *me*, then he's desperate."

Not "He" as in God, though Em's fiancé thought he was God's gift. His proper name was Joseph Betancourt, though Marisol rarely used it, mostly because she didn't care for the man. Thanks to her absentee father, she had deep-rooted issues with high-powered career types like Joseph, an executive banker. I, however, had more tolerance, simply because if Em loved him, there had to be some redeeming factor.

"Apparently," Marisol continued, "she was supposed to call him at nine this morning and didn't."

"So, she could just have gotten caught up at work and forgotten to call?"

"Undoubtedly. Doesn't he realize she's a doctor? That she's busy, too? He should get a clue."

Em was a second-year pediatric resident at Children's Hospital. She practically lived there. And what little time she had left she spent trying to rein in her mother when it came to planning the wedding. I hardly saw Em anymore, mostly keeping up through hurried phone calls and quick e-mails.

I tried to suppress the fact that Em and Marisol being doctors made me feel like a complete slacker. I could get a complex if I dwelled on my many career failures. "Did you call her?"

"Her cell is off."

"How about we not worry until around dinnertime?" I said, hoping Em would check in.

"Deal. Speaking of dinner . . . Last night."

I slipped on my boots. I had a good hour before I was due to meet with Raphael. I wanted to go see Jennifer Thompson's parents. Now that I was sure Michael had nothing to do with the skeleton, I could proceed in my plan to reunite the two. "Yeah, about that. Sorry."

"Don't be. It was a nice night. Dovie's an excellent cook. She told me about you looking for that little boy. So sad."

In the empty reception area, the fireplace crackled. The TV was muted, but the news stations were still carrying full coverage of the search. There had been no new developments.

"Very." Especially since I felt so helpless in finding him. But I couldn't share that with Marisol. Neither she nor Em knew about any of my family's psychic abilities. It hadn't been easy keeping that secret from them. "Tell me, what's Butch look like? I'm supposed to have dinner with him tonight."

"He's adorable. He looks a lot like Matt Damon."

"You love Matt Damon," I said, hoping she'd take Butch off my hands.

"Honestly, Butch and I hit it off, and in any other circumstances, I'd go for it."

Optimistic, I said, "What circumstances? Something that surely could be overcome."

"He's a butcher, Lucy. I can't date a butcher."

Marisol had been a vegetarian since first grade when she learned where veal cutlets came from. I thought about giving her the same speech I gave to Lola Fellows, but I knew Marisol too well. A butcher would never make the cut. I laughed silently at my own joke and decided that I'd been cooped up in this office much too long if I was cracking myself up with bad puns.

"Well, I guess I still have a date tonight."

"He's nice," Marisol said.

"I'm sure he is. Dovie wants great-grandchildren—she wouldn't pick just any guy for me."

"I wouldn't be too sure about that."

"You're not making me feel better."

"But I can vouch for Butch."

"Is that his real name?" I asked.

"No idea. You'll have to find out. Give him a chance. Maybe you'll finally find that someone special."

Marisol also didn't know about Cupid's Curse.

"Maybe," I said.

"How's Fluffy doing?" The noise of dogs barking filled the background. I could picture her in her lab coat, her dark bob swinging as she multitasked. During the day, she worked at a vet clinic in Quincy. At night, she volunteered at a free animal hospital downtown.

"Fluffy?"

"The hamster."

"I think he'd be outraged you named him something so embarrassing as Fluffy. His name is Odysseus."

She laughed at me. "You gave him a name—good."

"Yes, yes, I'm keeping him. You knew I would." I took another look at the TV and switched it off. "But no more pets!"

"You might not have to worry."

"Why?"

"The hospital might have to close. Lack of funding."

I wondered what would happen to all the animals they treated. "That's awful."

"We're going to hold a fund-raiser next month, but it might not be enough. . . ." Her voice trailed off as if she couldn't contemplate the consequences. "But that's enough of that. Call me if you hear from Em."

"Ditto."

We said our good-byes and hung up.

Immediately I called Em's cell phone. It was still off. I thought about trying the hospital, but there were so many negatives to that notion, I dismissed it immediately. I told Marisol I wouldn't worry until dinnertime, but honestly, I already was. Em was the most punctual, organized, type-A person I knew. Not calling *him* was out of the ordinary for her. And even if she was busy at nine, it was almost noon now.

Something didn't feel right.

The current address of Jennifer Thompson's parents was in Lynn, just north of the city. I couldn't think of it without singing "Lynn, Lynn, city of sin," part of a rhyme created when corruption and crime were prevalent years and years ago.

Sean had given me the address and the use of one of the SD Investigations cars housed in a parking garage down the street. He'd wanted to come along but had a client coming in and couldn't cancel.

The house was a nice two-story, not ostentatious, but upper middle class for sure. The lawn had yet to brown for the winter, and the shrubs had been freshly cut back. An autumn-colored wreath hung on the steel door. I used the brass knocker, the sound echoing down the block of similar homes.

I hoped that meeting Jennifer's parents face-to-face might sway them into passing my information along to her. Sean certainly hadn't had any luck on the phone.

The door opened an inch. "I'm not buying," a man said. Late fifties, graying, with a soft stomach and hard eyes.

"I'm not selling," I said with what I hoped was a disarming smile. I handed him a Valentine, Inc., card.

"What's this about?"

"Are you Martin Thompson?"

The door opened a bit wider. He had the looks

of a longshoreman. Weathered face, muscled body, snow-white beard.

"Yeah."

"I'm looking for Jennifer. Does she still live here? I have a client, Michael Lafferty, who'd like—"

Jabbing a finger, he said, "No, she doesn't live here, but you leave our Jenny alone. She's been through enough with Michael and those girls."

"But there was a misunder—"

He slammed the door in my face.

As I started down the steps I was beginning to think reuniting Michael and Jennifer was the worst idea I ever had.

"Look at what the cat dragged in," Maggie Constantine said with a big smile as I slid into a two-person booth in a bright, cheery corner of the Porcupine. I took a seat facing the kitchen door because I loved watching the hustle and bustle.

I set the files of Raphael's potential dates on the table, slipped my handbag from my shoulder, and smiled back. "It's good to see you, Maggie. Looks like business is doing well."

A line of people ordering lunch to go snaked toward the door. Most of the tables in the quaint dining room were occupied with those wanting to linger over their food. Food that smelled so good my stomach rumbled to life.

"I couldn't ask for much more," Maggie said. Her brown eyes shone with good humor and intelligence. Despite the cold, she wore a pair of knee-length brown shorts and a white T-shirt covered by a black apron that looped around her neck. Her dark hair was pulled back into a sleek

braid that swung halfway down her back. For the
sake of comfort, she wore a pair of fun, youthful
brown suede sneakers. A gold chain wrapped
around a delicate ankle. She stood a little over
five feet tall and was maybe one hundred pounds
(wet), yet her personality made her seem larger
than life. "Actually, any more and I'd need to expand." She added saucily, "Think your dad would
give up his space?"

"Not in this lifetime."

She snapped her fingers. "Then I guess I'll just
have to make do."

I was glad to hear it. It would be very easy for
Maggie to not renew her lease and move the
Porcupine to a bigger location. I often met my
father here during the lunch breaks of my various jobs. It had become a tradition—one I didn't
want to end.

Overhead, something classical floated from
speakers perched in the four corners of the room.
Bach, perhaps. Maybe Mozart. My father would
have known in an instant. I'd spent too much
time with Raphael—I could name that eighties
tune in one note, but anything else? I was a lost
cause.

Maggie had made the move from New York
City to Boston a little over three years ago, following her wheeler-and-dealer stockbroker husband after he accepted a job transfer. She'd
opened the Porcupine to keep herself busy while
her husband worked long hours.

Tragedy struck when her husband died of a
heart attack a year later, leaving behind a heart-
broken widow. At forty-four Maggie could have
done anything, gone anywhere. But somewhere

along the way she had fallen in love with the city and her restaurant and decided to stay. She worked long hours, often in before sunrise and never out before sunset.

I adored her even though she was a Yankee fan.

Some things just had to be overlooked.

"Eating alone today?" Maggie asked, handing me a menu.

"No, Raphael is meeting me."

"The elusive Raphael. I hear he has superhuman powers."

I laughed. "It just seems that way. My father tends to exaggerate where Raphael is concerned."

A cloud passed over her dark eyes. "How long will your father be gone?"

Over the past year, I'd wondered more than once if my father was seeing Maggie, but I'd never had the courage to ask either of them.

Personally, I hoped not. Maggie was special, and my father tended to break hearts without looking twice. "Two weeks as far as I know."

"Is this a working lunch? Making matches over mashed potatoes?" she asked, motioning to my files while filling a water goblet.

"Kind of." Wait a sec. "You knew my father has me looking after the business while he's gone?"

"He mentioned it in passing yesterday when he stopped in to say good-bye. I was surprised— I never thought you were interested in his work."

Wait staff bustled around the dining room, decorated in casual creams and decadent jewel tones. The line at the take-out counter stretched farther toward the door. Raphael was late.

I shifted, uncomfortable. Honestly? There was nothing I wanted more than to be a part of the family business. Making matches, finding true love, doing something meaningful with a gift passed on through generations.

But I couldn't. Not since that night when I was fourteen and talking on the phone with Marisol during a thunderstorm.

Life hadn't been the same since.

And fourteen years later, I still hadn't figured out what to do with myself.

"Let's just say I was persuaded," I said evasively, hoping Maggie wouldn't question my lame response.

"Am I interrupting?" Raphael asked, standing at a respectful distance.

"Not at all," I said. "You remember Maggie?"

"We've met a few times." He nodded in that old-fashioned-gentleman kind of way I found charming. "Pleasure to see you again, Ms. Constantine."

Maggie waved away his formalities and motioned him into the booth. "Call me Maggie."

Raphael nodded again.

Maggie filled his water glass as he set his napkin on his lap. "I'll let you two get to your lunch. If you speak to your father, please give him my best."

"I will."

As soon as she was out of sight, Raphael used his napkin to wipe a spot from his glass. "What?" he asked when he saw me arching my eyebrow at him.

"You just can't help yourself, can you?"

"Do you think she'd let me in the kitchen with my Mr. Clean?"

"No."

He leaned back against the cushioned booth and scratched at the stubble on his cheeks. "Charming place."

"You say that as though you have issues."

"Do not jump to conclusions, Uva."

"Mmm-hmm," I said.

He laughed. "Don't start with the 'mmm-hmms.' I'll confess I would do things differently."

"Such as?"

"The colors, first. So feminine. I'd decorate more neutrally."

"More boring, you mean." I loved Raphael with all my heart, but the man knew nothing when it came to décor.

He ignored me. "I'd renovate so the take-out line had its own entrance—too distracting to the sit-down diners." Scanning the menu, he added, "And I'd add a few more items to the menu as well. More flavor. And expand the healthy options, so men like your father would have more options."

That was a valid point. My health-nut father rarely chose anything other than the Mediterranean chicken salad. "It's a wonder you ever go out to eat."

"Which is why I rarely do. What's this?" he asked, poking the files on the tabletop.

"Possible matches."

"For whom?"

"You."

His eyes widened; then he winced, looking accusingly at the speaker above his head. "The music would also have to go."

Classical definitely wasn't Raphael's style.

A server came and took our orders. Raphael chose a fish-and-chips basket, made with the freshest cod and handmade fries, and I picked a gourmet BLT that had the most delicious roasted red pepper mayonnaise.

I grabbed the top file and flipped it open. "Marcia Bigelow, aged fifty-one. She's a seventh-grade science teacher. Loves autumn, chocolate-chip cookies, and taking cruises."

"Not piña coladas, getting caught in the rain, and making love at midnight on the dunes of the Cape?"

My cheeks heated. Lyrics of a song or not, I couldn't picture Raphael in that light. My father yes (despite the sand), him no.

Tells you a lot about my childhood.

"Don't mock. On paper she seems like a great candidate."

"Who are the others?"

We went through the other two files, and he decided to try a date with Marcia.

Maggie bustled around, flitting from one table to another, from the cash register to the kitchen. No wonder she was so trim.

"How long till spring training?" I asked Raphael.

"One hundred and seventeen days."

I smiled. There wasn't a man who loved baseball more than him.

"Spring training?" Maggie approached with a pitcher of ice water. "I go down every year to watch a couple of games. Have you been?" she asked Raphael.

Oh no. This could turn out badly.

"Never had the chance," he said. "I hear Fort Myers is very nice, though."

"Fort Myers?" Maggie said. "Oh no, I go to Legends Field in Tampa."

It was like watching a train wreck.

"Legends Field?" Raphael asked. "Spring-training home of the Yankees?"

The tone in his voice had Maggie's back stiffening. "That's right. Do you have a problem with that?"

I kicked Raphael under the table. His cursing out the Yankees was nothing new to me—however, I didn't want Maggie to fillet him.

Sparks flew from his eyes. "No, ma'am."

Maggie filled our glasses, cocked her chin, and sashayed away.

He huffed and puffed once she was out of earshot. "And you're friends with her?"

"What happened to all your lectures about fairness and equality?"

"Doesn't pertain where the Yankees are concerned."

Even though the Yankees hadn't been so good in the past few years, the rivalry between them and the Red Sox ran deep. "So stubborn, Pasa."

He grinned sheepishly. "Despite her bad taste in baseball teams, she makes a delicious fish-and-chips platter."

"I don't think now is the time to ask for the recipe."

I wanted to ask if he suspected Maggie and my father were an item, but Raphael would never tell, even if he knew for certain. It was one of the reasons he'd worked for my father for nearly thirty years.

As Raphael talked about the Sox's *excellent* chances next year (I think Maggie's comment had gotten under his skin), my mind wandered back to Max. If he'd been found yet.

It didn't take long for my thoughts to twist their way to the skeleton. And to Sean. And the vision I'd seen of the two of us.

"Uva?" Raphael asked. "You're a million miles away. What's wrong?"

Where to start? With a fear of failing my father? With the guilt of not being able to find a lost little boy? With my worry about Em? With having a vision of a dead body? With Dovie and her matchmaking and horrible eavesdropping?

I'd need a week to get it all out. Instead, I told him about the one thing I couldn't comprehend. I leaned in, across the table, and dropped my voice. "I had a vision."

He waited, as I knew he would.

"Of the future. At least I think it's the future. That is, if the vision isn't a figment of my imagination."

Lines creased his forehead as he frowned. "Of what?"

I was afraid he'd ask that. "Not important." There were some things he just didn't need to know.

"Are you sure it was of the future and not a recovered memory?"

"I'm sure." No way had I gone to bed with Sean and forgotten about it. That's like forgetting you won the lottery. Just didn't happen.

"This has never happened to me before. Why would a new," I dropped my voice, "*ability* appear now, out of nowhere?"

"I wish I could answer you."

He didn't know how much I wished he could, too.

I reached for my wallet to pay our bill, but Raphael stopped me.

"But this was my idea," I protested.

"But *my* pleasure."

"You're such a charmer. I'm surprised some woman hasn't fallen for you yet." I gathered up my files. Was that woman at my fingertips?

"A heart has to be willing, Uva."

True enough.

"I'll walk you out," he added, tossing money on the table.

I rose, turned toward the door, and froze.

Preston Bailey sat in the seat directly behind mine. She looked up and smiled.

"Hello," I said shakily.

"Why, Ms. Valentine, what a surprise. Who's your lunch companion?" She eyed Raphael.

"Just a friend," I answered vaguely.

The corner of her mouth quirked as she stared at me, a gleam in her perceptive eyes. "I see."

I hurried away, Raphael on my heels. As we stepped out into the sunshine, I took a deep breath. It wasn't what Preston Bailey had *seen* that bothered me.

It was what she might have heard.

TEN

At four thirty Sean picked me up at the commuter boat dock in Hingham, on his lap a tiny Yorkshire pup, sticking his head out the window.

"He's cute," I said, opening the car door. "Is he yours?" I sank into Sean's leather seats. He drove an older Mustang, two doors, sleek and black, a manly man's car.

"All three pounds of him."

"I wouldn't have pegged you as a lapdog kind of guy."

"The breed wasn't my choice," he said, rolling his eyes. "But the name was. Meet Thoreau." The dog bounded over to me, prancing on my lap.

"As in Henry David?" I asked, my heart swelling for a man I barely knew.

"Is there any other?"

"Awful literary of you." I scratched behind the puppy's ears. His fur was soft and shiny. Dark eyes peered up at me from under spiky brown bangs. A small pink tongue dangled from the corner of his mouth, panting slightly.

Sean maneuvered around the parking lot and

headed back toward Route 3A. "I minored in English back in the day."

"Oh," I said, falling that much harder.

In two hours I was supposed to meet Butch at the Hingham Bay Club for dinner, which was conveniently located in the same shipyard as the dock. I'd just have Sean drop me here after we were through. Raphael had somehow managed to get my car from the train station in Cohasset to the shipyard—maybe Maggie was right. He did have superpowers. I was glad—if my date with Butch was awful, then I had means of escape.

Inconveniently, I would have to wear my date clothes to Great Esker. It couldn't be helped. Before I left work, I'd changed into a wraparound dress and heels. It wasn't the ideal outfit to dig up a body, but then again, what was?

If that wasn't enough to worry about, Preston Bailey, the nosy reporter, had been outside the building when I left, snapping pictures of me. She wore a knowing look on her face, doubling my unease that she'd overheard my conversation with Raphael.

I was terrified to see her article.

"Do you have pets?" Sean asked.

"A three-legged cat and a one-eyed hamster."

He raised an eyebrow.

"Don't ask."

"Names?"

I hesitated.

"What? Are they something ridiculous like Fluffy and Muffy?"

I'd told Marisol Fluffy was a terrible name. "No. The cat is Grendel. The hamster is Odysseus."

He turned and looked at me. "You're serious?"

"Back in the day I minored in English, too."

Something resembling appreciation flashed in his eyes. "But now you're a matchmaker?"

"For a couple of weeks, at least. While my father recuperates."

"What did you do before that?"

Since the time change the previous weekend, night settled early in the evening. The setting sun was obscured by sparse clouds, darkness looming on the horizon. "This and that," I hedged. I wanted desperately to change the subject. There was no need for him to know I was a jack of all trades, master of nothing. "You were a firefighter?"

"Yeah."

"How long?"

"Nine years. Started right out of college."

"Suz said you were hurt?"

"Something like that," he answered vaguely.

It was obvious he didn't want to talk about it, so I let it drop. I directed him north on 3A, headed toward Great Esker Park. Thoreau turned twice and settled into my lap.

The little fur ball was adorable but not quite the type of dog I'd hoped Sean would bring with him. A big bloodhound would be more likely to "dig" up a long-buried body. But the puppy would have to do.

"Where are we going?" Sean asked.

"Great Esker Park in North Weymouth."

"Never heard of it."

"Mostly only locals know of it," I said. "It's hard to find."

"But you're not local to this area—how do you know of it?"

I looked out the window as we crossed the Hingham Bay Bridge. Boats bobbed in the choppy water. The Weymouthport condos rose up near Webb Park on their narrow peninsula, looking ominous in the murky evening light. "Through the grapevine." The supernatural grapevine, but I kept that to myself.

"That's quite an outfit to go to a park."

"Don't ask," I said, not wanting to explain about Dovie's matchmaking. I should have just canceled the date, but I wanted to act as normal as possible. As if I weren't about to unearth a murdered woman.

"Lucky guy," Sean said, eyeing me.

I shifted in my seat, scratching Thoreau behind his ears. "How do you know I'm meeting a man?"

He winked at me. "Don't ask."

Touché.

"Turn left at the next set of lights. It's a wonky turn—you need to get in the right lane."

"To turn left?"

"It's Massachusetts," I said. "The roads around here never make sense."

"Point taken."

There was a fierce breeze—the American flag at the Vietnam memorial was flapping so hard I could hear the reverberation from inside the car.

"Are you going to tell me what we're doing?" he asked, stealing a look at me.

For a second I was glad I'd taken time with my hair and my makeup. But then I remembered that I shouldn't be trying to impress Sean Donahue.

"You trust me, remember?" I didn't want to scare him away by telling him the truth right off the bat.

"I'm beginning to question my instincts."

He probably should.

Soon, he said, "I called Melissa Antonelli again today."

I tried to place the name, then remembered. Jennifer Thompson's older sister. "And?"

"A no-go. She wouldn't talk, either. Any idea why?" he asked me.

I shook my head, though I had two very good ideas. Elena and Rachel. "Turn left up here," I directed. "The park is at the end of the road."

At the bottom of the street in a residential working-class neighborhood, two metal gates closed off the park's lot. We parked in front of the gates, and everything darkened once Sean shut off his headlights. There was a small nature center off the parking lot, a picnic shelter, and a basketball court, its silhouetted hoops standing guard over the park. Beyond, a baseball field sat eerily quiet. There were no streetlights.

The wind rustled through the trees edging the wooded park from the lot, howling softly.

"It's gloomy down here," Sean said.

I shuddered. I was beyond glad Sean was with me or I knew I wouldn't be able to drag myself out of this car. "Yeah."

Sean leashed Thoreau and looked at me. "Should I bring the shovel?"

"Not yet. Just the flashlights. It's getting dark

quick." My ears stung from the chilly wind. I flipped up the collar on my trench coat. Sean stared at me.

"What?" I asked.

"You look . . . beautiful."

Heat flooded me, leaving wonderful tingling in its wake. "Um, thanks."

We walked through the empty parking lot to a paved pathway leading upward into the woods, Thoreau leading the way, tugging his leash, sniffing and marking to his heart's content.

I kicked at a stone. "Can I ask you something?"

"Sure."

"Who's Cara?"

His steps faltered. "How do you know—" He cut himself off. "The phone call in my office yesterday?"

I nodded. And waited.

"She's my . . ."

Just stick a knife in me and be done with it already. "What?"

"Ex-fiancée."

"If you don't mind me saying so, that wasn't a very ex-like conversation you were having last night. Grocery shopping implies intimacy."

He glanced at me, his gray eyes and dark lashes mesmerizing. "We've been going through a rough patch. On, off. Trying to see if we can make it work, and slowly realizing that whatever we had is gone. It's hard to admit we've both let go. We still share an apartment, but have separate bedrooms."

"Ah."

"I like you, Lucy. And meeting you has reinforced what I already knew—I have to cut the ties with Cara. For good. But like I said, it's hard. There's a lot of emotional baggage."

I liked him, too. Too much to tell him so. That could lead us to a place where I might not like myself in the morning. Especially if Cara still believed her relationship with Sean would work out.

My thighs burned as we crested a steep hill. No one was around. Just us, the wind, and my wishes for things that could never be. Because even if Cara weren't in the picture, I knew better than to get involved with him. "We missed the path."

"What path?"

"There's a dirt path with limestone steps." I'd been caught up in my conversation with Sean and hadn't been paying attention.

We stood on the paved path, along a ridgeline. Down to our right, the baseball field sat glumly silent, longing for little kids with baseball bats or a pickup game of Wiffle ball. Down on our left, the moon bounced off the Weymouth Back River. A beautiful image, but one I couldn't linger over.

I about-faced, but instead of heading back down the steep incline, I followed the pathway above where we came in, my flashlight aimed on the brush to my left. Soon, I spotted what I was looking for. A stone staircase leading back to the parking lot.

I led him down the stone steps, my heels catching every so often. About halfway down, I looked to my right. Thin-trunked trees dotted the hillside; a thick blanket of leaves covered the ground. I veered off the staircase and into the woods. About ten feet in, I stopped short.

"What?" Sean asked me.

"I'll stay here. Can you go get the shovel? You can follow the steps down into the parking lot."

As he stared at me long and hard, I could see the questions raging in his eyes.

"Please?" I added.

He handed me the leash, turned, and jogged carefully down the steps, disappearing into the inky night.

I knelt down, letting Thoreau lick and jump up on me. I wasn't a hugely religious person—my parents weren't the church type, but Dovie used to sneak me to services with her from time to time. It took me a good minute to remember one of the prayers. I said it low, quietly, forgetting words here and there. I was spooked to be disturbing the dead.

A minute later Sean was back, carrying a shovel, breathing hard. "What now?" he asked.

"We dig."

"Lucy, I think I need to know—"

"Trust, remember, Sean?"

He had this way of looking at me that made me feel he saw into my soul. I laid it bare for him.

"Okay," he finally said.

As I aimed the flashlight at the ground, I sat with Thoreau, quiet. The sound of shovel hitting earth echoed through the trees, mingling with the eerie howl of the wind.

After a foot or so, Sean asked, "How much farther?"

"I don't know."

Sean continued, his breathing labored.

"Are you okay?" I asked.

"Fine." Sweat beaded his brow. "Sometimes I get a little winded."

That didn't make sense—a former firefighter should be in great shape. Former. Oh. "From the accident?"

He didn't answer.

I didn't press.

Another few inches down, the shovel hit something solid. Sean pulled the shovel out. I flicked on a flashlight and shone it in the hole.

A chill went through me, cutting to the core. I started shivering.

A look of horror swept across his face as he stared at a length of human bone. "What is that?"

Through chattering teeth, I said, "The question should be 'Who is that?' And the answer is 'I don't know.'"

We were on our way back to the car, cutting through the parking lot, when our path crossed with an old man walking a tri-colored beagle. Sean and I tried not to make eye contact.

Sean dropped the shovel into the trunk and spread his arms wide. "What now? Should we rob a bank or something to make our day complete?"

Thoreau happily followed me to the passenger door. I lifted him up. "No need to be so sarcastic."

Sean ran a hand through his dark hair. "Forgive me, but I don't dig up dead people every day.

I'm not sure how I'm supposed to react." He held my door open for me. I sat, keeping Thoreau close to my chest.

As soon as Sean walked around the car and slid into his seat, I said, "I don't do this every day, either."

He didn't respond, but the skeptical look in his eyes said enough.

I took a deep breath, wishing I'd been of strong enough fortitude to have done this by myself. The inane thought of "next time" crossed my mind. Ha! There would be no next time. My job here was done. Well, almost. "Can you drive back to the Dunkin' Donuts on the corner?"

"You're hungry at a time like this?"

"I want to use the pay phone."

Pulling his cell from his pocket, he handed it over. "Here, use mine."

"No thanks. I don't want the trace."

His eyebrows jumped up, his gaze narrowing. Abruptly he looked away.

As he started the car, I prepared myself for a barrage of questions. To my surprise, Sean had none.

I supposed digging up a body could make a person speechless.

We'd stopped digging as soon as Sean hit bone. There was no reason to exhume the skeleton—just confirm there was in fact a body.

Sean pulled into the parking lot, angled his car near the pay phone. I jumped out. Using a tissue, I carefully picked up the receiver and dialed 911, making sure I left behind no fingerprints. My hands were cold and stiff.

The male operator sounded bored. "What's your emergency?"

"Hi, yeah, um, my boyfriend and I were just walking our dog at Great Esker and the dog broke free."

"We don't handle lost dogs," the dispatcher replied evenly. "I can connect you with Animal Control."

"No, no!" I said, trying to disguise my voice. "We have the dog."

"Then why are you calling? Is there an emergency?"

What defined an emergency in his book?

"Technically, no. But the dog, when it went into the woods, went crazy over a certain spot. My boyfriend, well, he had a shovel in his car and, well, he ran back to his car and got it and started digging, and about a foot down he hit a bone. A human bone," I added for good measure. "Someone's buried in Great Esker."

"How do you know the bone is human?"

What was with the trivia questions? "Medical school," I lied.

"What's your name, miss?" the operator asked a little more urgently.

I gave him directions to find the body. "There will be signs of fresh digging."

"Your name," he demanded.

I hung up and jumped into the car. "Go!" I said to Sean before the police tracked us to the pay phone.

Sean zipped out of the parking lot and turned south on 3A, headed back to the shipyard. I didn't know how I was going to make it through my date with Butch.

I'd *known* there was a body buried in that spot, but seeing . . . I shook my head. It was surreal seeing that bone.

Just over the Hingham Bay Bridge, Sean turned right, into a shopping plaza.

"Where are we going?" I asked, my heart thumping.

He backed into a well-lit parking space in front of Stop & Shop on the outskirts of the busy lot, shut off the engine, turned, and looked at me.

I tried not to shy away from his direct stare, but it was difficult. His piercing eyes were too much to bear. I stroked Thoreau's fur. "I need you to trust me. You said you would."

"Trust only goes so far, Lucy. You've got to trust me, as well. With the truth."

I closed my eyes. Did I dare? I had put him in a precarious position, but this secret had always stayed within my family.

Sean grabbed my hand. "Lucy—"

My head spun, visions coming deliciously slow, teasing. The two of us in my bed, skin to skin, Sean on top of me, kissing my cheeks, my lips, my neck, my breasts—

I yanked my hand away from his, and he cradled his close to his chest as if it had been burned.

"What the hell! That's the second time that's happened," he said, rubbing his palm.

"Wh-what?"

"I get zapped when I touch your hand." His gaze searched my face. "That's some static."

"Yeah. Static. I ran out of Downy," I said, dropping my head against the headrest. The dizziness was fading, but the sexy images were not

My body sizzled, begging for Sean to touch me more.

"Look at me, Lucy."

I couldn't. If I looked at him now, he'd read the desire in my eyes. He had a girlfriend. Kind of. Besides, there was Cupid's Curse to consider. There could never be anything between us. I shook my head.

"All right," he said, starting the car. "Just tell me one thing."

"What?"

"Did you have anything to do with that body being in the grave?"

Shock tamped down any lingering desire. I looked at him. "Are you crazy? No!"

He rolled out of the lot. "Okay. I'll let you keep your secrets for now, Lucy. But I will get to the bottom of all this. I'll figure out what's going on with you." He nudged my chin, so I'd look at him. "And between us."

ELEVEN

Heat warmed my hands, my face, my feet as I sat in my running car in the shipyard, frowning at the Hingham Bay Club. I was supposed to be having dinner with Butch in fifteen minutes.

I say "supposed" because I was considering standing him up.

Unfortunately, ingrained manners didn't allow me to seriously consider the thought.

But apprehension had me longing for alcohol.

Apprehension and what Sean and I had discovered.

It had been twenty minutes since he'd dropped me off at my car, then zoomed away.

I couldn't help that he was angry. I wanted to answer his questions, but I couldn't without putting my family's secrets at risk. Though I trusted him on some levels, how could I know for sure that he'd never tell anyone about my psychic abilities? That he wouldn't start questioning why my father was so successful? That he'd *believe*?

Leaving the safety of my car, I walked into the restaurant and headed for the bar. I was early;

there was little chance Butch was already here, lying in wait for me. I had plenty of time to wash down some anxiety.

I didn't do well with blind dates.

With dates at all.

"Something strong," I said to the bartender. Then I remembered I had to drive home. "But not too strong."

I slipped off my trench coat and made sure my wraparound dress stayed put when I sat, slipping my stiletto heel over the stool's rung. Above the bar the TV was tuned to the local news coverage of Little Boy Lost.

My drink, white wine, arrived and I took a grateful sip as I watched the TV, glad for the distraction from my thoughts. The TV showed John and Katherine O'Brien holding each other. Both wore that faraway look that cut to the heart of me. John O'Brien was a tall man, broad through the shoulders and hips, and looked like the type of guy you'd want to have around in an emergency. The strong type.

But the type to hurt his child?

I couldn't tell.

The camera cut back to the reporter. "Officials are now questioning whether Mr. O'Brien was under a doctor's care for his medical ailments. There's been no conclusive evidence Mr. O'Brien has a seizure disorder, but police are refusing to label him a suspect at this time. A source within the police department said that Mr. O'Brien has agreed to take a lie detector test and that possible charges may be filed. The test will be administered some time tomorrow. On a more disturbing note, the Hingham police have confirmed that a registered sexual predator has been living at the park's campground."

My stomach churned at this news. Max, Max, where are you?

My cell phone played a cheery version of "Jingle Bells" that didn't fit my mood. I took it and my wine to a far corner.

It was Marisol.

"Still no news from Em?" I asked her.

"No. And now I'm starting to get worried."

Out the window I watched as a commuter boat docked at the terminal. To my left, dozens of sailboats bobbed at the Hingham marina. Across a small strip of water on a thin peninsula, the Weymouthport condos stood proud and blocked the view of the vast waters beyond. Yellow squares of light dotted the complex's façade. "Maybe we should call the hospital, see if she's there."

"I did. She called in sick for today and tomorrow."

A knot formed in my stomach. "Did you check with her mother?"

"Just got off the phone with her. She hasn't heard from Em since yesterday afternoon. Said she sounded just fine, but thought it was odd Em hadn't checked in with her today."

"Have you talked to Joseph again?"

"Unfortunately. Em hasn't been home. Nothing is missing from the house. She's just gone. She has her handbag and her car. We can't go to the police yet—it's too soon."

I set my wine down. My stomach was

topsy-turvy and no amount of alcohol was going to settle it.

"I'm really worried," Marisol said.

"Me, too," I admitted.

"What do we do?"

"I don't know. Is there anything we can do?"

Out of the corner of my eye I saw a man walk in and glance around. He looked a lot like Matt Damon.

"Probably not," muttered Marisol. "But I don't like it."

"I think this is cause for me to cancel my date." I could skip out without Butch even noticing.

"No, don't do that. He's really a nice guy. I'm just—"

"Worried?"

"Yeah. I think I'll make a few more phone calls. I'll let you know if I turn up anything."

I hung up, took a deep breath, and headed back to the bar. It was times like these that I thought about cutting Dovie's branch off the family tree.

And putting it through a wood chipper.

"Hi," I said to the Matt Damon look-alike. "Are you—"

"Are you Lucy?" he asked at the same time.

I nodded. He smiled (he even had teeth like Matt Damon) and held out his hand. I took another deep breath and shook it. Images whirled, sending me to another place. One where I clearly saw a set of keys nestled in between couch cushions.

"Sorry I'm late," he said. "I couldn't find my keys. Needed to borrow my roommate's car."

Woozy, I sat on the stool. "Mine always fall between the cracks of my couch cushions. You might want to check there."

He looked at me oddly but said, "I will. Do you want to get a table?"

"Can we just sit here for a minute?"

Again the odd look. "Okay."

I ordered a ginger ale in hopes of settling my stomach, and he chose a Sam Adams. "Can I ask you something?"

"Sure."

"Is your name really Butch?"

He laughed. "No. It's—" He stopped, shook his blond head. "It's a long story."

Wearily, I said, "I have time."

"All in the interest of full disclosure?"

On his part, at least. No need to tell him that, though. "Sure."

"My first name is Hutchinson. Hutch to my family and friends. But," he went on, "I couldn't say my *h*'s when I was little and turned the *H* into a *B*."

"Hutchinson?" I asked.

"My parents owned a place on Hutchinson Island in Florida. It's where I was conceived."

"Ah," I said, rather wishing I hadn't asked. "Do you want me to call you Hutch or Butch?"

"Hutch is fine."

"Can I make Starsky jokes?"

"Maybe Butch would be better."

I laughed. It felt good. With one look I knew there was no romantic chemistry between us, but there were the makings of a good friendship.

"Are you really a butcher?" I asked.

He nodded. "For now."

I could relate. "Had many jobs?"

"Too many to count. Started out wanting to be a state trooper, but couldn't get through the academy. From there—"

Rudely I tuned him out as the flash of the TV caught my attention. A scroll at the bottom of the screen announced that John O'Brien would be taking a lie detector test the following day and that the police were questioning the sexual predator.

"I think it's great you went to help out last night," Butch said, following my gaze.

I sipped my ginger ale, feeling guilty. "Sorry I missed Dovie's dinner."

He grinned. "She has a way of strong-arming, doesn't she?"

"You could call it that. Was it awful?" This was good. This banter. Normal, even. I could almost forget about that bone. . . . I pushed the image aside. I'd found her. The police would do the rest. I could stop fretting. And get back to living a normal life without visions of corpses.

"Not at all. Dovie is a lot of fun, and your friend Marisol—"

He cut himself off, but not before I noticed the way his eyes lit when he said her name.

"She's nice," he finished lamely.

"That she is," I said, sorry that he didn't have a chance with her. They'd make a cute couple.

The image of Max O'Brien flashed on the screen. Next to it bullet points listed his height, weight, age. The reporter's voice-over described the clothes the little boy was wearing. The jeans, the long-sleeved blue T-shirt, and his father's Red Sox sweatshirt.

My glass slipped out of my hands.

Quickly I dabbed the bar top with napkins. "Did you hear that?" I asked Butch, wondering if I'd made up that last detail.

"What?" he asked, helping me swab.

"The little boy—he's wearing his father's sweatshirt?"

"I think that's what she said."

I signaled the bartender. "Have you had the TV on all day?"

"Yeah. No one will let me put it on ESPN," he grumped.

"Have you been listening to it?"

"Hard not to. Why?"

"The little boy who's lost—what's he wearing?"

He took a step back. "I dunno."

A woman two stools down tapped my shoulder. "Jeans, long-sleeved T-shirt, and his father's sweatshirt."

"His father's sweatshirt?"

She shrugged. "The police just disclosed that it was missing from the spot where the kid disappeared. Of course the media is hinting that the kid's buried in it somewhere."

Max was wearing his father's sweatshirt! This was the best news I'd heard in . . . forever.

I jumped up, grabbed my trench. "I've got to go, Butch."

"Now? So soon?"

"I'm sorry. Rain check, okay?"

I didn't give him time to answer. I dashed out of the restaurant and ran as fast as my heels would carry me to my car.

There was no time to waste.

I could help after all.
I could find Max.

By the time I reached command central, I was a nervous wreck.

My heart beat in triple time as I inched along the perimeter of the area in search of John O'Brien. I had to go through him—it was his sweatshirt.

I was a fish out of water, picking my way along the uneven ground in heels and a dress. Luckily, I still had my stocking cap in the car. It didn't quite go with my outfit, but I was more concerned with staying warm.

It also helped conceal my identity. There was no way anyone could tell I was blonde under the hat.

What was the proper way to go about this? I didn't know how to approach Max's dad. Or what to say to him. Or even if the police would let me near him. And I couldn't just shake his hand and hope to see the sweatshirt. Odds were he was fixated on finding his son, not the sweatshirt in particular. If I was going to be able to find it, he'd have be focused on the object.

If I went to the police first, how would I explain myself without giving away my abilities? And, in turn, my identity.

With my pulse thudding in my ears, I lurked, trying to look as though I fit in with the media personnel. Last night, my outfit would have blended right in with the roving reporters. But today everyone seemed to have switched to jeans and hiking boots as though they had been scouring the trails in search of the little boy themselves.

Adrenaline surged when John O'Brien exited the visitor center and headed toward the coffee tent. People cut him a wide swath.

And for the first time I had second thoughts.

What if I shook his hand and saw the body of his son? The son he had killed?

But what if I did nothing and the little boy was alive somewhere? Lost, lonely. Cold and hungry.

It was an easy decision, even if I had to put myself at risk to make it.

I moved forward, awkwardly, my heels catching on the grass. "Mr. O'Brien?" I said, cutting off his path.

He stopped, looked at me. "Yes?"

"Can I have a minute of your time?"

"Are you with the media?" he asked.

"No." My heart thudded in my ears.

"The police?"

"No."

"Then I'm sorry, I don't have time to—"

My voice caught. "I c-can find him."

John O'Brien's breath hitched. "That's not funny."

I looked him straight in the eye. "I'm not joking."

"What's your name?"

"I'd rather not say."

"You're wasting my time, miss." He dodged to his left, to walk away.

I cut him off again. "Am I? If your son is alive, I can find him. If you had nothing to do with his disappearance," I let the innuendo sink in, "then what do you have to lose? Nothing. And you've got everything to gain."

I didn't mention to him that I'd be able to see if little Max was dead, also. If John had killed his son, there was no need for me to become a target as well.

"How?" he asked.

"I'd rather not say."

He stepped in close. He was about two inches taller than me but looked much stronger. Pain and anger radiated from his eyes. It was much better than the faraway look that had been on the news. "If you're messing with me . . ." he threatened. "This isn't a game."

"Do you want to find him?" I asked, trying to keep my resolve. I couldn't help but feel I was in way over my head.

John O'Brien's voice broke. "More than anything."

"Go get a police officer. Any one will do. But only one. Do not tell him any details. Bring him to me, and you need to be here as well. I'll meet you by that tree," I said, pointing.

He took a hard look at me, blinked once, then sprinted toward the command center.

I hurried to the oak tree, partially hidden by the refreshment tent. The more privacy, the better.

Not a minute later, John O'Brien was back. "This is Detective Lieutenant Holliday with the Massachusetts State Police," he said.

"And who are you, ma'am?" Holliday asked me, a no-nonsense tone in his voice. He was older than me, probably by a good five or ten years, and stood about six feet, on the thin side. Probably a runner. His sandy blond hair was cut short. In the darkness, I couldn't make out the color of his eyes, just the penetrating way they looked at me. Sizing me up. He might've been cute if not for the annoying machismo radiating from his every pore.

"No names," I said.

"If you're interfering in this investigation," he began in that way only law enforcement could pull off.

I held up a hand. "Please, please let's skip the BS. I'm here to help. That's all that matters."

"Not if you've—"

"I'm here to help," I told the detective. "I don't have to be here, putting myself in this position. All I need is a minute. Okay?"

"I don't think—" Holliday began.

"Let her talk," John said, cutting him off. "What can it hurt?"

After a moment, the detective lieutenant gave a brief nod.

"Where is he?" John O'Brien asked. "Take me to him."

"It's not like that," I said, not sure how to explain.

"Maybe you should come with me, miss," Holliday said. The muscles of his jaw had clenched.

"Give me a minute." I looked at John. "Think about your sweatshirt."

"My sweatshirt?" he asked, dumbfounded. "Why in the hell—"

"Yes," I snapped. "Your sweatshirt. The one Max is wearing. The color, the size, any writing on it. Think about it. Now. Long and hard. Close your eyes and do it."

Holliday shifted foot to foot, clearly uncomfortable.

"Okay," John said. "What now?"

"Give me your hand."

"My hand?"

"Yes! And don't stop thinking about that sweatshirt."

The detective looked over his shoulder at the visitor center. Probably hoping for backup to help take down the crazy lady.

Reluctantly, John held out his right hand.

I swallowed hard, and reached out.

A cloud came over my vision as pictures flashed, images flying by. One by one, I took them all in. Frames of the boat ramp, of trees and trails and old stone bunkers. I zigzagged through the dark woods to a large oak tree, its trunk hollowed out. Inside, a little boy lay curled, wearing his father's sweatshirt.

My breath caught and my eyes fluttered open. John yanked his hand away.

Dizzy, I leaned against the tree. I'd seen enough.

I looked at the two men, who stared at me.

And I smiled. Big. So big my cheeks hurt. Tears stung my eyes. Just like the ones I'd seen in Max's eyes.

I could barely find my voice to whisper, "He's alive. Let me take you to him."

TWELVE

Detective Lieutenant Holliday had gone on guard. "I don't think that's wise. Why don't you tell me where he is? I'll go get him."

His tone had switched to an "I'm dealing with a nutcase" voice.

"I couldn't," I said. "The woods are too thick. I have to go by what's in my head."

"What are you?" John asked. "Psychic?"

I ignored the question. "He's alive. Maybe two, three miles from the boat ramp. In the hollow of a tree. He's crying," I added softly.

John grabbed me by my arms. "Show me!"

"Hold up!" Holliday said, pulling John from me. "Let me get some backup."

Panic set in. The fewer people who knew about me, the better. "No!"

"Why not?" Holliday asked.

"No more people. Please." I looked around. Two ATVs near the trailhead were being hovered over by a local cop. "Let's take those four-wheelers and go. Once we find Max, you can call for backup."

"I'm not comfortable with your plan."

"What about my wife?" John asked.

I couldn't give in now. "She'll see Max soon enough. I'm not comfortable with more people. We do it my way or I walk." It was a lame threat, one I'd never follow up on. Not with Max's life at stake.

"Jesus," John said. "Can we just go?"

"All right," Holliday conceded reluctantly.

Across the street, in the parking lot, Holliday waved off the local cop, and I climbed onto the ATV. It had been a couple of years since I'd ridden one on the dunes of a Plymouth beach.

John climbed onto the other one. Holliday stood looking at the two of us, obviously wondering who to ride with. After a minute, he climbed behind me and took a minute to figure out where to put his hands. He finally settled on gripping the seat.

I tucked my dress beneath my thighs and kicked off my heels. I'd rather be barefoot than get my heels caught.

I asked John to direct us to the boat ramp, since that's where my vision started. Weary-looking searchers stepped out of our way as we passed by. At the boat ramp, I took the lead. Soon enough we were deep in the woods, bumping over tree roots, squeezing through narrow paths, uprooting underbrush.

The headlights on the ATV cast an unnatural haze in the dark woods. Every once in a while the ghostly iridescent eyes of a nocturnal animal glowed at us from the brush.

I was grateful for the heat of Holliday's chest

against my back. Truth be told, I was freezing. I kept reminding myself that my discomfort was minimal in comparison to what Max had been going through.

I drove along, trying to follow the images in my head. The path seemed to narrow and I slowed.

"What is it?" Holliday shouted to be heard over the ATV's engine.

"I need a minute!" I yelled back.

"If this has been a wild-goose cha—"

"Shh!" I said, cutting him off.

Closing my eyes, I let the images wash over me. It was hard in the dark to pinpoint landmarks, but I knew instantly we'd gone too far. "We need to go back. We passed it."

"I thought you knew what you were doing," he said dryly.

"Shut up. Please." I went off-trail to turn the ATV around.

"What's going on?" John asked as we doubled back.

"We went too far!" I shouted.

I saw a look of disappointment cross over his face. Followed closely by doubt. He thought I'd led him out here on a whim, that I was some whack job messing with his head.

Before I dwelled, I motored off.

"Maybe I should drive," Holliday said, his voice rumbling against my ear.

"No."

"It wasn't a request! Pull over."

The beam of the headlamp shone on an old stump. I recognized it. Max wasn't far.

"In a minute," I said, over my shoulder.

Holliday's body tensed against mine. "Do it now. I'll use force if I have to. I don't want to hurt you, ma'am."

"Too late," I wanted to say. Why was I so sensitive to nonbelievers? Maybe it was wise my parents had always kept my gift a secret. From people who might label me a fake, a phony.

I drove another ten feet and angled the ATV across the path and got off.

John pulled up behind us.

"You've wasted our time," Holliday said. "What you did to this man was cruel beyond belief. You'll pay for this, mark my words."

I looked at him, tears in my eyes, and shook my head. Gooseflesh pimpled my arms, and a lump clogged my throat. My gaze went over his shoulder. "Mr. O'Brien?" I said.

"What?" Anger riddled that single word.

"I think your son is waiting for you." I motioned to where the headlights of the ATV lit the base of a hollowed-out oak tree about twenty feet from the trail. A little boy poked his head out of the tree, wide, scared eyes blinking against the bright light.

"Max!" John cried, stumbling into the brush, tripping in his haste to reach his son. "Oh my God, Max! It's Daddy!"

"Holy shit," Holliday said, reaching for his radio.

As he made his call, I watched the reunion between father and son. John O'Brien's sobbing nearly did me in, and I found I couldn't look anymore.

In the distance, a loud cheer echoed. Command central had just gotten the news. As waves of jubilation rolled through the darkness, tears welled in my eyes.

This.

This was what I'd been looking for most of my life. It made me feel, for once, that my life was worthwhile. That my gift had purpose.

Holliday alternately spoke into his radio and to Max. Eventually, Holliday looked over his shoulder at me. "Where the hell are we?"

Obviously, more emergency personnel were on their way. "I have no idea," I said honestly. "But I can probably get us back to the boat ramp."

He spoke into his radio again.

Max clung to his father's shoulder. Tear tracks streaked the boy's dirty face. I kept my distance, knowing intuitively there were some moments that just shouldn't be disrupted, though I wanted nothing more than to give Max a hug myself.

"Let's head back," Holliday said. He looked at me. "You can drive."

I had the feeling it was the closest thing to an apology I was going to get.

I thought of the woman buried in Great Esker and wondered if the police had exhumed her body yet.

Max's disappearance had a happy ending; hers would not.

I drove back slowly. The ATVs were loud, but not loud enough to drown out the cheers of the people gathered at the boat dock. Seemed like everyone in the park had gathered there.

As we neared, I veered off to the side and motioned for John to pull up next to me. "You go first," I said, nodding toward the opening at the end of the trail.

"Let's go see Mommy," John said to his little boy. Max clung to his father, his dirty little fists balled against John's back. The boy's eyes still held a lingering fear. I suspected it would be a long while before he let go—of his father, and the fear.

I waited a few beats, then followed. I'd like to say my letting them ahead was completely altruistic, but it wasn't. A diversion was needed if I was going to escape without trying to answer prying questions.

Just as I thought, chaos ensued as John and Max emerged into the clearing. I pulled the ATV off the path, on the fringe of the cheering crowd, and cut the engine. Holliday jumped off and offered me a hand. "I think I'll stay here!" I shouted to be heard. "My feet . . ."

They were a mess. Cut, bleeding, almost numb from the cold.

"Stay put," he said. "I'll find you a blanket and see if I can find your shoes."

"Aye, aye."

As soon as he blended into the crowd, I immediately started the ATV and skirted the throng, headed for the main camp. Once free of the celebration, I gunned the engine, driving as fast as I could.

The main gate area was completely deserted. I drove directly to my car, parked the ATV, and hopped off. My feet hurt like hell.

In my car, I pulled off my hat and turned the heat on full blast. I turned toward home. I was freezing, my feet were cut and bruised, and I was worried about having my identity discovered. Yet . . .

All I could do was smile.

I pushed open my front door and found Grendel standing there, yelling at me for being so late.

I listened for the creaking of Odysseus's wheel, but all was quiet. Grendel continued his tirade. I slipped off my trench coat and tried to placate him as I tenderly walked into the kitchen and turned on the light.

There was an empty bottle of wine on my counter. Obviously, Dovie had been here, probably lying in wait for me with another plan to set me up. I rinsed out the bottle and placed it in the recycling bin.

I opened and closed cabinets until I found something I wanted to eat (a Twinkie) and shook some of Grendel's kitty kibble into his dish. He ignored it, though he had to be hungry.

"Suit yourself," I said.

"For God's sake, could you be any louder?" a female voice called from my bedroom.

I dropped my Twinkie.

Grendel pounced on it.

"Em?" I called out tentatively.

She padded out of my bedroom, wearing a pair of my pajamas, her red hair pulled back in sloppy twin pigtails. Swaying a bit, she grabbed onto the kitchen counter.

Looking a lot like Pippi Longstocking on a bender, she said, "Do you always make so much noise?"

I didn't know whether to laugh or cry. She really was okay. Someone hadn't killed her and dumped her in the Charles River—a scenario my overactive imagination had created after Marisol's second phone call.

"What in the hell happened to you?" I asked. "You had us scared to death. And since when do you drink? I thought you stopped after what happened last time. Don't you remember the seal exhibit at the Aquarium?"

"Figured I was safe here." She hopped onto a stool and nearly slid off but caught herself before she landed on Grendel, who was in the process of dragging the Twinkie under the dining table.

"Safe from whom?"

"Myself," she muttered.

That was certainly a telling statement. It wasn't likely I'd get to the bottom of her binge tonight, so I let the comment go.

"How did you get here? I didn't see your car out front."

"Taxi. Here, kitty, kitty."

Grendel took a wide path around her.

I didn't need to ask how she got in—she had a key. We all did to each other's places.

I grabbed the cordless phone from the wall and called Marisol. She answered on the first ring, as though she'd been sleeping with the handset under her pillow.

"She's here," I said. "Drunk, but in one piece."

"I'm going to kill her," Marisol said. "Put her on."

I handed the phone to Em, who'd been waving it off. "Hi, Marisol," she said reluctantly, slurring her words.

I could hear the tone of Marisol's voice but

not the words. Her Latin temper was hard to keep under control.

After a minute of just listening, Em handed the phone back, slipped off the stool, and thudded back to my bedroom, swaying the whole way. I watched her go.

"Is she okay?" Marisol asked me.

"She looks all right, but something is obviously wrong."

I thought about putting coffee on and sobering her up but decided I'd let her be. Tomorrow would be soon enough to get answers from her.

"Should I come over?"

"Nah. No use. She needs to sleep it off, I think."

"All right. Call me in the morning, okay?"

"All right," I said, and hung up.

I foraged for another Twinkie and washed it down with a cup of milk.

My health-nut father would have a fit if he knew I ate this way.

It was late, past ten, but I took a minute to call Sean on his cell. I was surprised when he picked up—I'd intended to leave a voice message.

"It's Lucy," I said lamely.

"It's late," he countered.

I hopped up on my counter and tried not to look at my feet. They hurt, and the sight of blood turned my stomach. "I hope I'm not interrupting anything."

"Just doing surveillance."

"A stakeout? Is it as glamorous as it sounds?"

"Hardly. What's up?"

"I don't know. I just wanted to make sure

you're okay," I said, wondering if I had any Epsom salts to soak my feet in.

Or perhaps soaking them in hydrogen peroxide would be a better option. If I didn't give them a good cleaning I was bound to get an infection.

"I'm fine. Did you watch the news?"

"No." I'd been a little busy.

"The Weymouth police and state police from the Norfolk County DA's office are investigating skeletal remains found in the park. The reporter said an eyewitness placed a couple with a little dog at the scene. There was a vague description of us, but not much else."

I breathed deep. "Good."

"You okay? You sound tired."

"It's been a long day."

"Date didn't go so well?"

"It didn't go at all," I said.

"Good."

"Sean . . ."

"I know, I know," he said.

It was best to get off before thoughts of phone sex took over. I wished him a good night and hung up.

Gingerly, I walked into my bedroom and flipped on the light in the adjoining bathroom. It cast enough of a glow to illuminate my bedroom without being too harsh on Em's eyes.

She groaned and pulled a pillow over her head. I took stock. Her clothes were in a pile next to my bed, folded neatly. Lying curled in a ball in the corner of my bed, she looked comfortable. I hated to disturb her, but there was something I needed to know.

I sat down on the edge of the bed. "Em?"

"What?" she growled.

"Where's the hamster?"

She lifted the pillow from her face. "The rat is in the closet. Damn wheel made so much noise."

I smiled. She had such a way with words when she drank.

Lowering the pillow, she curled even tighter into a ball. "Good night," she mumbled.

For one of us, at least.

I rescued Odysseus from the closet, brought him into the kitchen, and fed him a couple of Cheerios. I offered some to Grendel, who refused until I dropped them on the floor so he could drag his "prey" away.

Glancing at the TV, I thought about turning on the news, watching the celebration of finding Max, but decided being there had been enough.

I finally dealt with my feet, cleaning the cuts and scrapes as best I could. I had to butterfly one particularly bad gash on my left foot. It probably needed stitches, but I figured Detective Lieutenant Holliday had probably spread word to hospitals to be on the lookout for a woman with foot injuries.

The irony of it all was that I had a doctor sleeping in my bed—but I refused to wake her up. Even if she were sober, I'd still let her sleep. In keeping with the Valentine family legacy of secrecy, I couldn't let anyone know I had been at Wompatuck tonight. I'd already risked a lot by going. I just had to hope no one would ever find out it was me.

With that thought, I finished cleaning up, changed into pajamas, and brought a pillow and blanket out to the couch. I was going to be getting up early and didn't want to disturb Em.

I shut off all the lights and crawled under my blankets, a smile still playing at my lips. Max was safe and sound. I'd found him.

Grendel hopped up on me and began kneading my stomach. Odysseus ran a marathon on his wheel. I tried to keep thoughts of the skeleton out of my head. Tonight was a night to bask in the glow of happiness.

As I drifted off to sleep, I couldn't help but agree with Em. That damn wheel did make so much noise.

THIRTEEN

Em was still out cold by the time I left the next morning. I knew she had called in sick, so I let her sleep in. Grendel had abandoned following me around as I got ready in favor of curling up with her.

His affection was easily swayed.

I retrieved Grendel's uneaten Twinkie from under the table, threw it away, and left a note for Em on the counter, asking her not to leave before we could talk. There was something going on with her, and I wanted to find out what it was, see if I could help; I'd be back in a couple of hours, planning only to work half a day. I wanted to check on Lola and follow up with Raphael to see if he'd made plans for a date.

My feet ached. I took two Advil and doctored my wounds as best I could, nearly using a whole tube of Neosporin in the process. I suppose I should be glad my toes hadn't been frostbitten, but it was hard to be grateful when every step I took hurt like hell.

I pulled a fresh pair of jeans from the dryer,

shimmied into them, and layered on a cami, a T-shirt, and a faux suede blazer Marisol had bought me for my birthday. Temperatures had dropped into the lower thirties and the heavy clouds on the horizon hinted at snow.

I drove to the commuter boat terminal, trying not to think about the night before. Today was a new day. I'd go to work, make a few matches, and hope no more clients would want to fire me.

Raphael was waiting for me at the Long Wharf Marriott. As I slid into my seat, he eyed me.

"Long night, Uva?"

"You could say that."

"Mmm-hmm."

There was no countering that.

He stopped to avoid hitting a jaywalker. "Were you limping?"

"Stubbed my toe this morning."

"Could be broken, want me to take a look?"

He'd bandaged almost every cut I'd had when I was little. "No. It'll be okay."

The radio was set to WEEI, a sports station. Callers were talking football, already boasting about the Patriots.

"Did you call Marcia last night?" I asked.

"I did."

"And?"

"She seems lovely."

Brake lights lined the street ahead of us. Pedestrians rushed by. Everyone in a hurry to be somewhere, the quicker the better. "Are you going out?"

"This weekend."

"You don't sound very happy about it," I said.

"Just nerves, Uva."

"You'll do fine!"

"It's been a long time."

"Just be yourself. She won't be able to resist."

We inched along with the traffic flow. The clouds hung low in the sky, and I wished it would snow. There was nothing more beautiful than the city covered in a blanket of white.

He adjusted the volume on the radio, turning it down. "Did you hear they found that little boy?" he asked casually.

Too casually.

"That's wonderful!" I said, carefully wording my response. "How? Where?"

"In the park where he went missing. A woman appeared out of nowhere, guiding the little boy's father and a police officer to where he was." He watched me closely out of the corner of his eye.

I swallowed hard.

15 times 3 is 45.

54 minus 6 is 48.

"How did she know where he was?" I asked, trying to sound curious.

"No one knows, Uva. The police want to talk to her. The parents want to thank her. The little boy says he'd never seen her before, so it seems she had nothing to do with his disappearance."

"Wow."

Raphael seemed intent to keep talking about Max.

"He'd been in the hollow of a tree trunk since realizing he was lost," Raphael said. "He remembered his parents told him to stay put if he ever became separated from them."

"Just like you always told me."

Smiling, he went on. "He'd heard voices calling for him but was too scared to talk to strangers."

"You always told me it was okay to talk to someone in a uniform. Do you remember the time I got lost in the art museum and couldn't figure out why the man in the uniform wouldn't help me?"

"I found you speaking to a wax replica of Paul Revere in full regalia. Yes, I recall. You were four. And a hellion."

"I was not!"

"Your memory, Uva. Not so good."

Rolling my eyes, I breathed in relief. I'd managed to change the subject away from Max O'Brien. I picked up the *Herald* lying folded in between the seat. The headline read: LITTLE BOY FOUND. I didn't read the story but did linger on the photos of Max and his parents. I flipped to the gossip page, my breath held, hoping Preston Bailey hadn't gotten her byline.

Several celebrities were in town, a socialite was out clubbing the night before, making a fool of herself, and there was a little paragraph about the King of Love, Oscar Valentine, taking his wounded heart out of town. Nothing about me—no pictures, no mention of me taking over the company. Nada. I was beyond glad. Maybe Preston Bailey had nothing on me at all.

My success at diverting Raphael's train of thought was short-lived. "They don't know where the woman is. Vanished after the boy was found. Supposedly she left behind her shoes."

Even as he said it, my feet ached at the memory. "Her shoes?"

"The detective is meeting with a sketch artist today to come up with a composite." He stopped at a red light and slid a knowing look my way. "Maybe someone will recognize her."

My stomach flipped. "That'd . . . that'd be good."

"Anything you want to tell me, Uva?"

It was obvious he knew it was me who'd found the little boy. Time to 'fess up. "You are superhuman, you know that? How'd you know it was me?"

"I suspected, but didn't know for sure until I saw you limping. Why didn't you tell me?"

"I don't know, Pasa. I guess I rather liked knowing I did this on my own. I wasn't ready to share it with anyone."

He nodded. "Understandable. But now tell me everything."

I laughed. And I did tell all—about finding Max. I didn't say a word about the skeleton. One revelation was enough for the day.

Raphael pulled up in front of Valentine, Inc. He leaned over, kissed my forehead. "I'm proud of you. You did good, Uva."

I smiled. "I know."

I asked him to meet me back here at eleven. That should give me enough time to get some files in order before heading home to talk to Em.

Preston Bailey was nowhere to be seen as I swiped my ID card. I climbed to the second-floor landing and paused, looking up.

Go up and say hi? Be strong and get to work?

The pull was irresistible.

I knocked on the third-floor door, calling out, "Sean?"

Cinnamon scented the air as he yelled, "Back here!"

His office door was open. I stopped dead in my tracks when I saw two official-looking men sitting in the chairs opposite Sean's desk.

"Honey, there you are. I was just telling these nice gentlemen all about you. Lucy, this is Detective Chapman and Detective Kolchowski of the Weymouth Police Department."

I tried to keep the surprise out of my voice. "Hello, Detectives. No need to get up," I said as they started to rise. The last thing I wanted to do was shake their hands. No telling what I'd see.

"Ms. . . ." One of the detectives—I didn't know which one—looked at his notebook. "Valentine, is it?"

"Yes?"

"We're here about the body you and your boyfriend found last night."

I glanced at Sean.

"Honey, I know you wanted to stay out of it, but a witness had my license plate number."

Again with the "honey." I took if for what it was meant—a hint that he had told the detectives we were a couple. Still, it twisted my heart into a confused knot.

"Why did you want to stay out of it, exactly, Ms. Valentine?" the bigger of the two detectives asked. He was thick—not fat—with keen eyes, thinning hair, and a chipped tooth on otherwise really nice teeth.

I stepped into the office. The chairs were all taken, and Sean offered me his. The seat was still warm. He sat on the edge of his desk.

"You may have heard of my father, Oscar Valentine," I said, making up an excuse on the spot.

"The matchmaker?" the other detective asked. This one was big, too, but his bulk tended toward fat. He wore rimless glasses, a long mustache, and a suit that had seen better days.

"Yes. He's had a bit of bad press lately. I didn't want to add any more stress to his weak heart. The gossip columnists would have a field day if they knew. So I wanted to keep it quiet. What did it matter who found the body?"

"Nothing," the one with glasses said, "if you had nothing to do with putting it there."

I opened my mouth, snapped it closed. It was probably best to say nothing at all, rather than be goaded into making rash comments.

The other detective tapped his notepad. "What breed of dog do you have?"

"A Yorkshire," Sean answered.

The mustachioed detective scribbled. "May I speak to you in the other room, Ms. Valentine?" he asked.

Rising, I said, "Sure."

They probably wanted to make sure Sean and I had the same story. I hoped he had stuck to the truth as much as possible.

"Could you run through the events of last night?" the detective asked, once we were settled in a conference room. He stood. I sat.

"Sure. Sean picked me up at the dock. We decided to go for a walk with Thoreau, the dog. Not long after we started walking, Thoreau broke free, dashed into the woods, and started barking. We tried to get him to come, but he wouldn't budge. Curious, Sean went and got a shovel from the car and started digging. When he hit a bone, we left and called the police."

"Does Mr. Donahue often keep a shovel in his trunk?"

I shrugged. "I don't often go looking in his trunk. We've only been dating a little while."

"Have you walked the dog at this park before?"

"No," I said.

"Why choose it?"

"A friend recommended it to me."

"Who?"

Shit! "Marisol Valerius." I'd have to call her ASAP.

"Do you find it odd that a dog would find a body buried so long?"

"How long has it been there?"

He hesitated, then didn't answer.

"Do you know a woman named Rachel Yurio?"

Rachel Yurio? A spark of memory lit a corner of my brain. Michael had mentioned her name to me the day we met. She'd been the sidekick of bad-girl Elena.

Rachel was the one in the grave? How? Why? And again, why did she have Michael's ring?

"I've heard of her," I said.

"How?"

"Through a client."

"Who?"

I hesitated.

"I can come back with a warrant, Ms. Valentine."

"Michael Lafferty."

"And how does he know her?"

"Old friends, I believe."

"Girlfriend, boyfriend?"

I shook my head. "I don't think so."

"How long has Mr. Lafferty been a client?"

"A couple of days."

"You've only known this man a couple of days, yet you and your private-eye boyfriend suddenly, *coincidentally*, dig up his dead girlfriend?"

It sounded horrible put that way. "They were just friends," I said lamely.

"How well do you know Michael Lafferty?"

I didn't like where this was headed. "He didn't have anything to do with her death," I stated.

The detective stared at me a long time. I let him.

Finally, he said, "And just how do you know that?"

How could I explain? I couldn't without revealing my abilities, and even then there was doubt the detective—or anyone—would believe me.

"I just—he's not the type."

Squinty-eyed, he scribbled in a notebook. "I think we're done for now. Is there a number I can reach you if I have more questions?"

I gave him my home number; then he walked me back to Sean's office. Dropping a business card on the desk, he said, "Don't leave town. Either of you."

Sean saw them out. I was sitting in his desk chair when he returned. "Charming, aren't they?"

"The body apparently belongs to Rachel Yurio," I said.

"Yeah. They found a purse with ID in the grave, and apparently she's been missing for years."

I toed the rug. "She's a friend of a client. Or she was."

Sean's shoulders stiffened. "A client? Who?"

I told him pretty much what I told the detective, including all Michael had told me about Elena Hart and Rachel tormenting Jennifer.

"And you just happened to know where this girl was buried?"

I said, "Strange coincidence, right?"

"Coincidence."

"Yeah."

He shook his head. Trying to evade his stare, I dialed Marisol at her clinic. She didn't answer her cell. I left a message.

"If any detectives come asking about me, you told me that Great Esker Park was a good place to walk a dog. And you might want to think about how you know the park. And you might want to erase this message, just in case."

I was going to face twenty questions when she listened to that voice mail.

"Lucy," Sean began.

I held up a hand. "I can't explain it."

"You're going to tell me how—"

I cut him off. "Maybe someday. For now I need more help."

"You've got some nerve, Lucy Valentine."

I knew.

"What did you need?"

"I need to hire you."

"For what?"

"I think I may have just implicated my client

as a murderer. I've got to fix this mess before my father gets back."

Before I caved under Sean's intense scrutiny, I hurried out of his office. Downstairs, I shoved open the door to Valentine, Inc., and found Dovie sitting at Suz's desk, a stack of files in front of her.

"No Suz?" I asked.

"She called and will be in later today."

"You're not matchmaking, are you?" I pointed at the files.

"Nah. Just looking to see if there are any good candidates for me."

I laughed. "I thought you'd sworn off men after Grandpa died."

"I swore off getting married—not men. It might be time to start taking dating seriously. I'm not getting any younger."

Not true—thanks to her plastic surgeon.

"First Raphael, now you. Seems like love is in the air."

She held up a few folders. "Want to have a look-see for yourself? I heard your date with Butch didn't go so well."

News traveled fast. "I had to leave. I took a rain check. But he's not my type, Dovie."

"And who is?"

Sean.

I avoided the question. "There's no point in dating at all. Not with our family's track record in the marriage department."

"Who said anything about marriage?" she asked. "It's okay to have a little fun once in a while. A little va-va-voom once in a while."

"I'll pass." I didn't think I could va-va-voom if I tried.

Bangle bracelets jangled harmoniously as she shook her arm at me. "I met a man the other day. He's perfect for you. I'll bring him by sometime."

There was no sense in arguing. I headed for my office. "Oh, and no eavesdropping today."

"Spoilsport."

I was stopped in my tracks by the image on TV. It was a split screen, one side showing a composite sketch of someone who looked remarkably like me and the other side showing a picture of the shoes I'd left behind in the woods.

I shut off the TV, hoping Dovie hadn't seen. "How about we listen to CDs today?"

"Fine, fine," she said, deep into reading a file.

Flipping on the stereo, I pushed the CD button. My father had five discs set to go. As soft jazz filled the office, I tried telling myself that the sketch didn't look that much like me. Just a little. Through the mouth mostly. And I'm sure hundreds of women owned heels like mine.

In my office, I sat behind my desk and pulled Michael Lafferty's phone number. I reached his answering machine at home. I hung up before leaving a message and tried him at work, an auto body shop near Weymouth's Jackson Square. Whoever answered told me Michael was busy and would have to call me back. I left my name and cell number and told him it was urgent.

I had to warn him before the police got to him.

Trying to bide my time, I pulled the file for Lola Fellows. Nervous, I dialed. She answered on the third ring, with a harried and terse, "Yes?"

"Hi, Lola, it's Lucy Valentine, just calling to check on you. Did you contact Adam?"

"I did."

"And?"

She sniffed. "I suggested we go to dinner."

I wanted to say, "Good for you," but thought it might sound condescending.

"And?"

"He declined."

My head dropped. "He did? Why?"

She cleared her throat. "He said something about my attitude."

Karma was a bitch.

"I was going to call you later," she said. "You have to talk to him. Get him to change his mind."

Leaning back in my chair, I said, "Why, Lola?"

"Because. What if he is my true love? We have to at least give it a try. Plus, I don't like that he thinks I'm a bitch. Yes, even though I am one." She sighed.

I couldn't help my smile. "I'll call him and give you a call back."

"Thank you," she said grudgingly.

I hung up and dialed the number I had for Adam. It took some doing, a lot of cajoling, and a little bit of guilt, but he finally agreed to meet Lola at Faneuil Hall for dinner the next night.

To my surprise, I found I was having fun running interference between the two.

Lola seemed relieved when I called her back with the news. Maybe there was hope for the pair after all.

I met with two more clients, both women and both of whom were new to the company. I had them fill out all the forms. I was determined to find them good matches. I could do it—I just had to believe I could do it, as Raphael advised.

Maybe matchmaking was inherently in my blood, even though I couldn't read auras. I was coming to believe anything was possible.

My cell phone rang. It was Michael Lafferty.

FOURTEEN

"Ms. Valentine? Did you find Jennifer?"

I spun in my chair, stared at the building across the alley. "Not quite yet." Clearing my throat, I said, "But I did find Rachel Yurio. She's dead, Michael, and has been for years."

Silence stretched. "What are you talking about? Rach? What does she have to do with anything? And what do you mean you found her? If she's been dead for years . . ."

"Have you been listening to the news? About the body found in Great Esker?"

"Yeah. Creeped me out. I walk Foo there all the time. You don't mean . . . Rachel?"

"Unfortunately, yes. And unfortunately, the police have linked me to you and you to Rachel."

"What are you saying?"

"I'm saying that because I found Rachel you're now a suspect in her death because you're my client."

"You're joking! I didn't have anything to do with her death."

"I know."

"How did all this happen? How did you find her? I'm lost."

"I can't explain it, Michael. I just wanted to warn you the police would probably be contacting you."

"Two guys, bad suits, one balding, one with glasses?"

"They're already there?"

"Yeah."

"Do you have a lawyer?"

"No. Jesus, do I need one?"

"My advice? Get one fast. And don't talk to the police without one."

"But I didn't do anything! I don't have anything to hide."

"I know. But you're now their focus, and they're not going to leave you alone until they hear what they want. Get the lawyer. I'll get you out of this mess, I promise. Give me time to sort it all out."

I hung up, dropped my head onto my desktop. I doubted anything like this had ever happened to my father. If the papers thought it shocking that my father had an affair, they'd go ballistic if / when they heard about this. How long did I have? Not long, I figured, before my name was plastered all over the newscasts as having been the one to find Rachel Yurio's body. It was necessary for Valentine, Inc., to go into full damage control mode. It was not good that Michael was being questioned. He had come to me to find him a mate—not send him to jail.

Talk about bad for business.

Don't panic, don't panic.

I dialed my mother's cell first. There was no

signal whatsoever, no voice mail. I called my father's cell next—again nothing. I knew they both had international calling, so either they didn't have service on the island or their phones were dead.

I had no idea what new hotel they were staying at, but I needed to get in touch with them. I was in over my head.

When I dialed Raphael's cell, he answered on the third ring. Pots and pans banged in the background.

"Where are you?" I asked.

"Downstairs."

Downstairs? "At the Porcupine?"

"Long story, Uva. I'm filling in for the head chef."

This was a story I had to hear.

"I can't talk now," he said.

"Real quick—do you know where my parents are staying in St. Lucia? The new place?"

"No, Uva. Is something wrong?"

"No, no," I lied. "I'll see you soon."

I hung up and dialed Sean's cell. "I need you," I said as he answered.

"I like the way that sounds."

Desire flared, hot and heady. I tried my best to tamp it down. "Your help," I clarified.

"Anything you need," he said, "I'm your man."

Closing my eyes, I tried not to think about us in bed. Breathe. "I, uh, need you to track down where my parents are staying in St. Lucia."

"I'll get back to you," he said after I gave him some basic information.

"Call my cell. I'm leaving for the day."

Taking a deep breath, I reminded myself that

the police were more than capable of solving this crime. I knew I wasn't guilty. And I knew Michael wasn't, either. I had to hope that the police would find the evidence to clear both our names and bring Rachel Yurio's killer to justice.

But as much as I wanted to stay completely out of the investigation, I couldn't. I'd promised Michael I'd try to find Jennifer, and it was the least I could do after what I'd done to him. But my number one goal wasn't matching him. It was clearing his name. And if Jennifer could answer a few questions about Rachel Yurio, too, then all the better, right?

Downstairs, I hobbled into the Porcupine. It was filling with the early lunch crowd. I was dying to hear how Raphael had ended up in Maggie's kitchen. The pair of them hadn't exactly gotten along yesterday.

I glanced around for Maggie but didn't see her. I stopped a server and asked for her.

"Out back," he said, gesturing toward the kitchen. "Be careful. Our head chef quit this morning. It's chaos back there."

I pushed through the swinging doors into the kitchen. I'd been warned. Six people hurried between long benches and stovetops, ovens, and fryolators, chopping, dicing, sautéing.

No Raphael. Or Maggie.

One of the sous chefs glanced at me. I grabbed the opportunity. "I'm looking for Raphael?"

"Freezer." He nodded with his chin to a doorway near the Sub-Zero refrigerator.

I passed through the door. To my right, long plastic flaps hung over the open door to the freezer. I glanced in. Raphael and Maggie were locked in a kiss so passionate, I was surprised the goods inside weren't melting.

My mouth dropped open and I backed away. Raphael and Maggie?

I hurried back through the door.

"Find him?" the sous chef asked.

I shook my head.

His brow wrinkled. "Really?"

"It's okay," I said. "Just when you see him, can you tell him that Lucy doesn't need a ride?"

"Yeah. Sure."

"Thanks."

I left, still bewildered. Never in a million years would I have matched Maggie and Raphael— yet there was obviously something between them.

Discouraged, I hailed a cab.

Maybe I wasn't cut out to be a matchmaker after all.

Em looked up from her spot on the couch as soon as I walked into the house. She set the book she was reading on her lap and made an attempt to sit up but looked to be in too much pain. Resting her head against the sofa pillow, she rolled to face me. Her sky blue eyes were puffy, but she'd wrestled her wild hair into a lovely braid.

"You're looking better," I said to her, setting my things down next to the door.

"Funny, because I feel worse."

"How much did you drink?"

"Too much. Thanks for letting me stay."

I sat in the chair opposite her. Grendel jumped into my lap. "You don't have to thank me. You're always welcome here."

"About that . . . Could I possibly stay here for a while?"

Grendel purred loudly. Odysseus was asleep in his cage, balled in a corner, nearly buried by pine chips. "Sure. How long are you thinking?"

"A week. Maybe two."

"Em, what's going on?"

"I don't want to talk about it."

"All right," I said, wishing she would. "You can stay as long as you'd like."

"I should just grow up and go home."

"It would help if I knew why you'd left. . . ."

"I really don't want to talk about it," she said, resting her forearm over her eyes.

This wasn't getting me anywhere. "Have you eaten?" I asked. "I can make an omelet."

"Not hungry."

"Okay." I was suddenly starving. I limped to the kitchen.

"Are you limping?" Em asked.

I gave her the same lame stubbed-toe excuse.

"You stubbed toes on both feet?"

Leave it to a doctor to realize both my feet were hurting.

"They're fine," I said.

She sat up. "What's going on?"

I pulled eggs, diced ham, and a green pepper from the fridge. An omelet was one of the few things I could make well. "I could ask you the same thing."

"I don't want to talk about it."

Tipping my head saucily, I smiled. "Neither do I."

"Not fair."

I cracked three eggs into a bowl. "I was thinking the same thing."

She pulled a pillow over her face.

A pad of butter sizzled in a small sauté pan. I added the green pepper and ham and stirred.

I was looking forward to getting my life back to normal. No more missing boys. No more visions of dead bodies. I simply had to stop touching Sean's hand and try my hardest to forget the images I'd seen of us in bed.

All I needed to do before normalcy could return was clear Michael's name. And to do that I had to figure out who had killed Rachel.

I laughed. No problem.

"What are you laughing at?" Em asked.

"Nothing."

I whisked the eggs with more force than needed, added a bit of water, and poured the mix into the pan with the pepper and ham. As I worked the edges of the omelet, my cell phone rang.

It was Butch.

"I just wanted to make sure you were okay," he said.

I had one guess as to who gave him my cell number. "I'm fine. Sorry about last night."

"Me, too. I was actually calling about that rain check."

A refusal perched on the tip of my tongue. I should say, "No thanks, we're better as friends," blah-blah, but I'd left him hanging twice already. And besides, he might be a good diversion from Sean.

Before I said anything, he added, "I was thinking we should double-date."

There was something in his tone that made me suspicious. I shook some grated cheddar cheese on top of the omelet and watched it bubble. "Oh?" I said.

"Yeah. I thought my roommate might want to meet your friend Marisol."

I couldn't help but smile. Sometimes men were so transparent. It had been obvious to me last night that Butch had liked Marisol. This was his way of seeing her again. Since I had the feeling she liked him as well, butcher or not, I agreed.

"Tonight?" he said. "Same time, same place?"

"I'll have to check with Marisol, but sure." Why not? It could be fun, even if he was using me to get to Marisol. I'd need to call her and ask if she was free for dinner.

We said our good-byes just as Em made her way to the kitchen island, pulling herself up onto a stool.

I flipped the omelet and shimmied it from the pan to a plate, where I cut it in half. I handed a plate to Em, and grabbed a fork for my half.

"I said I wasn't hungry," she said around a mouthful of omelet.

"I know."

"How long have we been friends?" she asked.

"Twenty-five years."

"We tell each other everything, right?"

I didn't want to answer that. "Do we?"

She frowned, poking fork holes in the omelet. "I guess not."

"I think that's okay." I grabbed some orange juice from the fridge.

"Is it? Aren't friends supposed to be closer than that?"

"I think everyone has secrets."

"Do you?" she asked, her blue eyes hopeful.

"Of course. Do you?"

"Yeah. But I wish I didn't."

I wished I didn't, too.

She took another bite. "Did you know that I never wanted to be a doctor?"

"What? No. You don't?"

"I wanted to be a kindergarten teacher. But my parents thought teaching five-year olds was beneath a Baumbach. 'Always the best for a Baumbach,'" she mimicked her mother's voice. Pain shone in her blue eyes. "I still want to be a kindergarten teacher. I've always envied the freedom you have, Lucy. Doing what you want, whenever you want."

I laughed. "I've always envied that you knew what you wanted. That you had goals. I felt like such a slacker next to you and Marisol."

Em's mouth dropped open. "Really?"

"It's true. Do you really want to be a teacher?"

"Yeah. But my parents . . ."

"What does Joseph say?"

"That he'll support me no matter what."

Points for Joseph. "It's not too late, Em. You can be a teacher if you want to be a teacher."

She rubbed a finger over the granite countertop, tracing a vein of gold. "It's not that easy. But I swear if I have to see one more child die . . ." Her voice caught.

I went around the counter and gave her a hug. "Listen," I whispered. "You can do what you want, Em. You'd make an amazing teacher. Your parents will come around."

She rested her head on my shoulder. "I just

need some time to work it out. Are you sure I
can stay here? I just need a little vacation from
my life for a while."

"For as long as you need."

"Thank you."

The phone rang as I wiped the tears from her
cheeks.

"If that's my mother, I'm not here," Em said,
sniffling. "I'm going to clean myself up."

As I picked up the phone, I watched her go.
"Hello."

"Ms. Valentine? This is Preston Bailey. I have
a couple of questions for you before tomorrow's
story goes to print."

Wonderful. I heaved a sigh. "I don't have anything to say to you, Ms. Bailey."

"I think you'll regret that decision."

I hung up on her, hoping I didn't.

FIFTEEN

Déjà vu.

I was once again sitting outside the Hingham Bay Club in need of alcohol.

To say I was a nervous wreck was an understatement.

Not because, like last night, I was due to meet Butch, but because of the five o'clock newscast I'd seen.

Most of the coverage had to do with Max and the mysterious woman who'd found him. There had been a taped piece with Detective Lieutenant Holliday holding a composite sketch of me.

There were no two ways around it.

I was a wanted woman.

How long? How long did I have before someone pieced together the information? Before someone recognized my picture?

Could I bluff my way through an interview? I certainly couldn't explain the condition of my feet, if they asked. Did they need a warrant for that?

Suddenly joining my parents in St. Lucia sounded like a fabulous plan.

Ironically, there had been a small sound bite on the news about the body found in Great Esker, believed to be that of Rachel Yurio, who'd gone missing five years ago. Little did the newscasters know the two stories had one similarity—me.

Thankfully, the media hadn't mentioned I was the one who found Rachel Yurio. Not yet at least.

Someone tapped at my window, and I nearly peed myself.

"What are you doing out here?" Marisol shouted.

I opened the car door. "Waiting for you."

"You could have waited inside," she said, kissing both my cheeks.

She looked incredibly beautiful, her short black bob shining in the moonlight. The scrap of skirt she wore showed her legs, but a high-necked top hid her ample cleavage. Stilettos finished the outfit.

Looked to me as though she was trying to impress someone.

Myself? I'd worn straight-legged black trousers, a black turtleneck, a thick silver chain Dovie had given me for Christmas, and black high-heeled boots that put me at just under six feet tall. And hid my feet, though the pain was just about intolerable.

"We should go in before you freeze," I suggested.

"Is that a comment on the size of my skirt?"

I laughed. "Yes."

"You're just jealous," she said.

"That must be it," I returned easily. "I'm glad you could make it out here tonight."

"You know I'm always willing to do a favor for my best friend."

A favor for me. Right. It had nothing to do with Butch and his likeness to Matt Damon.

We sat at the bar and I filled her in on what was going on with Em.

"I never thought she was one for medicine." Marisol signaled for the bartender and we ordered. "I'm surprised she lasted this long."

"I thought she made a great doctor." The TV, I noticed, was tuned to ESPN. Good. I didn't want to see a sketch of my face flashed on the screen all night.

"She doesn't have the heart for it. Too compassionate. Too empathetic."

"Aren't those good qualities to have for a doctor?"

She sipped her wine. "In moderation. If you give and give and give, then there's nothing left. And no way to deal with the heartbreak of the job."

"Em is staying with me for a while, to sort it all out."

"Do her parents know?"

"No. And she wants to keep it that way."

"Mrs. Baumbach isn't going to be happy."

Gillian Baumbach was just about the most controlling person I'd ever met. Sweet on the outside, steel on the inside. She had a say in just about everything Em did, including donating money for a new wing of the hospital where Em worked, to secure her a job.

If Em quit . . . There were going to be fireworks.

"I know."

"What was with your phone call today?" Marisol asked. "Detectives?"

"Long story," I said, wondering what on earth I was going to tell her.

"Let's get a table," Marisol said, hopping off her bar stool, eager to hear the details. It was all I could do to keep up with her as she followed the hostess.

"It was nice of Butch to think of me for this double date," Marisol said, skirting tables.

"Yes. Very selfless," I said, dryly.

She slid into a booth. "What's that supposed to mean?"

I sat opposite her. "He likes you. This whole night is a ruse so he can see you again."

Her brown eyes went wide. "No way."

"Yes, way."

"Do you really think so?"

"Why do I feel like I'm back in high school?"

"But he's a butcher!"

I shrugged. "Stranger things have happened." Just look at Lola Fellows and her "trashman."

"Now about those detectives?" Marisol asked.

"It'll have to wait. Here they come."

"How do I look?"

"Stunning as usual." It was nice to see her flustered for a change. Usually she was so calm, cool, collected. I almost wished my father were here, just to see if there was a chance in hell for Marisol and Butch, or if it was all part of a cruel dating game.

I looked up at Butch, smiled, and reintroduced him to Marisol. From my angle, I couldn't see the man standing behind him until he stepped forward to slide into the booth.

"Aiden, this is Lucy Valentine and Marisol Valerius. Did I say that right?" Butch asked her.

She blushed. "Perfectly."

I'd never known Marisol to blush. She must have it bad for Butch.

"Ladies, this is my roommate, Aiden Holliday."

My stomach dropped to my toes as I met the gaze of *Detective Lieutenant* Holliday. His eyes met mine, lingering. Recognition sparked just as Butch sat next to me, trapping me in the booth.

"Well, now," Aiden said. "If it isn't Cinderella."

Oh shit.

Shit, shit, shit.

"Do you two know each other?" Butch asked.

"Through work," I managed to say, my voice tight.

Marisol asked. "What do you do, Aiden?"

"He's with the state police," Butch said.

Aiden stared at me. "Working with the detective unit of the Plymouth County DA office."

Marisol's eyes grew wide as she glanced at me. "Is this the detective who might call me?"

I shook my head.

"There's more than one of us?" Holliday asked. "Interesting."

Shit.

"And what do you do, Lucy?" Butch asked. "I couldn't get a straight answer from your grandmother."

"I, ah—" The least amount of information I gave out, the better. Though, shit, Butch knew where I lived.

I wasn't going to escape so easily this time.

"She's a matchmaker," Marisol said proudly. "At Valentine, Inc."

"You're related to *the* Oscar Valentine?" Butch asked.

"Guilty," I said.

"Interesting choice of words," Holliday said.

Marisol leaned forward. "Did you do something wrong, Lucy?"

"And what was that Cinderella crack?" Butch asked.

I grabbed my purse and nudged Butch. "If you'll excuse me, I've got to go to the restroom."

Concerned eyebrows dipped. "Are you okay?"

"Yeah. Great. Wonderful."

"Do you want me to come with you?" Marisol asked.

"No, no! Stay there. I'll be right back."

I cringed at the pain in my feet and hobbled my way to the empty restroom. I wanted to pace, but there was no way. I leaned against the wall, wondering what to do.

I'd been caught, plain and simple. All that planning gone to waste. How was I to explain myself?

"This isn't funny!" I said aloud to the Fates. Because who else but the Fates would have orchestrated this? That Detective Lieutenant Holliday was Butch's roommate?

Cruel, cruel fates.

Leaning against the tiled wall, I knew I couldn't stay in here forever. But I wasn't ready to leave. I pulled my phone from my bag and noticed that I had two missed calls from Sean. Maybe he had information about my parents' whereabouts. Perfect timing, too, because I needed to talk to my mother.

I listened to Sean's voice mails. Both asked me to call him back as soon as possible. I dialed.

He picked up on the first ring. "You're a hard person to track down."

"If only that were true."

"What's that?"

"Nothing. Did you need me?"

Silence came over the line. Then I realized what I had said. Bad choice of words.

"I've been looking for you, yes. You're not home."

"No kidding. Are you there?"

"I was."

Hope bubbled up. "Are you still in my area?"

"Headed north on Three A."

Salvation! "Could I ask a huge, humongous, enormous favor?"

"Something other than digging up dead bodies?"

I didn't have time to get into that. "Yeah."

"What?"

"Could you pick me up?"

"Where are you?"

"Hingham Bay Club, in the Hingham Shipyard."

"I know of it," he said. "I would, but I'm going the other way from your place. I can't be late."

"Take me with you. I don't mind if you don't."

"What's going on?"

"I'm not sure you'd believe me if I told you."

"You always know how to pique my interest. I'll be there in five minutes."

"I'll be waiting outside."

I clicked my phone closed and drew in a deep breath. I just needed to sneak out without anyone seeing me.

Namely, Aiden Holliday.

Unfortunately, as soon as I opened the restroom door, the man I didn't want to see was waiting for me.

"I was beginning to doubt you were in there."

I tried to pull off a laugh. "You'd think I'd run?"

"You've done it before."

"True enough," I said.

A hint of softness entered his blue eyes. "How're your feet?"

"They hurt like hell."

"I can imagine. Tell me, how did the daughter of the world's most famous matchmaker find little Max O'Brien?"

I should have known Holliday wasn't one to beat around the bushes. "It's complicated."

"You're going to have to answer a few questions, Lucy."

"You know I didn't have anything to do with Max's disappearance."

"We'd like some answers. Only you can give them to us."

Why wouldn't he let this be? Why couldn't I catch a break? Why had I agreed to go out with Butch tonight in the first place?

Why?

"You make a lousy date, you know that?" I said.

He cracked a smile. "So you knew Butch wanted to be with Marisol all along?"

"He was a little obvious. She likes him. I just hope he has a chance with her."

"Okay, I'll bite. If she likes him, what's the problem?"

"He's a butcher. She's a die-hard vegetarian."

He laughed.

"What?"

"His family owns the market. Butch manages it and all their other stores. He likes to work in each department to keep a hand in the running of the place—he's not a butcher at all. I don't know if that will make a difference to Marisol."

It might. It might not. One never knew with Marisol.

I shifted my weight, wincing at the pain in my feet. "I think we've avoided the subject long enough, don't you?"

"I'm all out of small talk."

"I'm trying to figure out if I need a lawyer."

"You're not under arrest," he said.

"Said like a detective luring a suspect to the police station. Barracks. Headquarters. Whatever."

He smiled. It did wonders to his face, softening all the hard angles. "You seem like a nice person, Lucy. We just need to straighten all this out. We can do it the easy way. Or the hard way."

Marisol came around the corner. "Lucy? Are you okay?" She eyed Holliday.

"I'm fine. Hungry."

"The server is waiting to take our orders," she said.

We started walking back to the table. I stopped at the bar while Holliday and Marisol continued on. "I'm going to get something a little stronger than wine. I'll be right there."

I ordered a bourbon straight and slid a twenty across the bar. I waited until the good detective looked at his menu before I bolted for the door, my feet screaming in pain the whole way.

Sean was waiting. Thoreau, too. "What happened to being outside?"

I slunk down in my seat and the Yorkie bounded over, licking my face. "Can we talk about this later?"

As soon as we reached the main road, I sat up, buckled my seat belt, and took off my boots. I didn't dare peel off my trouser socks to see what further damage I'd inflicted. Sean might ask questions.

We slowed at a red light. "What are you running from, Lucy?" Sean asked.

I let out a breath. "Everything."

SIXTEEN

"I don't suppose you want to elaborate?" Sean asked.

"No. Did you find where my parents are staying?"

"Not yet. I've got a contact on the island tracking them down. I should know by morning."

I couldn't believe I'd run.

Like father, like daughter, I supposed.

Talking to the police was inevitable. But what would I tell them? Certainly not the truth. I needed time to concoct a story. A good one.

The car was comfortably warm. I snuggled into my seat, breathed deep. Sean's alluring scent hung in the air. A mix of something spicy, cinnamon maybe, and clean—Irish Spring, I guessed. He wore jeans, brown casual shoes, and a blazer over a blue button-down.

His hair was mussed, as if he'd been raking his fingers through it, his cheeks freshly shaven.

He looked good enough to eat.

Thoreau settled in my lap just as my phone rang.

"I still can't get over the Christmas song this time of year," Sean said.

I silenced "Jingle Bells" and sent a quick text to Marisol saying I was okay and would call her tomorrow with all the details.

Then I turned my phone off.

"Have you watched the news?" he asked as we crossed the Fore River Bridge.

"Yes."

"They've pegged Michael Lafferty as a person of interest."

"I knew they would. I told Michael to get a lawyer. Stall for time. We've got to clear his name. Did you have a chance to do any work on the case?"

"Some. You never did say how you found Rachel's body."

"No, I didn't say."

He passed a slow-moving T bus headed toward Quincy Center. "You're not going to tell me anything more?"

"No."

"Look, after all I've done, you owe me some answers. If the police think I'm somehow involved in this murder, all my work toward getting my own PI license is at risk, and so is Sam's, since I've been working off his license. I've gone above and beyond for you, Lucy."

"Yes, you have. And I'll make sure you're paid well for it. I should never have brought you into this mess. If I'd known . . ."

But I had known. And I'd asked him anyway. All my life I fought for independence, trying to prove I was capable. One little skeleton comes along and I go running for help.

I am woman—look at me run.

He slammed his hand against the steering wheel. "I don't want your money. I want answers."

Thoreau's head jerked up. I rubbed between his ears to settle him back down.

My heart twisted. I hated not being able to tell Sean. "I'm sorry."

"Not as much as I am."

"You can drop me at the Quincy Center T station. I'll take a bus home."

"I'm not going to let you do that this time of night."

"Then I'll take a taxi."

"Don't."

"Don't what?"

"Don't go," he said softly.

"Why not?"

He clenched the steering wheel. "I like your company."

I laughed. "I can tell."

Sheepishly, he glanced at me. "Please. Stay."

I was such a sucker. "Okay." We drove in silence.

He pulled into an empty bank lot near Milton Hospital and let the car idle, lights off. It was close to eight o'clock. A bright sliver of moon peeked through the clouds. The snow I thought would fall never had.

"What are we doing?"

"Surveillance."

"What are we surveilling?"

Smiling, he pointed across the street.

"Dominico's? I could go for some Italian."

"We're looking for John Roddrick Dominico.

J-Rod to his friends. I call him John Roddrick Dominico."

I laughed. It felt good. "What's he done?"

"He's a construction worker who claims to have been injured on the job."

"What did he hurt?"

"Back. He's been collecting workers' comp from his insurance company for over a year now."

"But?"

"His insurance company hired SD Investigations to make sure he really is injured. There," Sean said, "right on schedule."

I watched as a bulky young man came out of the restaurant carrying a pizza box in one hand, a two-liter in the other.

"Dinner break," Sean said. "Comes here every night for free food."

J-Rod got into an older-model Dodge and peeled out of the parking lot.

After a minute, Sean flipped on his lights and followed.

J-Rod cut through Quincy Center and picked up Route 3 near the Quincy Adams T station. We followed at a distance.

Soon we were exiting the highway somewhere in Norwood, winding through back roads.

"How long have you been watching him?"

"Going on three days."

"And you haven't gotten the goods on him yet?"

He smiled. "The goods?"

"Too *Law and Order*?"

"I think you're insulting the show."

Laughing, I said, "Okay, well, you know what I meant."

"I've got the goods," he said.

"Then why are you still following him?"

"Nail in the coffin."

"Coffin" reminded me of Rachel Yurio. I shuddered.

J-Rod pulled into the driveway of a two-story colonial in a small neighborhood. A large Dumpster sat at the curb, debris nearly spilling over its side. We sidled up to the curb in front of a neighbor's house about three doors down. As soon as J-Rod walked in the front door, Sean drove past the house, turned around, and parked diagonally from the house and turned off the car.

The moon's glimmer provided little light, just enough to see his features—which were tight and focused. He took out his camera, adjusted a lens, and took several pictures of the house, the car.

He dropped the camera in his lap and twisted his body to reach in the backseat, pulling forward several manila files. Moonlight shimmered in his gray eyes. "I apologize for earlier. I tried to strong-arm you into telling me what I wanted to hear. If my job is at risk, it's because I willingly put it there. Not because you did."

"That's not true."

"It is. I knew what I was getting myself into."

"Why *did* you agree to help me?" I wanted to know what had been in it for him.

"Honest?"

"Of course."

"I miss the adrenaline of being a firefighter. The excitement. I've been pushing papers for six months now. And doing routine surveillance. Sam won't let me do much else."

"That doesn't sound like Sam."

"He has some absurd notion that he's protecting me."

"From what?"

He ignored me. "I wanted the excitement, Lucy. A body in the woods . . . I'm a danger junkie, Lucy. Plus, you're gorgeous. Who wouldn't want to spend time with you? I'd have been an idiot to turn you down."

I wasn't sure where he was going with all this. "You've lost me."

"I don't want you thinking you're alone in all this. I'm not going anywhere. I want to see this case all the way through." He handed me the files.

"What are these?" I asked.

He aimed a pair of fancy binoculars at the house. "Everything I could find out about Rachel Yurio at the time of her disappearance, a file on Elena Hart, and one on Jennifer Thompson."

I flipped through the pages of Rachel's file, reading by moonlight. Rachel Yurio had been twenty-three when she disappeared. She'd been working as a waitress at a Quincy IHOP and living with Elena Hart in an East Weymouth apartment. Rachel had been fired from her job shortly before she disappeared.

Rachel had been raised by her grandmother and grandfather. He had passed away more than a decade ago, and Rachel's grandmother now resided in a retirement home in South Weymouth. There were no other living relatives.

Rachel had a police record—shoplifting (twice), writing bad checks, assault after a bar fight. There was a picture paper-clipped to the file.

"It's the best I could find. Her senior year at Weymouth High."

Sean had blown up the color yearbook photo of the young woman into a five-by-seven. It was grainy, the pixels stretched, but still easy to see Rachel had been beautiful—even beneath the heavy eyeliner and spiked black hair.

"What happened to her parents?" I asked.

"Don't know."

"Her eyes . . ."

"I know."

It was hard to tell what color they were. Maybe a dark blue. Or brown. But it wasn't the color that captured my attention. It was the sadness in their depths. A deep, dark sadness.

"I contacted the school and spoke to her old guidance counselor. She described Rachel as intelligent and well-spoken but sensitive, with poor self-esteem and no friends except Elena Hart. To say the counselor didn't have fond memories of Elena is an understatement. Elena cut class, used foul language, never did any work. She brought Rachel down to her level, and there was nothing the counselor could do about it. Rachel was so desperate to have a friend, she didn't care that the friend was getting her into trouble. Nothing could be done."

"What about Rachel's grandmother?"

Across the street, a light came on in the living room. The window was bare—no blinds or curtains. J-Rod was carrying a ladder.

Sean snapped a few pictures. "When I asked the counselor, she wouldn't say, but I got the impression that something's going on there."

"We need to talk to Rachel's grandmother, co-workers, any friends she may have had," I said.

Sean smiled. "We?"

"I mean, well, yeah."

He laughed. "Okay."

"There's no telling exactly when Rachel went missing," Sean said. "The police traced her last known movements to her working a shift at a Quincy IHOP at the end of October, a few months before she was officially reported missing. Her grandmother was finally the one who filed a missing persons report."

"Did Rachel have a landlord?"

"Yeah, but rent was automatically withdrawn from her bank account. It wasn't until she was reported missing that they found the apartment vacant."

"Vacant? What about Elena?" Where was her best friend? Why hadn't she filed a missing persons report?

"She's now Elena Delancey." Sean motioned to the file on my lap. I opened it.

Elena Hart had grown up in Weymouth, barely graduated. Her arrest record was an arm's length long. Fraud, trespassing, theft, assault, destruction of property. The list went on. She'd also worked at the same IHOP as Rachel and had been fired on the same day.

"She left Massachusetts about the time Rachel went missing," Sean said.

I arched an eyebrow. "Running?"

"Maybe so," he said. "Here's the good part. She moved to Rhode Island, went to college. Got a job as a social worker with a nonprofit kids' group, got married, and now has kids of her own."

"You're kidding."

"No. Completely turned her life around. Not so much as a speeding ticket."

"What caused such a drastic change?" I asked. Thoreau stirred. I petted him and he yawned, stretched, licked my hand, and went back to sleep.

"My best guess? Guilty conscience."

"Penance? For what? Killing Rachel?"

"Makes sense, doesn't it?"

It did. But could we prove it in order to clear Michael's name? That was the question. Well, that and why Rachel was wearing Michael's ring. I still couldn't figure out that one.

I absently flipped through Jennifer Thompson's report. There wasn't much in it I didn't already know, other than that she'd once had a restraining order against Elena Hart. Jennifer had essentially fallen off the map after graduation from Boston University. Gone. Poof. And her parents and sister weren't talking.

This didn't bode well for Michael's future with her.

Sean twisted again and pulled another file from his backseat. His eyes locked on mine. In the moonlight, they seemed grayer than normal. Bright and alluring. "How's your toe?" he asked, dropping the file on my lap.

Actually, my feet stung and ached, but I didn't want to complain. I opened the file and my breath caught as I looked at the composite sketch of myself that had been broadcast all over the Bay State.

My head dropped.

Sean reached over and nudged my chin so I'd look at him.

Breaking through my panic was the wonderful feel of his hand on my skin as his palm cupped my cheek. I leaned into it. There were no images when he touched my face, just delicious sensations I didn't want to end.

From beneath lowered lashes, I looked at him. It was powerful, the connection we had. An inexplicable pull dragged us together.

I leaned in. He met me halfway. Just as our lips were about to touch, the porch light of the house we were watching snapped on.

My heart pounded with disappointment. Sean fumbled for his camera.

J-Rod came out the front door, a roll of carpet slung across his shoulder. Sean snapped away as the man lifted the carpet and tossed it into the Dumpster. He wiped his hands on his jeans and headed back into the house.

"John Roddrick Dominico has been renovating houses for over eight months," Sean said.

"While still collecting workers' comp?"

"Yeah." He held up his camera. "I think I have enough proof to take to my client. You ready to go home?"

"Not really." Because I didn't know if the state police would be there waiting for me.

"No?" he asked, his eyes questioning.

I bit my lip as I looked at the sketch in my lap. If I wanted Sean's help, he needed to know the truth. It was time to take the leap.

I just hoped he wouldn't let me fall.

SEVENTEEN

One good thing about IHOP was that it stayed open late.

Another was that they served Belgian waffles.

Nothing made me feel better like Belgian waffles.

It wasn't a coincidence that we were here. This was the restaurant where Rachel and Elena had worked.

There were two men at a table in the back, but other than them and us, the place was deserted at nearly midnight. Thoreau was happily snoozing on a blanket in the car.

We'd just sat down when Sean's phone rang. He frowned at the ID screen and silenced the call.

"Cara?" I guessed.

"Yeah." He didn't sound too happy about it.

I didn't want to overtly pry, so I carefully unfolded my napkin, laid it on my lap, and bit my tongue.

A waitress shuffled up to the table and greeted us with menus, chatting about the crazy weather and the little boy who'd been found.

As if I needed a reminder.

Her name tag read: "Tess," and she shoved menus at us before swinging ample hips toward the other occupied table.

"Chatty," Sean said.

"Might work to our advantage."

"You sure you never worked as a PI?"

I smiled. "It's one of the few things I *haven't* done."

"True."

I scanned the menu, though I knew what I wanted. Then what he said hit me. "What do you mean, true? Did you do a background check on me?"

"Of course I did."

"That's not fair. Now you know everything about me and—"

"Hardly," he scoffed.

"And I know hardly nothing about you," I said, ignoring his comment.

"Seems fair to me."

I rolled my eyes.

Tess came back, and Sean and I both ordered waffles. After she brought our orders to the kitchen, she was back with two glasses of ice water. I looked up at her. "How long have you worked here, Tess?"

"Too damn long, darlin'.."

Sean slid a business card across the table. "We're investigating the death of Rachel Yurio. Did you know her?"

Tess made the sign of the cross.

I took that as a yes.

By the amount of wrinkles, I guessed Tess's age around seventy-five. It was hard to grasp

that she was as old as Dovie. They were different
as night and day, looks-wise. The difference between those who have and those who have not.

Tess's uniform clung to her many curves; loose
dyed red curls fell over her full face. She stood at
an angle, as though her back hurt. Thick ortho-
pedic shoes made no noise as she shifted foot to
foot, the eyeglasses hooked to a chain around
her neck swaying.

"Honey-pie," she said, openly admiring him,
"some people you just don't forget."

I smiled as he blushed. It was adorable.

"I was so sad to hear about her on the news.
What do you want to know?" Tess asked.

"Anything," I said. "How long did she work
here? Did she have any friends? Did she ever
talk about anyone? Did anyone not like her?"

"She was quiet, that one. Worked here about
two years. Her and Elena started about the same
time. She's the one you need to be talking to."

"Elena Hart?" Sean asked, pulling a small
notebook from his coat pocket.

"That's the one, honey-pie. She and Rachel
were best friends, roommates, thick as thieves,
those two, and had been since middle school;
leastways, that's how they told it. Well, they were
until . . ."

"Until what?" I asked.

"They had a huge falling-out. A doozy." Her
eyes took on a faraway look. "I remember clear
as day. Me and Rachel were working late. Elena
came storming in, fire in her eyes, looking for Rachel. They got into it so bad the manager called
the police."

"What was the fight about?"

"I'm not sure. All I remember was that Elena kept sayin', 'How could you? How could you?' Both of them were crying up a storm, slapping at each other. The manager fired both of them on the spot."

That had to have been the fight Michael told me about. The one where Elena had found out Rachel betrayed her by telling Michael the truth about the night he passed out.

"After they walked out the door that night, I never saw hide or hair of either again." Tess looked over her shoulder and said, "Be right back; your food's up."

When she came back Sean leaned in. "Tess, do you think Elena might have had something to do with Rachel's death? Gut feeling?"

She rocked back on her heels. "I've had myself a rough life. I've been through a lot, seen a lot more. But I ain't ever seen anyone as evil as Elena Hart. Now Rachel, she's a tough cookie, that one, but with a heart of gold. I never knew why they were friends."

As Tess walked away, I looked at my plate of food and realized I'd lost my appetite. What a waste of perfectly good waffles.

The men in the back finished their meal, dropped money on the table, and ambled out.

Sean poured syrup. "How about tomorrow we go see Rachel's grandmother and see if Elena will talk to us?"

"Sounds good," I said. "I also want to go see Jennifer's sister, Melissa. A face-to-face meeting might get us more information on why Jennifer has fallen off the radar."

I poked at my waffles as a long silence

stretched. I was lost in thoughts of Elena and Rachel and Michael Lafferty and Jennifer Thompson. And, of course, Sean. He knew I had found Max and was waiting for an explanation.

Sean pushed his food around his plate but must have been thinking along the same lines, because he said, "Are you going to tell me?"

Was I ready to tell?

Leaning back in my seat, I took a good, hard look at him. I didn't have the heart to keep pushing him away. And he had a stake in this now, too. He'd trusted me, and now it was time I returned the favor. I was going to tell him everything. About me, about Michael, the ring, and little Max. I wouldn't tell him about the auras—some secrets weren't mine to tell. Taking a deep breath, I said, "It started when I was fourteen. . . ."

"Who's the hottie?" Em asked from her spot on the couch as soon as I walked into the house at 2:00 A.M. She clicked off a rerun of *Frasier*.

"How do you know he's hot?"

"Dome light when he got out to give you a hug. Plus, he followed you home to make sure you arrived safe. That's a hottie in my book."

Sean followed me home after I picked my car up at the shipyard. It had been really sweet of him. Especially since I was nervous the state police would be at my door waiting for me. Thankfully, they weren't.

"So . . . who is he?"

"Sean Donahue, PI."

"What are you doing with a private investigator?"

"Not as much as I want," I said, flopping into the chair next to her.

Em sat up, drawing a blanket to her chin. Her eyes were completely clear—there had been no drinking tonight. "That sounds interesting!"

"I wish it were."

"Is he not interested? Is he blind? Stupid? Gay?"

"Just getting out of a relationship."

"Messy," she said.

I nodded. Plus, I had to deal with Cupid's Curse. It would be best if I could just keep my hands off Sean altogether. Nothing between us would—could—end well.

Grendel leapt into my lap, starting sniffing. His fur rose on end, and he gazed up at me as though I'd betrayed him. "Yes," I said to him. "I was with a dog. His name is Thoreau, and he's very cute." I scratched Grendel's ears. "But not as cute as you, and you could easily take him."

Seemingly placated, he sat down on my lap, rolling onto his back so I could rub his stomach.

"You're like the cat whisperer," Em said.

I laughed. "I just know what he likes to hear."

"What's with the PI?"

"Long story." From my bedroom, the sounds of Odysseus running on his wheel carried. "And it's late. How about I tell you in the morning?"

"Okay," Em said. She rose and gave me a hug. "I'm here if you want to talk."

I eyed her suspiciously. "You've been talking to Marisol."

"She's just worried about you. Something about detectives . . ."

My nerves leapt. "The tall blond one didn't show up here tonight, did he?"

Her eyes widened as she shook her head. "What have you gotten yourself into?"

"Tomorrow," I promised.

I checked the phone before I headed into my room. Ten new messages.

They could wait.

I brushed my teeth, washed my face, and climbed into bed.

By the time I cracked open my eyes at five thirty, I wasn't entirely convinced I'd ever fallen asleep.

Pulling the covers over my head, I wished I could stay in bed all day, forget everything going on in my life. But I couldn't hide—as much as I wanted to.

A minute later Em tiptoed into my room. I drew down the edge of my blanket, cracked open an eye.

"Did I wake you?" she asked, clutching a pile of clothes.

"No. What're you doing?"

"Showering. I'm working today. But I'm also going to turn in my two weeks' notice. If I haven't already gotten fired for my little sabbatical."

Suddenly Em's motives were clear. "You were trying to get fired."

"Well, yeah. I hoped it would be easier for my parents to accept that way. But I should have realized that their donations pretty much guaranteed my place on staff. I need to do this the right way, even if it's the hard way. I'm enrolled next semester at Boston College. Going to get my teaching degree."

She'd been busy yesterday. I smiled. "I'm proud of you."

"I'm proud of myself." She waved to the bathroom. "I'll call for a cab when I'm done in here."

"You don't need a cab. Take my car."

"You don't need it?"

"Not today." Sean had volunteered to do the driving. He was picking me up at nine.

"I'll take that offer," she said.

"What time do you have to work?"

"Seven to seven." She ducked into the bathroom. "But I still want to hear about everything going on with you. Dinner tonight?"

"Sure."

The pipes knocked in the wall as Em turned on the hot water. Grendel swatted my face playfully. I scratched under his chin as someone pounded on the front door.

My bedside clock glowed 5:48.

Who on earth?

I dislodged Grendel, who burrowed under the warm covers, and yelled, "Coming!" Which was followed closely by, "Ow, ow, ow," as I walked. My feet had gotten worse overnight. I looked down at them—swollen and bruised. I was going to have to let Em look at them.

More knocking. "Coming!"

I switched on the front light and pulled open the front door.

Detective Lieutenant Holliday smiled down at me, tapping a rolled newspaper on his palm. "Good morning, Lucy."

I groaned. "What, no crack about Sleeping Beauty?"

"I don't want to become predictable with the fairy tale references. Can I come in?"

I knew he'd come eventually. I hadn't suspected it would be so early. I held open the door and motioned to the couch. "Can you give me a minute to throw on a robe?"

"You're not going to run, are you?"

"With these feet?" I said, gesturing downward.

He whistled low. "You should have those looked at."

"I plan to. I'll be right back."

When I came out, I found him sitting in the chair next to the couch. "Is someone here with you?" he asked.

Em had already folded her blanket and tidied up the couch. "A friend is staying with me for a few days. She's in the shower—has to work today," I said lamely, rambling.

He was wearing loose-fitting jeans, running shoes, and an athletic pullover. Not what I'd considered cop-wear.

"Coffee?" I asked.

"Please."

In the kitchen, I poured some beans into the grinder. The smell of fresh coffee filled the air. As I worked, I could feel his gaze on me. For once I wished my kitchen didn't open into the living room. He was making me uneasy. "Cream? Sugar?"

"Black."

A few minutes later, I brought him a mug. I sat on the couch.

He took a sip. "It's good. Thanks."

"You're welcome." His blond hair was disheveled—bed head—and dark circles marred the skin around his blue eyes. "Are you here on official business?"

"Technically, no."

"Then why are you?"

The bathroom door creaked open and Em came out, dripping wet, wrapped in a towel. "Is that coffee I smell?" She froze when she spotted Holliday. Her gaze darted to mine.

"Em, this is Detective Lieutenant Aiden Holliday." To him, I said, "And this is Emerson Baumbach."

"Uh, hi," she said, slowly backtracking to the bedroom.

The detective smiled, his eyes glued to her. "Pleasure."

"I'll just, um, be, ah, right back." Droplets of water flew as she spun around.

Even after she'd left, his gaze remained fixed on the doorway. He blinked slowly, as if he were questioning whether Em had been real.

I decided to burst his bubble. "Em's staying with me for a few days—she needed a break in between planning her wedding and working nonstop."

"Wedding?" he asked, finally turning to look at me.

"On Valentine's Day."

"How sweet," he said, sounding as if it was anything but.

"Why are you here again? It's early, you know."

"I'm here because contrary to what you may believe, I'm not a jerk."

Coffee burned the back of my throat. "I never said you were a jerk."

"You thought it."

I smiled into my mug. "Once or twice."

"I suppose I deserved it, but you have to admit, you came across as a crazy loon."

"Is that professional cop-speak?"

He laughed. "Yes."

I leaned forward. "What made you change your opinion?"

"First, you found Max. Second, I met you."

"Third?"

His face crumbled into a frown. "Let's just say I feel as though it's my turn to help you."

"What do you mean?"

He unfolded the paper he'd been holding—the morning's *Herald*. The headline filled the whole left side of the page.

MATCHMAKER'S PSYCHIC DAUGHTER FINDS
LITTLE BOY

On the left side, there was a picture of me in my wraparound dress and heels, with an inset showing they were the same heels found at Wompatuck State Park.

Preston Bailey had gotten her byline.

EIGHTEEN

Somehow I managed not to drop my coffee. I slowly set it on the table and picked up the paper. Preston Bailey had written the whole article with little to go on but assumptions and circumstantial evidence.

She had, in fact, overheard my conversation with Raphael at the Porcupine—she'd referenced what she heard in the article, with my words about having a vision in quotes.

Once the composite of the person who'd found Max came out, she'd put two and two together, using the snapshots of me leaving work as further proof.

The way the article was written cast doubt on whether my abilities were real while also hailing me as some kind of hero. The juxtaposition was confusing to say the least.

"You could have told me you were psychic. I've worked with people like you before. It would have saved a lot of trouble."

People like you. As if I were some kind of mutant. I dropped my head into my hands, stared at the words in the article, the print blurring. "The point was no one was supposed to know I found Max. I didn't want people to know it was me."

Turmoil churned in my stomach.

"I figured that out on my own, Cinderella. That's why I'm here. I came as soon as I saw the headline to warn you. Why not just acknowledge you found him?"

I wrapped my arms around my stomach, trying to hold the pain at bay. "Not many people know I have psychic abilities."

"Why? Why not tell? Think of all the good you could do. You found Max."

I jumped up, paced, trying not to wince at the pain in my feet. "It's not that easy! I wish it were; really I do. The reasons are complicated. And contrary to what this article leads people to believe, I don't have random visions. My gift is very specific."

"How so?"

"I can only find lost objects. Inanimate objects. Not people. Not pets. And there are rules," I fairly cried. "The object has to belong to the person who lost it, and only that person can ask me to find it."

He set down his coffee. "But you found Max—"

"No. I found his father's sweatshirt."

"Ah. That's why you asked John O'Brien to think about his shirt."

"Exactly. I feel the objects' energy through people's palms. I can't explain it. I don't know why it happens. It just is. I hate shaking hands, because I don't ever know what I'm going to see.

Like the other night when I met Butch and saw his car keys in his couch."

"Wow."

Tears welled in my eyes. The phone rang. I answered without thinking. It was a reporter from the *Globe* wanting a comment.

"I have none," I said, hanging up.

Not a second later, the phone rang again. I disconnected it from the wall; no doubt about it, I'd need a new phone number.

"Lucy?" Em came out from the bedroom dressed in a light blue sweater and gray trousers. Her hair had been towel-dried and her curls left loose and wild. Her blue eyes widened when she took a good look at me. "What's wrong?"

What could I say? Do? Em had known me for almost my whole life and I'd kept this from her. Would she ever forgive me? Would Marisol?

"I don't know where to begin," I said softly, my emotions thickening my words.

She turned on Holliday. "Does this have to do with you?"

"No, Em. It's not him. It's me. I . . . I'm—"

"What?" she asked.

Holliday rose. "Here," he said, handing her the paper.

Em sank onto the couch.

"The media are gathering at the bottom of the drive," Holliday said, peeking out the window. "And there's an older woman running across the lawn from the main house."

A second later, the front door flew open. Dovie rushed in, arms wide. I went into them willingly.

"There, there," she said, stroking my hair. "It'll be okay. We'll get through it."

"Mom and Dad are going to have a fit."

"Let them," Dovie said.

Em finally looked up from the paper. "Is this true, Lucy?"

"A lot of it is hogwash," Dovie said, letting me go.

"But most of it is true," I said. Once again I went through what had happened when I was fourteen, how I could only find lost objects. By the time I was done, I was sick of hearing myself talk. "Are you mad at me?" I asked Em, my heart in my throat.

"Mad? No!" Em said, hugging me. "How could I be?"

"I never told you. Or Marisol."

"Or anyone," Dovie added, scooping up Grendel, who finally had decided to leave the warmth of the bed to see what the ruckus was about.

"Oh, Lucy. Didn't we just talk about this yesterday? We all have secrets. Yours, though, is a cool one. I always wondered how you knew where I left my driver's license that one time. . . ."

I was so relieved I couldn't speak.

"I warned the reporters not to trespass or they'll be charged," Dovie said. "But I don't think they're going anywhere any time soon. I've called the Cohasset police—perhaps they can do some crowd control."

Em looked out the window. "There's a car coming up the drive."

Two doors slammed in tandem. I looked out and groaned. Could this day get any worse?

* * *

I plastered myself against the door. "We are not opening this door."

"Who is it?" Dovie asked.

"No one I want to talk to."

One of the Weymouth detectives pounded on the front door, the knock vibrating against my back.

"Do you want me to get rid of them?" Holliday asked.

"More than anything," I whispered.

"Ms. Valentine," one of them shouted, "it's Detective Kolchowski. We'd like to speak with you."

"A detective?" Holliday glanced out the window. "With which department?"

"Weymouth," I answered, my back vibrating again with the force of the detective's knock.

"What do they want with you?" Dovie asked.

"It might have something to do with a dead body I found."

"What!" Em screeched.

"We know you're in there, Ms. Valentine! Let us in or we'll come back with a warrant."

I reluctantly pulled open the door. The two men stood on my wraparound porch, peering into my living room. "Are we interrupting?" the detective with glasses asked.

"If I said yes, would you go away?"

"No."

"Then come on in."

"I'll be right back," Em said, grabbing her purse and heading toward my bedroom. "I have to make a phone call."

"Detectives, this is my grandmother, Dovie

Valentine, and this is Detective Lieutenant Holliday, Massachusetts State Police."

"Plymouth County," he said.

"A little out of your jurisdiction," the tall one said.

"I'm not here on business," Holliday said tightly. "What's this about a dead body? You working with the Norfolk County detectives?"

The Norfolk County State Police detectives. Weymouth, like Cohasset, was situated in Norfolk County, while Hingham, sandwiched in the middle, was in Plymouth County. Massachusetts was known for roads and boundaries that didn't make any sense—it extended to counties as well.

"Yeah. I'm Curt Kolchowski," the balding one with the chipped tooth said.

"I'm Patrick Chapman." The chubby one with the mustache and glasses shifted his weight.

"I'm sure you're here about the *Herald* article, Detectives."

"We saw it. But we've been trying to reach you since yesterday. Didn't you get our messages?"

"No," I said truthfully.

"What is this about?" Holliday asked.

"She didn't tell you?" Kolchowski raised his eyebrows.

"Tell me what?"

"She and her boyfriend dug up a body in Great Esker."

"That was you?" he asked.

I sank into the couch. My feet were killing me. I put them up on the table. Grendel hopped in my lap.

"Boyfriend?" Dovie asked hopefully.

Yes. Yes, this day could, in fact, get worse.

"Seems awfully coincidental you're suddenly psychic after becoming a person of interest in a murder case."

"A person of interest! I found the body, if you haven't forgotten. I didn't put it there."

"Is it just coincidence you found your client's dead ex-girlfriend?"

"Client?" Dovie squeaked.

"Michael Lafferty," I said to her. "And Rachel wasn't his girlfriend."

"What is this, Lucy?"

I closed my eyes. "Here's what happened." I told them the whole story, from when Michael walked into my office to when I shook his hand and saw the vision of the ring. And of how that led me to do a little digging in Great Esker.

"Convenient," Chapman said.

"What are you implying?" Dovie demanded.

"I'm implying you're a phony, Ms. Valentine," he said to me.

I gritted my teeth, sat up. "Have you two ever lost anything?"

"What?"

"Have you ever lost anything? Keys, wallet, et cetera?"

"Yeah," Chapman said hesitantly.

"Think about that object. Don't tell me what it is. Just think about it. Are you thinking?"

"I don't see what this has to do—"

I grabbed his hand. It was as big as a catcher's mitt and just as leathery. Images whirled through my head, a tornado of information. Pulling my hand away, I looked at him. "Your wedding ring."

I tsked. "I'm not sure where you lost it, but it's currently in a pawnshop in Southie."

His mouth tightened.

"You?" I said to Kolchowski.

He held out his hand. After a dizzying second, I shook my head clear. "The item you lost is a shirt. Looks to be an old Aerosmith concert shirt, but it's seen better days. It looks like someone hacked at it with a pair of scissors."

"I knew she did something to it! Where is it?"

"In a black garbage bag with dozens of ripped-up baseball cards in the Holbrook landfill."

"Son of a bitch!" he mumbled. "I didn't know about the baseball cards. Man, that hurts."

"Phony, my ass," Dovie said.

The two detectives stared at me as if not quite believing, but believing just the same.

"Michael can't be guilty. He didn't know where the ring was." I gave them a second to process. "He's innocent. You see that, right? You only went after him because of me—because he was my client. But now you know how I found Rachel's body."

Chapman shook his head as if trying to sort it all out. "If you two don't mind," he said to Dovie and Holliday, "we'd like to ask Ms. Valentine some questions in private."

"No," Dovie said.

"I'm sorry, ma'am, but it's not up to you."

"Lucy," Em said, coming from the bedroom, "Marshall says not to say another word. Oh my God! What happened to your feet?" She crouched down and looked at my wounds. "Holy shit, you did a number on them."

"Detectives, it's time for you to leave," Dovie said, in full protective mode.

"Who's Marshall?" Kolchowski asked, not budging.

Marshall was suddenly my savior. He was also Joseph's father, Em's future father-in-law. And one of the best attorneys in the city.

"Marshall Betancourt," Em answered. "Lucy's lawyer. If you want to speak with Lucy, you'll need to go through him first. Here's his number." She handed Kolchowski a scrap of paper.

It didn't escape my attention the way Holliday looked at her, impressed.

"You sure that's the route you want to go?" Kolchowski asked me.

"Yes," I said. It was obvious they didn't want to release Michael as a suspect. Maybe because he was the only one they had. Had they tried to find Elena at all?

Dovie marched to the door, held it open. "Good day, Detectives."

As the two detectives walked toward the door, Chapman looked back at Holliday. It wasn't a friendly look that passed between them.

As soon as the door closed, Holliday said, "I don't think I'll be getting a Christmas card from them."

"Will they cause trouble for you, Lieutenant?" I asked.

"Please call me Aiden. And nothing I can't handle."

Em rooted around her bag and came up with a prescription pad. "You need antibiotics, Lucy." She looked at her watch. "I can go get them."

I glanced at the clock. "You're going to be late for work."

"I'll go," Dovie said, taking the prescription.

"Could you get some fresh bandages and some Polysporin, too? Lucy, stay off your feet today. Doctor's orders." Em gathered up her things.

I fished through my bag, tossed her my car keys. "Thanks, Em, for everything. I'll see you tonight."

"I'm going to go, too." Aiden strode to the door. "I'll run interference for you at the street," he said to Em.

She gazed up at him and smiled. "Thanks."

"I'm going to let you rest today, Cinderella, but I'll need to take a statement from you," Aiden said. "If you want to have your lawyer with you, that's fine, but it's mostly just tying up loose ends. I don't know what's going on with this other case—and honestly, I don't want to—but I suggest you listen to your lawyer. And stay out of the detectives' way. They're gunning for you."

As Em drove off, Dovie waved, then closed the door. She looked at me expectantly and smiled. "What boyfriend?" she asked. "Details!"

NINETEEN

It was a day of firsts.

It was the first time I'd "lawyered up."

The first time I'd been outed as a psychic.

My first time riding in the trunk of a car.

Fortunately, I was way past the age of losing my virginity—good thing, too, since Sean was in close proximity. He was just the kind of boy Raphael had warned me about.

Slivers of light cut through the darkness of the trunk. My legs were bent to my chest, and I rested my head on an old musty blanket. Every time the car bounced over a dip in the road, pain radiated from my spine and I sucked in gasping breaths traced with mold spores. It had been just five minutes since the trunk had closed, and already my heart raced, my palms dampened.

To say I wasn't a happy camper would be a complete understatement.

"Three times three is nine," I said, trying to distract myself.

Sneaking away in the trunk of Sean's car had seemed like a great idea ten minutes ago.

Until I realized I might be the slightest bit claustrophobic. Who knew? It wasn't as though I was trapped in trunks every day.

"The square root of one-forty-four is twelve."

"Are you talking to yourself?" Sean shouted.

"How much longer?" I yelled back.

The car slowed, then stopped. A second later, the trunk popped and Sean was there, holding out his hand. "You don't look so well."

I looked at his palm. No way. My heart was already palpitating—it would probably go into complete arrest if I saw more images of Sean and me in bed together. "Don't want to zap you," I said, hauling myself out.

Sean had parked in the empty lot at Sandy Beach. The dark gray whitecapped ocean stretched out before us as far as eye could see. Hungry seagulls squawked overhead, circling beneath ominous storm clouds. The sharp briny smell of low tide stung my nose as angry waves slapped at the rocky shore.

"You okay?"

"Nothing a little fresh air won't cure." I took in deep lungfuls. The crisp breeze cooled me off. My heartbeat settled into a steady rhythm.

The wind ruffled his dark hair, raising the short strands on end. "You should have told me you were claustrophobic. We'd have come up with another plan."

"I didn't know." I stretched my legs, working out the kinks, while inhaling deeply. Rain hung in the crisp autumn air. A strong gust of wind took hold of my ponytail, thrashing it against my face. "We should go."

"You sure you're ready?" Sean looked completely comfortable in a pair of jeans, sneakers, and a button-down striped blue and white shirt, the sleeves rolled up to his elbows. In this light, his eyes were the same color as the churning ocean.

Shells crunched beneath my sneakers as I walked tenderly toward the car door. "I'm good."

As long as I didn't walk, I was just fine. I had one dose of antibiotic and two Extra Strength Advils in me. Hopefully enough to get me through the day.

As I buckled my seat belt, I said, "I'm sorry about Dovie earlier."

"What was with that?"

"When the detectives came, they mentioned you were my boyfriend. She was sizing you up to see if it was true, because she didn't believe me when I said you were."

His head snapped to look at me. "You what?"

"The road! The road!"

Jerking the wheel hard left, he swerved back into his lane. He'd just barely missed a telephone pole.

So much for my steady heartbeat.

"Does being my boyfriend panic you so much you want to run us off the road?" I teased.

"I just, I mean—"

"You should see your face." Panic furrowed his brow; apprehension darkened his eyes. The sharp sting of rejection pinched my chest. It was ridiculous to feel that way. I knew—knew!—we couldn't be together. I had issues. He had issues. Then there was the whole Curse thing to deal with. But still, his reaction smarted.

"Did you really tell her that?" he asked.

"Yes, I did."

"But Lucy . . ."

My heart fluttered at the way he said my name. I tried to pass it off as having drunk too much coffee that morning. "Yes, I lied to her. And I'd do it again. She's on a mission for me to have children and is setting me up with every single guy on the South Shore. Enough is enough. I saw an opportunity to save my sanity, and I took it."

"So you're using me."

"Essentially."

"I'm okay with that."

I smiled at his teasing tone. "Unfortunately, she's suspicious. Be prepared for more questioning."

"Consider me forewarned."

Fat raindrops splashed the windshield. Our first stop was to meet Ruth Ann Yurio, Rachel's grandmother. She lived in South Weymouth, a good half-hour drive from my cottage.

"Did the detectives try to get in touch with you?" I asked.

"They called—I didn't answer."

"How long do you think we can avoid their questions?"

"Not much longer. Stonewall as long as possible. Or until they believe we had nothing to do with Rachel's death other than recovering her body."

I'd spoken to Marshall Betancourt for almost an hour, telling him the whole story. He didn't seem the least bit put off at representing a psychic, though he kept joking about me being able to "see" that the detectives had no case against me. I had to set him straight—that my abilities were limited.

"Too bad," he'd said. "I was hoping to hit the lottery tonight."

I didn't find the joke the least bit funny.

So far I'd found the hardest part of being outed was explaining my gift to people. No one quite understood that psychics came in all shapes and talents. Some could simply read auras, like my ancestors. Some had ESP, telepathy, clairvoyance, channeling. The list was actually quite long. My talent was a specific form of ESP. I was convinced there was a medical explanation behind being psychic—how else to explain why an electrical surge transformed my abilities? Something in my brain had been altered.

"Have you been able to locate my parents?"

"They checked out of the main resort because it was undergoing some unexpected renovations."

That explained a lot. My father wouldn't have put up with the noise. When he was on vacation, he strived for peace and quiet.

"They moved to an exclusive private villa on a remote part of the island. No phones, no electricity."

Sounded like something my father would engineer—and my mother, an original flower child, would wholeheartedly support. "If there's no electricity, their cell phones are probably dead."

"Exactly. I hired a messenger to track them down and have them call you and check their e-mail as soon as possible."

"E-mail?"

"I sent them the link to the *Herald*. The story is front and center on their Web page."

"Great."

In the chaos of the morning, I managed to find time to call Raphael, who'd slept in and hadn't yet seen the paper. It wasn't like Raphael to sleep late, and it had me wondering if he was alone.

And I'd have to keep on wondering, because that wasn't a question I was going to ask him. He'd been first horrified at the article, then mad, cursing like I'd never heard him before—in both Spanish and English. He'd wanted to come to the cottage, but I insisted I was okay. He finally relented, but not before cussing out Preston Bailey one more time.

I let him. Preston was probably lapping up accolades this morning while my life was falling apart.

My hands balled into fists. Anger bubbled in my chest, pounding against my rib cage like a prisoner trying to escape a cell. Closing my eyes, I tried to relax.

8 times 6 is 48.

The square root of 4 is 2.

10 to the second power is 100.

Better. But not quite there. I always thought I had a forgiving nature, but apparently not where nosy reporters were concerned.

"Want to hit me?" Sean asked.

My eyes flashed open. "What?"

"Want to hit me?" He nodded to my clenched fists.

I released my fingers, flexing them. "Not you."

"Might make you feel better."

Sex might, too. I wondered if he was willing. Therapeutical sex. I might be on to something.

"I'm sorry," he said, as if reading my mind.

"About?" I questioned. Did *he* have ESP? Was he turning me down when I hadn't technically asked?

"Everything you're going through right now."

My heart tripped over itself. Why did he have to make it so easy to fall for him? "Thanks."

Sean pulled into the parking lot of a massive retirement community off Route 18, not far from South Shore Hospital. We parked in the main lot and Sean cut the engine. Rain tapped melodically against the roof as he shifted to face me.

Before I could react, he had encircled my left wrist with his fingers.

"What are you doing?" Curious more than anything.

"What happens when you touch me?"

My mouth went cotton-ball dry. "H-happens?"

"Do you see something I've lost?" With a little bit of pressure, he turned my hand over, palm up. The heat from his fingers sizzled against my skin.

"I've never seen something you've lost." There. Not a lie.

With his other hand, he traced the outline of my fingers, like he was a little kid drawing a Thanksgiving turkey. He touched everywhere but my palm, which tingled uncomfortably.

"Does your touch zap everyone?" he asked.

"No, I don't zap everyone." Water! I needed water. "Just you."

"I must be special."

I focused on his lips, my own aching. "You must be."

"But you do see something when you touch me."

"Nothing." I kept staring at his lips. The way they moved when he spoke. The way his tongue flicked against his teeth. The way they pulled me in.

"Liar," he said softly, leaning in to me. "What do you see, Lucy?"

I nearly jumped out of my skin as his fingers trailed across my palm.

Images came slowly, languidly. Lips. A bed.

"Nothing," I said, closing my eyes against the lie.

"Nothing?" Again his finger drifted across my palm.

Mouths meeting. Hands exploring. A bare breast. A heated gaze.

My eyes flew open. I snatched my hand away, tucking it protectively under my arm.

The rain intensified, sheeting the windshield. Rattled, I tried not to look at him but couldn't refuse when he nudged my chin. His thumb brushed my bottom lip. I think I groaned.

"I can't see it, Lucy." He held up his fingers. "But I *feel* it."

"I don't understand it," I said, tears clouding my eyes from the sheer need of wanting him. "I can't explain it. And there's no point in talking about it. We should go."

Shoving open my door, I didn't give him a chance to argue. Ignoring the pain, I dashed toward the main building, dodging puddles.

Under the safety of the awning, I brushed at my eyes, chastising myself for being so emotional. Sean jogged across the parking lot, his shirt darkened with moisture. He finger-combed sopping hair, sending spikes into the air. His labored breathing caught my attention.

"You okay?" I asked.

"I'm all right."

I looked long and hard at him. Outwardly, he was in perfect condition. I'd give him a 10 on a how-hot-is-he? scale. What had happened to him? What injury had caused him to leave the fire department? Had left him fighting for breath?

We followed an outdoor corridor to Ruth Ann's apartment. By the time we rang her bell, we were dripping wet.

"Do you think she'll talk to us?"

Sean shrugged. "You never know."

Slowly, the door opened. Gentle folds of wrinkles lined the woman's heart-shaped face. Sharp green eyes focused on us. "Yes?"

"Mrs. Yurio?"

The woman shook her head. "No, dear."

"Is she home?" I asked.

"May I ask what this is concerning?"

Dripping, I said, "I'm Lucy Valentine and this is Sean Donahue. We'd like to talk to Mrs. Yurio about Rachel."

"Valentine?" the woman said hesitantly, the crow's-feet at the corners of her eyes deepening.

"Yes, ma'am."

"Are you the girl in the paper today?"

Breathing deep, I said, "Yes."

The door opened. "Come in."

The foyer opened into a surprisingly spacious

living room. It was an open layout, with one room blending into another with only columns as dividers. Vanilla scented the air as she led us to a pair of brocade-covered sofas facing each other. The scent couldn't quite cover a lingering antiseptic smell.

"Let me get some towels," she said, hurrying down a narrow hallway.

A door opened and closed. When she returned, she placed two bath towels across the sofa. "I'm Marilyn Flynn. I take care of Ruth Ann."

"Take care?" I asked.

She nodded to an open door down the hall. Through it I could barely see the frame of a hospital bed. "She had a stroke many years ago and never fully recovered. She's not quite . . . there," she said softly.

"How long ago?" Sean asked.

"Eight years, give or take."

Eight years? "Wasn't she the one who reported Rachel missing?"

The woman smiled wanly. "Technically. Six years ago when Rachel didn't come by for Christmas, I knew something was horribly wrong. It just wasn't like her to miss a major holiday with no word. I took Ruth Ann to the police station and filed a report. Back then she was still able to get around, but I provided most of the information."

"Are you a relative?" Sean asked.

"All but blood," she said. "Ruth Ann and I grew up together. Neither Rachel nor I had the heart to put her in a home after the stroke, so I volunteered to move in and take care of her, even though she doesn't remember me."

The love in the woman's voice broke my heart. "I'm sorry."

"Thank you. Coffee? Tea?" she asked. "To warm you up?"

"No, thank you," Sean and I said in unison.

She slowly lowered herself onto the couch facing us, delicately perching on the edge of a cushion. Her crooked posture and sallow skin hinted at health problems, but her eyes were clear. White, shoulder-length poofy dandelion-style hair framed her face.

"You knew Rachel well, then?" Sean said.

"I was like an auntie to her. Like I said, no blood, but love doesn't know the difference."

Very true. "We're sorry for your loss."

She nodded.

"I don't really know where to begin," I said, twisting my hands. "We, Sean and I, were the ones who found Rachel's body."

Her paper-thin eyelids drifted closed. "It's still hard to believe it's her. She's been gone for so long. It's both a blessing and a curse," she said softly. "How did you find her?"

Slowly, I went through what had happened with Michael and the ring, leading us to the body. It was surreal to be talking about my abilities out in the open.

Marilyn tipped her head, the wrinkles stretching into smooth skin along her jaw. "I mourned her, years ago. I knew she was gone. She was an independent one, but her grandmother meant the world to her. When she didn't come calling at Christmas, I checked her apartment and reported her missing. The police never wanted to believe something may have happened to her, but I was certain."

"Why?"

She blinked twice. "I found her locket on the floor of her apartment—the clasp had been broken, as if someone ripped it from her neck. Rachel never removed that locket. It was a gift from her parents the Christmas before they died. She never would have willingly left it behind."

"Did the police find any signs of a struggle?" Sean asked.

"No. There weren't any. Except the locket. There was no evidence she was gone, none at all. But I knew . . ." she said, trailing off.

"How old was Rachel when her parents passed?" I asked.

"Six. A car accident. From then on she was a changed girl. Sullen, sad. It was to be expected, the psychiatrists said. As she grew into a teen, she became more withdrawn." She shook her head. "If not for her friends, I'm not sure what might have happened to her."

"Elena?" I asked.

"And Jennifer," she said.

Coincidence? "Jennifer Thompson?"

"Yes. Three peas in a pod, all through middle school."

I was suddenly reminded of my friendship with Marisol and Em.

"Unfortunately, the girls' friendship with Jennifer fell apart in high school."

"Over Michael," Sean stated.

She smiled. "So silly. Jennifer had what Elena wanted. Elena never got over the supposed betrayal. And held on to her fixation of Michael much too long in response. There's nothing worse than being jealous of your best friend, or wishing for something that you felt should have been yours. Rachel sided with Elena, mostly because she didn't want Elena to have no one."

Marisol, Em, and I had never let a boy come between us. I can only imagine the ugliness that would have ensued if one had.

"Do you know what happened to Jennifer?" I asked.

She shook her head. "Last I heard of her was when she and Michael had broken up. Rachel was ashamed of her role in that and eventually confessed to Michael."

"You knew about the huge fight between Elena and Rachel?" Sean asked.

She nodded. "Elena moved out of their apartment that same night."

"How did Rachel take it?"

"Devastated." She smoothed an already straight skirt. "I have to be honest. I wanted to like Elena. But she was . . . hard. Raised by a single alcoholic father. Dirt-poor. I never could trust her. Her eyes. So very disturbing. She was clearly damaged, if that makes sense. Rachel, being of a kind heart, latched onto her. Was certain Elena was good underneath the surface, even though she continually tested that faith."

"How so?" Sean asked.

"You name it. Stealing, fraud, assault, harassment. Poor Jenny Thompson took the brunt of it. Elena held a mean grudge."

"Do you think Elena would hurt Rachel?" I asked.

"I'd like to think Rachel meant too much to

her. But I also feel that Elena would lash out if she was hurt. All this I told the detectives from the state police."

Sean asked, "Is she an official suspect?"

"I don't know. The only name I heard mentioned was Michael's."

Raindrops skimmed my spine. "Does Elena's father still live around here?"

"Her father passed away when she was just eighteen, a fire. She had no other family that I know of."

"What did you do with Rachel's belongings?" Sean asked.

"They're in storage."

"Did the detectives confiscate anything?"

"They never asked about her belongings. They looked through her things after the initial missing persons investigation, but not recently."

Sean said, "Do you mind if we have a look?"

"Why?" she asked.

I explained about my ring theory. "Therefore, Michael can't be guilty. And if he's innocent . . ."

"Rachel's killer is still out there."

I nodded. "Yes. There might be something in her things that will point us in the right direction. Do you happen to know why Rachel would have his ring?"

She shook her head. "I honestly don't know. Are you sure you don't want something hot to drink?"

We shook our heads.

"I'll get the storage key for you," Marilyn said. "I don't know why I kept her things. I suppose a part of me always hoped I was wrong. That one day Rachel would come home." She grabbed a key ring from a kitchen drawer and handed it to Sean.

I clasped my hands. "I can't thank you enough, Miss Flynn, for speaking with us. I feel . . . almost responsible for what happens."

She moved quickly, giving me a hug. "Thank you for all you've done. I can now put her to rest properly."

"If we find anything," Sean said, holding open the door. The rain had stopped. "We'll let you know."

"Wait!" she said, grabbing my hand.

Images flew through my head. I swayed, grabbing onto the doorjamb. Through the swirling haze, I heard:

"When you're going through Rachel's things, if you find a small jewel-encrusted trinket box, will you please bring it to me? I couldn't find it when I went through her things before. It's the one thing I've given her that I'd like to keep."

The images took me along highways, down back roads, over railroad tracks, finally stopping on a small yellow house. On a nightstand next to a queen-sized bed sat a small jewel-encrusted trinket box.

"We will," Sean said.

I pulled my hand loose, holding it close to my chest. The images stopped.

"Ruth Ann helped me choose the box as a gift for Rachel's high school graduation. I know she treasured it. I would love to give it to Ruth Ann. Perhaps it will spark a memory or two. Are you all right, dear?" Marilyn asked me. "You've gotten pale."

"Yes, I'm fine, thank you. We'll be in touch."

As soon as we were out of earshot, Sean wrapped his arm around me. "What happened back there?"

"I saw the box. And it wasn't in storage."

TWENTY

"How could you see the box," Sean asked, "when it belonged to Rachel?"

"It was a gift from Marilyn. Gifts are the only time I can get a reading from two people. It's how I saw the diamond ring."

"But wasn't it Michael's ring?" Sean said, starting the car.

I smiled. "Said like a man. Engagement rings belong to the woman after they're given. They're considered a gift and don't have to be given back if the relationship fails. The man is out of luck, unless the woman takes pity and gives it back."

Sean's face clouded. He zoomed out of the parking lot, heading south, toward the highway.

I realized what I'd said. Nothing like sticking my foot in my mouth. He had to be thinking about his own failed engagement. "I'm sorry. I wasn't thinking. . . ."

"You were just answering a question."

"I know, but . . ." I bit my lip. "I, ah . . . Shit. I don't know what to say."

He suddenly laughed.

"What's so funny?"

"You. You're adorable when you swear."

Sean took the Route 3 north ramp onto the highway. We were on our way to see Melissa Antonelli. I was hoping I'd be able to tug at her heartstrings a bit.

"I'm glad you think so."

"I moved out of my house," he said suddenly. "I'll stay with Sam until I can find a place."

"Are you okay?"

"I'll get through it."

I couldn't help the happiness that swept over me, though I'd like to think I was a better person than that. After all, he was hurting.

But he was free. Available. I didn't have to feel guilty if I flirted with him.

As if the heavens were giving me their blessing, the clouds parted. Thin sunbeams streamed down from the gloomy skies, dappling the road with light. I fully expected to hear the "Hallelujah Chorus" any second now.

Though I didn't want to hear all the details, I figured I'd be a good friend and ask, "Do you want to talk about it?"

"No."

Thank goodness. But . . . "What about Thoreau?"

Sean smiled as he merged onto Route 93, heading into the city. "I have him."

"Good."

"Tell me about the box," Sean said, clearly wanting to change the subject. "Where is it?"

"I think it's with Elena."

"What?"

"It's in Rhode Island. Where's the file you have on her?"

"Backseat."

I reached back and grabbed a stack of manila folders, rifling through them until I found one with Elena's name.

I closed my eyes, letting myself see the images again, slowing them down. I blinked. "I didn't see a house number, but the street is the same. Pawtucket, Rhode Island."

"It can't be a coincidence."

"No," I said. "Which leads to the question—why does Elena have Rachel's box?"

"If it was as sentimental to Rachel as Marilyn believes, then she never would have given it away."

"I have a hard time believing that, too."

"Maybe she stole it?" Sean ventured. "When she moved out?"

"Maybe."

"Or maybe she wanted a keepsake after she killed Rachel, and took something she knew Rachel treasured because Rachel took something she treasured—her trust? Am I reaching because I'm desperate to find out who killed Rachel?"

"Maybe a little," Sean said. "But it's good to talk things out."

The city loomed ahead, tall buildings scraping the clouds. Rough harbor water tossed boats against their moorings near the Dorchester Yacht Club. "If Elena was as mad as we've been hearing, she was plenty angry."

"Enough to kill?"

"Maybe. People have killed for less."

Traffic slowed to a near stop. We inched along.

He looked at me, his eyes searching. "Could you?"

"What?"

"Kill someone in anger?"

"Until today, I would have said no, that there had to be something mentally off to kill. But since that article came out this morning, I've been fantasizing about that reporter having an unfortunate accident. Is that wrong?"

"I think we need to work on refocusing your fantasies."

Heat shot through me like a bullet. My mouth went dry; my heart hummed with desire. "What do you have in mind?"

Traffic lightened as we entered the tunnel. "I think you've seen what I have in mind."

If we'd been anywhere but the car, I probably would have thrown myself at him. As it was, I was grateful I couldn't.

Sean merged onto 1A, heading for Lynn. "You're speechless. I see I've succeeded in refocusing your thoughts."

"Preston who?" I said, playing along.

"Exactly."

He was single.

Officially.

It was a good day, all things considered.

Melissa Antonelli didn't live too far from her parents. We pulled to the curb in front of a lovely Cape Cod–style house with a brick walkway leading to the front door.

She opened the door before we even knocked. To my surprise, she said, "You must be the PIs. Come on in."

I didn't correct her. Sean was the PI. I was merely . . . what? A matchmaker on a quest?

I glanced back at Sean, who shrugged and nudged me toward the house.

Inside, the scent of a roast filled the air. My stomach rumbled. Two small boys chased each other up the stairs, nearly knocking us over.

"Hold on to the rail!" Melissa yelled. Then sighed. "They never listen. Come in, come in."

"I'm Lucy," I said, holding out my hand to her. No images flashed.

"Sean," he said, shaking.

"You're here about Jenny."

I nodded.

"My parents told me to be on the lookout for you. That you were looking for her and might stop by. They also told me not to talk to you, but I want to hear what you have to say. Sit, sit."

Sean and I sat in matching club chairs. She sank into a floral couch. The room was tiny, with a huge TV taking up most of the space. Pictures cluttered the top of the TV set. A large Monet print hung above the sofa.

I stared at the photos on the TV. In one of them Melissa wore a wedding dress, and on one side of her stood her father and an older woman, and a young woman who looked a lot like Melissa stood on the other. Same long dark hair and dark eyes and tall, thin frame.

"Is that Jenny with you?" I asked. "On your wedding day?"

Melissa stood and went to the TV. She took down the frame, handed it to me. "Seven years ago."

Up close, I could see Jennifer's eyes were haunted. "She's lovely."

"Still is. Mom also said you were working for Michael. Is that true?" From upstairs, a crash rang out. She tipped her head, listening. "No crying. A good thing."

"Michael is my client," I said, explaining how I worked for Valentine, Inc. "When I interviewed him, one thing was clear. He's still very much in love with your sister. I offered to try and find her, see if she would speak to him." I told her what Michael had said about his night with Elena— how it had been a setup.

Melissa said, "She's evil, that one." The two boys, about six and four, rushed back down the stairs.

"Let's go for a walk," she said, and shouted her plans toward the kitchen. "He's watching football. Completely oblivious."

The last of the leaves had been washed off the trees by the rain. They squished under our feet as we walked along, the muted oranges, reds, greens, and yellows blending together.

"Your parents are protecting Jennifer," Sean said. "From Elena?"

"And Rachel Yurio. They put her through hell, those girls. And no matter how many times we went to the police, nothing could ever be proven."

I walked in the middle, Melissa on my right, Sean on my left. "What did they do?"

"Nasty phone calls, slashed her tires, followed her. Sent dirty e-mails to her professors posing as her. Jenny's cat disappeared and she found its bloody collar on the back step."

I shuddered.

"Yeah," she said. "Jenny loved Michael. With all her heart. But she couldn't take much more of the harassment. She felt like Elena would stop at nothing to get her out of the picture."

"Including setting Michael up with those pictures," I said, wincing with each step I took.

"Those photos were the last straw. When Elena showed them to Jenny, she added a threat. That if she didn't break it off with Michael, then Jenny might disappear just like her cat."

Scan must have sensed I was in pain, because he slowed his pace. Melissa was forced to fall back or walk way ahead of us. "And she didn't go to the police?"

We'd made it to the end of the street. Melissa turned to head back. "No. By that point she thought Michael had cheated on her. She just wanted to get on with her life. Even after she broke up with him, Elena would pop up here and there to taunt her. She's sick. After Jenny graduated, she decided to move west. And my family became very overprotective."

"Understandable," Sean said.

"I'm not sure if you're aware," I began, "but Rachel Yurio is dead. And has been for over five years. Murdered."

Shock widened her eyes. "I didn't know. Did the police catch who did it? Was it Elena?"

I was beginning to suspect it was. "By all appearances Elena has turned her life around. She's a social worker in Rhode Island. Has a husband and a couple of kids."

Melissa shook her head. "Those poor kids."

"Michael is under suspicion for Rachel's death."

She stopped suddenly. "Michael? Why?"

I swallowed hard. "It's complicated. Can I ask you something?"

"Sure."

"Do you know what Jennifer did with her engagement ring?"

"She mailed it back to Michael. FedEx, I think. Why?"

A gust of wind sent leaves scrambling down the street. "Rachel was wearing it when she died."

"You didn't have to see me in," I said, passing Sean as he held my front door open.

I'd given Melissa Antonelli my cell phone number and asked her to pass my information along to Jennifer. Whether she would call me was anyone's guess. The more I heard about Elena Hart, the more I suspected she'd killed Rachel. I was exhausted, so Sean and I both agreed to put off seeing Elena until the next day.

"Do you want me to look at your feet? I do have paramedic training."

"I'm okay. Em doctored them this morning. The antibiotics will kick in soon enough."

"You sure?"

"Do you have a foot fetish?"

He laughed.

"Coffee?" I asked, not wanting him to leave just yet.

"Sure."

Grendel came streaking out of the bedroom, twisting himself around my feet until I picked him up. He pawed my face while I murmured sweet nothings to him, trying to soothe his injured feline feelings.

"He hates when I leave him," I explained.

Sean smirked.

"What?"

"Nothing. Nothing at all."

I passed Grendel to Sean so I could make the coffee. Weak sunlight filtered through the living room windows. Outside, the ocean rose and fell with the steady rhythm of a sleeping chest.

"How long do you think the media will stay?" Sean asked.

"Hopefully they'll go soon." I'd refused to shield my face from the flashbulbs and was still seeing spots because of it. "But I have the sinking feeling they won't leave until I talk to them."

"Are you going to?"

"I don't know."

I'd like to get my parents' opinions on the matter, but they had yet to call.

I ground some coffee beans, watching Sean play with Grendel, who was lapping up the attention. We'd set our plans for the next day— early on we were going to head to Marilyn's storage unit and look through Rachel's belongings; with any luck we'd find a clue as to who killed her. After that, we were going to head to Elena's house in Pawtucket. I was curious to see what she had to say about the trinket box and about Rachel's death in general.

"This is a really nice place you have," Sean said, taking a look around.

"I love it here. My grandfather bought the estate for Dovie when they were first married. Dovie renovated about a decade ago, bringing back the original beauty of the place."

"It's like something off of a postcard."

I glanced at Dovie's enormous house on the bluff. Lights blazed from the downstairs windows. "The main house is too much house for one woman, but she adores it too much to ever downsize." She'd grown up in a New York tenement, one of three kids who owned nothing but their names. She hadn't had an easy childhood, and I think the house represented security to her, more than anything sentimental. Even though my Grandpa Henry had given her the place as a wedding gift, the marriage was crumbling before the honeymoon was over.

"And she has me down here to keep her company. Which is one of the reasons rent is so cheap."

"Rent?" he asked, surprised.

The scent of freshly ground coffee beans filled the kitchen. "About ten years ago, I renounced my trust fund, wanting to prove that I could make it on my own. I put myself through college, bought my own car, and pay my own bills."

"Why?" he asked, stroking Grendel's fur.

As the sun dipped lower in the sky, the room grew darker. Intimate. I tried not to think about him and me, me and him, all alone in my house. It was a hard thought to banish. I retrieved two mugs. "At the time I was feeling guilty that I couldn't—"

I was about to say "read auras." I'd gotten so comfortable sharing myself with Sean that I'd forgotten he didn't know the Valentine secret. I needed to be more careful.

"Couldn't what?"

I thought fast. "'Couldn't' is the wrong word.

Didn't want to go into the family business. I figured I didn't deserve the money and should make my own."

"Noble. But crazy."

I laughed. "Trust me, I've kicked myself a thousand times since. But I like my life—for the most part. I like taking care of myself. I'm not going to lie—it helps that I know the money is still there, waiting for me."

"Will you ever take it?"

I shrugged. "Who knows?"

He set Grendel down as I turned on the coffeepot. I watched Sean wander through my living room, looking at the pictures on the mantel—of me, my parents, Raphael, Dovie, Em, Marisol, and Grendel. My family.

"Is this you?" he asked, holding up a shot of me at four, pigtails flying in the wind as I built a sand castle.

"Yes."

"Adorable."

"Thanks."

"Is that Dovie?"

"Which shot?" I asked, coming around the island.

"No." He pointed out the window. "Is that Dovie headed this way?"

Darkness cloaked a silhouetted figure walking down the slope toward the cottage.

"Yep. Probably making sure I took my medicine."

"Should I prepare for twenty questions?" he asked, smiling.

"I'd forgotten! She's going to quiz you until you break. Maybe you should go."

His gray eyes glinted flirtatiously. "Do you want me to?"

"No, but Dovie—" I had a sudden thought.

"What?" he asked. "What's that devilish look in your eye?"

"I know a way to get her off our backs."

"How?"

I hooked my thumbs in my pockets and rocked on my sore heels. "Prove to her that we are together."

"And how do we do that?" he asked, a grin curving the edge of his mouth.

Very deliberately, I turned to look at my bed, just visible through the bedroom doorway.

"You're not suggesting . . ."

"I'm suggesting we pretend—to get Dovie to leave us alone. Are you in?" I asked.

His eyes darkened, and he looked at me in a way that suggested he'd been thinking of more than just pretending. "I'm in."

My mouth went dry as heat pulsed through my body.

It was going to be easy to fake it.

"Come on! We've got to hurry. She'll be here in a minute." I tugged him toward my bedroom.

My heart beat wildly. This was a dangerous game.

"Shirts," I said, slipping my sweater over my head.

Sean stared at me, eyes hooded, as I pulled back the covers on the bed.

"Your shirt! Hurry!"

Slowly, he unbuttoned. I pulled off my cami, hesitated with my bra. I could feel Sean's searing gaze.

Suddenly chicken, I kept the bra on, slipping the straps off my shoulders. I jumped into the bed, pulling the sheet up to my chin. I patted the space next to me. Dovie would be there any second.

Sean's shirt opened to a white tank beneath. Solid, enticing muscles defined his arms, his chest. Slowly, he pulled the tank over his head.

My mouth dropped open. "What happened to you?"

A thin red five-inch surgical scar stretched downward from his left collarbone. It was a recent scar—it hadn't fully healed.

There was a knock at the door.

Sean dove into the bed next to me. He drew the blankets to his waist, covering his jeans, and leaned up on his elbow. His gaze locked on mine. I couldn't look away from the sadness in his gray depths. Instinctively, I leaned into him.

He cupped my face, his thumb sliding along my cheekbone, my lip.

Drawing in a shaky breath, I wanted to question, to say something, but the look in his eyes asked me to wait. Besides, there was nothing I wanted more at that moment than his kiss.

As if in slow motion, his head lowered to mine, his lips a whisper away from my own. "Shall I kiss you?" he asked.

His husky voice pulled me closer to him, leaving me suddenly wishing this wasn't pretend at all.

"Do I need to beg?" I asked.

Dovie knocked again and yelled, "LucyD?" The doorknob jiggled; the front door creaked open.

His lips quivered in a faint smile just before his mouth met mine.

The kiss was slow and sensual, wrapping me in spirals of desire, leaving me wanting more, more, more. He shifted on top of me, his elbows bracing his weight. The heat of his body against mine nearly did me in.

I tried to think of all the reasons why this scenario was a bad idea.

At this very moment I couldn't think of one, though there were probably many.

In the back of my mind, an alarm was going off, warning bells blaring, but I pushed an internal snooze button.

Through my sheer pleasure, I heard footsteps approach, then fade away. A second later, the front door closed.

Sean's kiss slid from my lips to my ear, my neck, then back up again.

"She's gone," he whispered.

"I know."

Neither of us moved. His chest beat against mine, our hearts in rhythm.

Eyes closed, he rested his forehead against mine, our noses touching. The rest of us nestled together in the most intimate of ways, making me want him more than ever.

"This isn't pretend," Sean whispered.

"No," I agreed.

His eyes flashed open. "We should stop?"

There were so many reasons to. But I didn't want to think about them. I just wanted this moment to last. But I had to be realistic and protect my heart.

Stupid Cupid's Curse.

Slowly, I nodded.

He gently kissed my forehead and levered himself off me.

I closed my eyes, wishing for things that could never be.

TWENTY-ONE

I was changing Grendel's kitty litter when I suddenly realized my visions of Sean and me had come true. My breath caught, held.

Slowly, I let it out in a long exhale.

How? Why?

Not having the answers frustrated me.

As I tidied the rest of my cottage, I tried not to think about saying no to Sean. My heart was aching. There were so many reasons Sean and I shouldn't get together. Cupid's Curse, for one. Cara, another. We worked together. We barely knew each other.

It was true Sean and I had met a few days ago. . . . But I did know him. And he knew me. It wasn't something I could explain—I could just feel it.

Which made this a very tricky situation indeed.

Because I could see myself falling in love with sexy Sean Donahue.

It was the last thing I wanted to do. Because losing him would tear me apart. And there was no doubt I would lose him eventually. We Valentines just weren't made for long-lasting commitments.

I tried to look on the bright side. I could enjoy what we had while it lasted. Dance the dance and all that, and simply ignore the dark cloud hanging over the slippery dance floor.

Blowing out a breath, I wondered about the scar on Sean's chest. I wished he hadn't left before we could talk about what had happened to him. He'd obviously had a serious operation. Was it why he left the fire department?

As soon as Sean had left my cottage, I'd noticed I had several missed calls on my cell. One from Em (she was meeting with Joseph and would be late), one from Raphael (checking in), one from Marisol (who was working the graveyard at the animal hospital but wanted details ASAP and oh, by the way, was going with Butch the next day to the Patriots game), one from Dovie ("Hubba, hubba! He's a good choice, LucyD. Your babies are going to be beautiful!"). Babies. I almost choked. The last call was from Aiden Holliday (he would be stopping by tonight at eight to take a statement from me). Still nothing from my parents.

I'd wondered about Raphael and Maggie. Were they together?

One thing I knew for sure—if Raphael was with Maggie, it meant that she and my father had never been an item. Raphael was too loyal to overstep those bounds.

I changed into a navy blue tracksuit, pulled my hair back in a headband, and tended my feet with the supplies Dovie had bought. The pain was subsiding, much to my relief.

I was doing my best to not think about Rachel or who may have killed her, though Elena was the only one on my list.

Before I thought better of it, I called Michael Lafferty to check on him. He didn't answer.

Flipping on the TV, I channel-surfed to see if any wealthy Americans had gone missing in St. Lucia (none had). I shut the TV off when I heard a car on the crushed-shell drive outside.

Pulling open the door, I saw Aiden Holliday standing near his sedan as another car pulled up behind him.

"There's someone who wanted to see you," Aiden said. "I didn't think you'd mind."

The back door of the second car flew open. Max O'Brien bounded out, took one look at me, and came running.

Tears welled in my eyes as I bent down to catch him. He landed with a thump against my chest, his little arms squeezing me tight. I lifted him up, not letting go.

Finally, he pulled back and looked into my face, a smile stretching ear to ear. He was missing a bottom tooth, I noticed, thinking he was the most adorable little boy I'd ever seen.

"Thanks for findin' me," he said.

"You're welcome."

A flashbulb popped to our right. Aiden took off after the cameraman who'd trespassed.

"Are you famous?" Max asked me.

"Not as much as you are."

He giggled.

I soon found that four-year-olds were heavier than they looked. My arms burned, and I had to put him down. Katherine and John were next, hugging me and thanking me.

The ocean melodically crashed against the cliffs, and sundown had brought a chill. I invited everyone inside and was surprised when they declined.

"We're off to Disney World. To recover," Katherine joked. "Our flight takes off at midnight. We just couldn't leave without seeing you first." Her eyes, I noticed, were filled with life, with joy. It was such a difference from the images on TV.

"Thank you," I said. And meant it. I didn't know how much I longed to see Max until he came barreling toward me.

"I think we can stand here all night, thanking you," John said, "but we should go."

I gave Max another hug.

"And here's this," Katherine said, pulling an envelope from her bag and handing it to me.

"What is it?"

"The reward money."

I pushed the envelope back to her. "No, no. I don't want it. I didn't find Max for the money."

"We know that, Lucy. But it is what it is. The people who raised it would want you to have it. You'll put it to good use, I'm sure." She pressed it into my hand, gave me another hug.

I waved as they drove off until I couldn't see them anymore.

"Thanks for bringing them," I said as soon as Aiden was close enough to hear me after returning from his chase.

"Thought you might like that." He strode to

his car, opened the door, and pulled out a leather briefcase. "I have some paperwork to go through with you."

"You didn't have to come out here. I would've come to you."

"I don't mind." He followed me into the house, looked around. "You alone?"

"Em's out till later," I said.

His face fell. Ah. The real reason he'd come here—not to see me, but to see Em. Poor guy. He didn't stand a chance—not with Joseph in the picture.

We worked until nine, going through all the events leading up to finding Max.

"You'll have to come in and sign the official statement, but that should only take a minute or so."

"I'll do it on Monday."

He gathered up his things and rose. Then abruptly sat back down. "I—"

"What?"

Grendel dragged himself out of bed and stretched his way into the room, paw by paw, stopping at his food bowl to see if there was anything in it worth his interest.

Aiden pulled another file from his bag and dropped it on the coffee table. "There's another unsolved case . . ."

I stared at the file on the table as if it would jump up and bite me.

"And I spoke with some colleagues. We'd like to discuss hiring you as a consultant to the state police."

"You know I'm not psychic in the traditional sense. There's little I can offer."

"Not true, Lucy. Your ability to find lost objects can help us tremendously. Maybe not everyone, but a majority."

"How?"

"The same way you found Max. Focus on what the missing person has with them when they disappear. An iPod, a cell phone, earrings, a sweatshirt. Anything that was a gift from someone else."

The weight of what he was asking hit me, knocking me backward into the couch cushions. The file on the table tempted me.

Aiden tapped the manila folder. "This is the case of Jamie Gallagher, one of many missing person cases. She was sixteen when she disappeared on the way home from school one day last winter."

A lump lodged in my throat. "You do know most of the cases won't end up as Max's did."

"I'm aware. But any lead is helpful. And if it's a body we recover, you can't imagine the relief for the family just *knowing*. Being able to have closure. Let me leave the file here. You can bring it when you come by headquarters. Just think about it, Lucy."

"I will."

He held out his hand. I shook it. Images swirled, flying past at a dizzying speed. I wobbled, pulled my hand away, and narrowed my gaze at him. "Was that a test?"

He blinked innocently.

"Your camera is on the ocean floor, somewhere off Nantasket Beach."

He grinned. "You pass."

The front door opened and Em strode in. Her cheeks reddened when she spotted Aiden.

Wasn't that interesting?

"Am I interrupting?" she asked.

"I'm just leaving," Aiden said.

"Me, too, actually." Em held out car keys. "I just came back to bring you your car, Lucy."

"You're leaving?" I asked.

"Going home."

"You sure?"

"Yeah. I gave my notice today. Time to face the music and go see my mother tomorrow. Could you give me a ride to the rail station?" she asked. "I think I can catch the last train into town."

"I can take you," Aiden volunteered quickly.

"I couldn't ask—"

"I'm going that way," he insisted.

"Okay, then."

I watched the way the two of them looked at each other. Joseph better watch out.

Her face suddenly crunched into a frown. "I'm being selfish! Are you going to be okay here alone, Lucy? I can stay awhile; we can talk."

Honestly, I was talked out. "I'm fine. Plus, Dovie's not far."

"All right." Em hugged me. "Get some rest, okay?"

I locked the door behind them. My cell rang and I hurried to answer. It was Sean.

"Hi," I said. "Is Thoreau okay? He was alone a long time today."

"Yeah, but I hope Sam can get the stains out of his dining room rug. Anything going on there?"

I laughed, but it was hard with the lump in my throat. I glanced at the file on Jamie Gallagher. I had a big decision to make. "This and that. Em just left, going home. Holliday came by with papers. Oh! And I got to see Max." I shared all the details.

"Wish I'd been there to see that," he said softly.

"Me, too."

I wished he was here, period.

TWENTY-TWO

If there was sainthood for patience, I'd have achieved the status by now.

Sean and I were in his car, going 75 miles per hour southbound on I-95.

I'd been with him for nearly five hours straight, and he hadn't brought up his scar once.

Sean had picked me up early, and we'd confined Thoreau to my kitchen so Grendel could taunt him from atop the refrigerator. Then we'd driven to the storage unit to look through Rachel's belongings. Now we were on our way to Rhode Island to see Elena . . . not a word.

I should just ask.

But I wanted him to tell me, to share.

"You're quiet," he said.

"Just thinking."

"About Rachel?"

"Yeah," I lied.

"She didn't have much, did she?"

The storage unit had been smaller than I would have thought. All her belongings had been neatly boxed and labeled. There had been very little—a small dinette set with two chairs, a couch, a full-sized bed and frame, a couple of end tables, a thirteen-inch TV set, and a chunky coffee table. Three boxes held her clothes. A fourth contained assorted kitchen things. Personal items had been packed into one small box.

Within a jewelry box lay a couple pairs of cheap earrings, a gold bracelet, and a heart-shaped locket that held two pictures, a man and a woman, who I assumed—based on the conversation with Marilyn yesterday—were Rachel's parents.

Traffic slowed on the highway. I'd taken this route many times with Raphael to see the Pawtucket Red Sox play at McCoy Stadium. Elena didn't live far from the field, on a picturesque side road dotted every half mile with 1950s-style ranch houses and lined with tall maple trees. The only drawback to the neighborhood was the commuter train track that ran behind the houses.

Elena's house was the last on the street, a dead end. Trimmed hedges formed a natural L-shaped fence that followed the shared property line with the closest neighbor and also blocked the view of the train tracks at the rear of the property. The other side of the yard dead-ended into a six-foot-tall wooden fence separating the yard from a thick copse of woods, probably to protect the nicely landscaped yard from hungry deer.

There was a Honda Civic parked in the stone driveway. As we walked up the cobbled path to the door, the Providence commuter train shrieked past, headed to South Station in Boston. The earth quaked.

My legs were shaking a little, too. Mostly because I didn't know what to expect from Elena Hart. I also noticed Sean had brought his gun with him today. I, apparently, wasn't the only one nervous.

Sean rang the doorbell.

The house had been freshly painted in a cool shade of yellow. Green shutters bracketed the front picture window. Freshly swept steps and two planters of potted mums welcomed us. Everything was neat, tidy. Perfect.

The door opened. A woman peered out. Sleek blonde hair fell in waves, framing her oval face. Dark blue eyes narrowed. "Yes?"

"Elena Hart?" Sean asked.

With a wary smile, she said, "Actually, it's Delancey now."

"I'm Sean Donahue, a private investigator, and this is Lucy Valentine." He passed her a business card. "If you wouldn't mind, we'd like to ask you a few questions about Rachel Yurio."

Elena's eyes widened. "Rachel? I haven't seen Rachel in," she paused, "probably five or six years now. Wow, what a blast from the past."

Sean said, "Do you mind if we come in?"

Stepping aside, she held the door open in invitation. She wore dark jeans, a pink cable-knit sweater. Barefoot, her footsteps didn't make a sound on the oak floor. Her toenails were painted a sedate pale pink.

She wasn't as I had imagined her—hard and rough around the edges. A badass mean girl. I supposed everyone grew up sometime.

"Not at all, but I can't imagine I have any information useful to you. Like I said, it's been a long time. What exactly are you investigating?"

Sean and I glanced at each other. She didn't know. Or was pretending she didn't know.

The most had been made of the small living room. Two cushy love seats faced each other, a glass-topped coffee table sandwiched between them. A brick fireplace was fronted with a wrought-iron screen. Creamy gold colored the walls. Several photos of Elena with a dark-haired man and two babies, a boy and a girl, decorated the mantel, and there had to be a dozen framed pictures of children's artwork hanging on the wall. It was a cozy room, friendly and welcoming. The furniture, the art, the photos—all were such a far cry from what Rachel had possessed. It was a depressing comparison.

"Cute kids," I said. "How old?"

"Two and three. They're at the park right now with their dad," she added. Twisting her wedding band, she glanced at the sofa. "Please sit down."

On guard I sat in the love seat facing the picture window. Sean sank down next to me. I cleared my throat. "Rachel had been missing for years. Her body was found a couple of days ago. She'd been murdered and buried in Great Esker Park."

Elena's hand shot to her mouth to cover a gasp. She sat on the opposite love seat and stared at us. Tears gathered in the corners of her eyes. "And you're here why? You think I did it?"

"Interesting you'd jump to that conclusion," Sean said.

"It's not a hard leap, Mr. Donahue. I wasn't exactly a pillar of the community in my youth. And the last I saw Rachel, we had a huge fight— it's been almost six years to the day I last saw her. It's a logical jump to make. If you've tracked me down, someone must have told you about me. Maybe even about the fight Rachel and I had. There were quite a lot of witnesses."

"Did you kill her?" Sean threw out.

Her eyes widened, and she shook her head.

I took another route. "You're a social worker now?"

She gave a sad smile. "Talk about leaps, right?"

I nodded.

"That day I walked out on Rachel, I knew I had to change, that she was right."

"About what?" I asked.

"That I was a worthless human being."

Harsh, I thought.

"And I was. I decided then and there to change. I moved to Providence, went back to school. I met my husband, Mark, not too long after. I haven't looked back."

"You never wanted to show Rachel that you changed?" I asked, relaxing a bit. There was nothing threatening about Elena Hart at all. Had she really changed? "You didn't try to contact her in all these years? She was your childhood best friend, stuck with you through thick and thin. Didn't you think she'd be happy for you?"

She leaned forward, bracing her elbows on her knees. "I thought about it a time or two, but figured it was for the best I didn't. I'd come a long way in terms of changing my life. I work part-time with a nonprofit adoption agency; I have the kids, my husband. I volunteer in the community every chance I get. I figured if I went back and Rachel was doing better than me, then I might feel inferior, that I could never be good enough to meet her high standards, and start slipping into that worthless person I used to be."

"Yet Rachel wasn't perfect. She had an arrest record. She was your partner in crime," Sean said.

Elena winced. "I suppose I deserve that. Rachel was a follower, Mr. Donahue. She was so intent on changing my ways, she went along with whatever I said and did to make sure I didn't get myself into too much trouble. And sometimes that backfired on her."

My knee brushed Sean's leg, sending a sizzle clear up my spine.

"We're trying to gather as much information as we can to turn over to the police," I said. "Michael Lafferty is the prime suspect in the case."

"Michael? Why?"

"Motivation is a little fuzzy," I said, not moving my knee. I liked the sizzle.

I left out the part about me finding Rachel's body, which in turn implicated Michael. I didn't want to dwell.

She frowned. "I'm sure you already know I had an infatuation with Michael Lafferty. One I'm not proud of. One thing I know for sure— Michael wouldn't hurt anyone. He's not the type."

"Did Rachel have any other enemies?"

She shook her head.

"No old boyfriends?"

"She was always too busy working or trying to keep me in line."

"Rachel was found wearing the engagement ring Michael had given to Jennifer Thompson. Do you have any idea why she'd have the ring?"

Elena's head dropped. "Because of me."

"How?" I asked.

"I'm so ashamed. I've tried to contact Jennifer several times to apologize and tell her the truth, but I can't find her. Her family won't tell me where she is."

I didn't blame them a bit.

"The truth?" Sean asked. "About what?"

Taking a deep breath, she said, "Michael and I were never intimate. He passed out one night from drinking too much, and I had Rachel take a few snapshots that made it look like he and I had been together. I showed them to Jennifer and that's what caused their breakup." She pressed her fingers against the bridge of her nose. "I was horrible. Just horrible."

I didn't disagree. And it was nice to get confirmation of the story Michael had told me—that he had stayed faithful to Jennifer.

"Let's just say I intercepted Michael's mail one day."

"You stole his mail?" I asked.

"Yeah, I did. When I saw it was from Jennifer, I couldn't help myself. The ring was inside. On the spur of the moment, I took it."

"How did it end up with Rachel?" Sean asked.

"I left it in the apartment when I moved out. I figured she'd get it back to Michael. Obviously she didn't get the chance."

The explanation made sense but still didn't cover why the ring had been on Rachel's finger.

"What happened to Jennifer's cat?" I asked, not sure why I had to know.

Her eyes slowly fluttered closed. They re-opened, bright and shiny. She held up a finger, then walked out of the room. She came back a minute later holding an overfed tabby cat. "His name is Mikey," she said, rolling her eyes. "As a tribute to Michael. I was going to return him to Jennifer, too, but like I said—"

Sean cut in. "You couldn't find her."

She nodded.

I was relieved the cat hadn't been hurt. But I suddenly questioned whether Elena had been as dangerous as she came across. Were hers empty threats? Or was she really a sociopath in dis-guise?

I leaned forward. "Can I ask you a question?"

"I guess."

"You have a trinket box that belonged to Rachel."

Suspicion clouded her eyes. "How do you know about the box?"

I ignored her. "How did you get it? It was given to Rachel by a family friend—a sentimen-tal item. Rachel would never give it away."

"You're wrong about that," she said, chin raised. The cat hopped out of her arms, trotted away. "She gave it me. It was my twenty-first birthday, and she couldn't afford a present. She wanted me to have it."

I couldn't think of another question. I looked at Sean, who stood. "I wouldn't be surprised if you heard from the Massachusetts State Police soon," he said, pulling open the screen door.

"You have my card if you think of anything else."

I added, "Like if you can think of anyone who would want to do Rachel any harm."

She stood in the doorway, a frown tugging the corners of her mouth downward. "I've been thinking. I can't think of anyone except . . ."

I paused on the top step, looked back at her. "Who?"

"The only person who truly hated Rachel was . . ."

It suddenly hit me. "Jennifer Thompson."

Slowly, Elena nodded. "She hated us both. With good reason."

Marilyn Flynn was waiting for Sean and me.

As soon as I knocked, she quickly pulled open the door. "Come in, come in," she offered.

"We can't stay," I said, holding out the storage key. It had been a long day, and I wanted to go home.

I couldn't stop thinking about Jennifer Thompson. What if she had kept a low profile because she was living in fear? Not of Elena but of being found out. What if she was guilty of killing Rachel?

Was that why her parents were protecting her, too? From murder charges?

"Did you find anything amidst Rachel's belongings that will help the investigation?"

I shook my head. "Not really."

"Did you find the trinket box?" Marilyn asked, her eyes hopeful.

"Yes and no," I said.

She cocked her head in confusion.

"The box wasn't in storage. Elena has it."

"Elena?"

"She claims Rachel gave it to her for her twenty-first birthday. Do you know if that's true?"

Marilyn's face fell in disappointment. "I don't know. I simply cannot believe Rachel would give the box away." Tears welled in her eyes. "How could she?"

"I don't know," I said softly, wondering if Elena had in fact stolen it. "I'm sorry."

"It would have been nice to have the box back, but if it's Elena's now, it's Elena's."

"Maybe you can ask for it back," I said. "She would probably understand."

"I could never!" Marilyn shook her head. Soft white hair trembled.

"I'm sorry. We should go." I nudged Sean. "Thank you, Miss Flynn, for your help. I wish we could have been of more help. I hope this situation will be resolved soon."

She smiled grimly, as if knowing resolution would not bring any peace to her or to Ruth Ann Yurio.

As Sean and I walked to his car, he reached out to hold my hand.

Images rolled in front of my eyes lazily, and I closed my eyes against the vertigo as my body swayed.

He pulled his hand away, steadied me. "Sorry, I forgot that happens. What did you see?" he asked flirtatiously.

My heart beat crazily in my chest as if it was

running scared. Can't say I blamed it. Not after what I'd seen.

"Lucy?" He nudged my chin. "What did you see?"

I swallowed hard. "You and me in bed."

"I like the sounds of that. Why the frown?"

"It was a hospital bed."

TWENTY-THREE

Sean had been noticeably silent since I told him of my vision. We were almost to my cottage, and I had to admit the images I'd seen had freaked me out as well.

"Are you okay?" I finally asked.

"I'm fine."

I drew in a deep breath. I didn't like not knowing where we stood with each other. I didn't like not being able to speak my mind or to ask him questions without getting vague answers.

Maybe Cupid's Curse was already at work.

Which made me that much crankier.

I hated that curse.

I drew in a deep breath, trying to put it out of my mind. Streetlights came on as dusk fell. I pulled out my cell phone, checked the screen to see if my parents had called. If they had, I wouldn't know—my batteries were dead.

I shoved the phone back into my bag, chastising myself for not charging it, and focused my attention out the window.

7 times 6 is 42.

144 minus 24 is 120.

99 plus 99 is 198.

297 times 3 is . . .

I frowned, trying to calculate in my head, for some inexplicable reason getting stuck on what 9 times 3 was. I huffed.

"Are you angry?" Sean asked.

"Yes."

He laughed.

"What's so funny?"

"You. Most women would have passively-aggressively answered that question."

"I'm not most women."

"So I'm learning. Are you mad at me?"

"Yes."

He winced.

"And at my parents, and at Preston Bailey, and at Michael Lafferty, and at the numbers nine and three."

Taking his eyes off the road, he glanced at me. "Nine and three?"

"Don't ask."

"And you're mad at me, why?"

I shifted to face him. "You're a clammer."

"A clammer?"

"It's what Marisol, Em, and I call guys who don't share. They clam up, leaving us guessing, leaving us to invent how they may or may not be feeling."

"Could I at least be a fried clam? I don't like them steamed."

I punched his arm.

"Hey!"

"Avoiding is just another tactic a clammer uses. You won't tell me about your scar, and you're bothered by the vision I had, and won't tell me why. Is my being psychic a problem for you?"

He pressed his lips together. The flash of oncoming headlights highlighted the inner debate raging in his eyes.

Finally, he said, "It has nothing to do with you, Lucy. I'm amazed by the ability you have."

"Then what is it?"

"I hate hospitals." He tapped the steering wheel with his thumb as he turned onto Route 3A. "When you said you saw us in a hospital bed it . . ." He shuddered. "I hate hospitals, so it would have to be something serious to get me there."

"The scar?" I asked.

"About a year ago, while I was still with the fire department, I was on scene at a car fire. One minute I was pulling a hose; the next I was being rushed to the hospital. My heart had stopped. I blacked out. The guys on the scene had to shock me back to life." He passed a slow-moving hatchback. "The doctors ran test after test. None of the news was good. I was diagnosed with cardiomyopathy, specifically ventricular tachycardia— a dangerous arrhythmia. The only way to keep me alive was to implant a defibrillator just under my collarbone. Electrical leads are attached to my heart, keeping me alive."

I longed to reach out, hold his hand, comfort him, but the last thing I wanted was to see the images of us in a hospital bed again.

"My life changed that day. I changed. I was a firefighter and suddenly I couldn't be. I was athletic, but now sports could kill me. My whole identity changed. Cara couldn't deal with my mortality any more than I could, so that started falling apart. Sam's the only one who seems to understand me, but even he treats me with kid gloves. And now that you know, you'll probably do the same."

"Are you okay now?"

"I have limitations, a hell of a scar, and have to see cardiologists every so often, but other than that . . ."

Yeah, other than that. "I won't treat you any differently."

"Yes, you will."

"No," I protested.

"I don't want to be another stray you take in and rehabilitate."

"You'd rather be euthanized?" I joked.

"You know what I mean."

I sobered. "Yes, I do. I'll do my absolute best not to treat you any differently than I have been. I promise I won't even think twice the next time I ask you to dig up a body."

He laughed. "I'm going to hold you to that, Lucy." He paused a beat. "I've been thinking. What I want to know is what we were doing in the same hospital bed and whose bed was it? Mine or yours?"

"I don't know. You took your hand away before I saw the whole picture. I have a feeling there are some things better off not known."

"Do these visions scare you?" he asked.

"The unknown scares me. I don't know why I see visions of our future. It doesn't fit with what I've known most of my life."

Flashbulbs split the air like lightning as we turned into Aerie's private drive.

Reporters crowded the car. Sean steered steadily, while I tried not to look at any one thing in particular.

I would have thought the media would have abandoned post by now. Surely something else in this world was more exciting than my life.

Shouting filtered through the window. Questions about Max, could I see if the Patriots would win the SuperBowl, if my father knew about my ability.

The crowd closed in on the car. Someone off to the side caught my attention. My heart jumped into my throat, beat crazily. I craned my neck, but the person had disappeared. A tall woman, her long brown hair pulled back into a ponytail that spilled out of a ball cap. She looked a lot like Melissa Antonelli. Had it been her . . . or her look-alike sister, Jennifer?

Either way, what was she doing here?

"What's wrong?" Sean asked.

I took a deep breath. "Nothing." Were my eyes playing tricks? It *had* been a long day. A long, enlightening day.

As Sean pulled up to my cottage, I said, "I'm amused by the irony."

"Of?"

"Us. Here I am, a commitment-phobic matchmaker who's—" I caught myself before saying "falling for." Nothing like tempting Cupid's Curse. Or the Fates.

"Who's what?"

"Who's with a man with a broken heart. Literally."

He dropped his head back and laughed. "Thank you, Lucy."

"For what?"

"For not tiptoeing around the heart talk. Nobody . . . no one talks about it. Ever."

"I don't know any better," I said, shrugging. "So if I offend at some point, just let me know."

My front door opened, the light from inside framing Dovie's graceful silhouette.

"She's probably put rose petals on the bed and has champagne chilling," I quipped, opening my door. "Baby booties have probably already been ordered."

"She's not knitting them herself?"

I laughed until tears flowed at the thought of Dovie knitting.

"What's so funny?" Dovie demanded as we walked up the flagstone path.

"You. Knitting."

Thoreau bounded out of the house, yapping and prancing around Sean's feet. Sean bent and scooped him up.

Dovie laughed. "That's a good one."

She air-kissed our cheeks. "I came by to walk the pup. Noticed you hadn't been home all day. I'd have made dinner, but didn't know when you'd get back. You're not answering your phone."

"The batteries are dead," I said, pulling my phone out to recharge. Grendel sauntered around the couch, his tail straight in the air. He bypassed me completely and went straight to Sean, who'd sat down, Thoreau in his lap.

This was a first. Usually Grendel attached himself to me immediately.

"Your cat's in love," Dovie said. "Doesn't take a matchmaker to see that."

"What?"

"Look."

Grendel inched his way along the back of the chair, down the arm, and sidled into the crook of Sean's arm, where he lovingly tapped Thoreau's ear, purring.

"Species *and* gender confused," Dovie said. She gave me a hug and headed for the door. "I'll let you two lovebirds be. There's champagne in the fridge. Enjoy!"

Sean said, "No rose petals?"

"Pardon?" Dovie asked.

He smirked. "Nothing."

Dovie pulled open the door. "Oh, LucyD, your parents called me. They couldn't reach you."

"They called! When?"

She waved a hand. "Earlier. They're on their way back. Should be in sometime tomorrow."

It was as though a weight had been lifted.

Dovie blew us a kiss. "Ciao!"

"I've got to get back to Sam's," Sean said. "He's due home later, and he'll be wondering why my stuff is at his house."

"Not to mention the mysterious stains on the dining room carpet."

"Those, too."

An awkward silence filled the space between us. He rose and tugged me to him.

My heart beat wildly as he looked me in the eye, lowered his head, and kissed me.

It felt so right, being with him. Why was I fighting against it? Why not give in and simply enjoy? Dance that dance? At least for a little while. What harm could that do?

We tumbled backward onto the couch, kissing, touching, exploring. I loved every minute of it.

When we broke for a breath, Sean said, "I should go."

I didn't want him to go. Yet . . . if he stayed, that might be the beginning of the end of us.

"Lucy? I should go?"

Reluctantly, I nodded.

He gave me one more earth-shattering kiss that promised more could be had if I'd just say yes. Tears clouded my eyes.

I rested my head on his shoulder. "What are we to each other? Does it even need a definition?"

"I don't know," he said, running his hand through my hair. "We're something."

"I have commitment issues," I said in a rush.

His eyes shone with humor. "Noted."

"I just felt the need to warn you."

"Consider me warned." The corner of his mouth lifted in a faint smile. "I guess that saves me my 'I can't make any promises' speech."

I should be happy about that. Oddly, I wasn't.

He dipped his head and caught my bottom lip between his teeth, released it. "How about we take it slowly?"

I lifted my chin, pressing my hungry lips to his. "Some things should be savored?" I said between pressing my lips to his.

"Exactly."

"I like the sound of it."

"Me, too, Lucy."

Our bodies molded to each other. I was all for slowing down. Some things shouldn't be rushed.

As my toes curled, I tried to let all my thoughts go, just enjoy the wonderful kiss, the way I felt as though with him I'd come home.

But in the back of my mind I couldn't let go of

the worry. About losing him. Now not only because of Cupid's Curse but also because of his heart.

I tried to block it out. Dance the dance, I reminded myself, wrapping my arms around his neck.

A loud purring broke us apart. Grendel was licking Thoreau's face.

"I think my cat is molesting your dog."

Sean laughed. "Thoreau doesn't seem to mind."

"It's not going to be pretty when you two leave."

"You're going to miss me that much?" Sean teased.

Truth was, yeah.

But I'd see him tomorrow at work. After I stopped in to see Aiden. And met with Marshall Betancourt. I didn't want to think about Elena or Michael or Rachel or Jennifer. I wanted to forget I was even involved in that case.

Except . . . Marilyn. I couldn't stop thinking about the trinket box. She couldn't ask for that box back . . . but I could.

As Sean went in search of Thoreau's leash, I rummaged through my bag for Elena's address and phone number. I borrowed Sean's phone since mine was charging and the house phone was still disconnected.

"You're calling Elena?" he asked, leash in hand.

I explained about the box.

His gaze softened.

"Don't look at me like that," I said, dialing.

"How's that?"

"Like I'm a big sap."

Elena answered on the third ring. Kids squealed with happiness in the background. I explained why I was calling.

"So you'd like me to give the box back to Marilyn?" she said.

"It would mean a lot to her." I watched Sean trying to get Thoreau away from Grendel.

There was a long pause on the phone. "It's the least I can do for Marilyn. It means much more to her than it does to me."

"That's great! She's going to be thrilled. Do you mind if I pick it up? I wouldn't trust it not to get broken in the mail."

"Not at all. Tomorrow morning?" she ventured.

Grendel hissed at Sean. I covered the phone and made kissy noises, but Grendel ignored me. "I can't in the morning."

"I work Monday evenings; how about lunchtime?"

"Sounds great. Thank you again," I said.

As soon as I hung up, I slipped the phone back into Sean's pocket, letting my hand linger.

"Keep doing that and I won't be going anywhere," he said.

"What are you suggesting?"

"You know exactly what I'm suggesting." In case I forgot, he whispered it in my ear, making my knees weak.

"That, Mr. Donahue, can't be good for your heart."

He slowly backed away, toward the door. "Maybe not, but it would be a good way to go."

TWENTY-FOUR

By the time I hit the road to meet with Elena, I was glad for the reprieve.

And reprieve it was. I'd been on the go most of the day.

My meeting with Aiden had only taken a few minutes. Marshall Betancourt had met me at work to go over my role in the Rachel Yurio case. He'd set up an appointment for me to meet with the Norfolk County State Police detectives and the Weymouth detectives later that day, to be interrogated and to give a statement. After that, I would hold a press conference at the police station.

After I had demonstrated my abilities, the Weymouth detectives were less inclined to believe I had anything to do with the murder, but wanted to put me through the paces nonetheless. Lucky me.

Suzannah had welcomed me this morning with a big hug and a reprimanding, "You could have told me!"

I'd puttered around the office, avoiding phone

calls from the local media outlets, and finally decided to head to Elena's. Sean would have come with me, but he was due in court to testify in a divorce trial.

"Jingle Bells" filled the air, reminding me that it was almost time to pull out my Christmas lights and decorations. I checked the screen. It was my mother. I'd never been so happy to see "Mum" pop up on my display.

"Lucy?" she said, the line crackling.

"Are you there?"

". . . connection."

"Hello!" I shouted. "Where are you?"

"Air—"

The line cut out. I immediately dialed her back, but it went straight to her voice mail.

When my phone rang a minute later I thought it was her, but much to my surprise it was Jennifer Thompson.

"I'd like to meet with you if possible," she said.

"When? Where?" Had it been her in front of my house yesterday? Obviously she was in town.

"Somewhere private," she answered.

A disturbing thought emerged. What if she thought I was the only one who could prove her guilt? Would she try to get rid of me? Was she the one who had killed Rachel?

Simply, I didn't know.

And because I didn't, she was on my suspect list. Adrenaline surged, prickling my skin. "Why privately?"

"I'd like it if no one knew I was in this area."

I read between the lines. "You mean Elena?"

"Yes. I'm sure you can understand."

I could, based on what Elena had done in the past, and I couldn't, based on the Elena I met yesterday. The mother, the social worker . . .

Before I agreed, I had to know if Jennifer had been at my house yesterday. I asked.

She seemed genuinely surprised. "Your house? No." She laughed. "Though I'd liked to have been. My sister conned me into babysitting the terrors. My nephews. And I have to do it again today. Missy has yet another mysterious appointment."

"Mysterious?"

"Ever since I got to town she's been in and out. It's not like her. Feels like she's up to something. Maybe a surprise welcome home party for me."

I turned onto Elena's street.

Jennifer and I obviously weren't thinking along the same lines. Because I suddenly realized that Jennifer's motive for getting rid of Rachel extended to Jennifer's family as well. Every member from her father down to her sister—all who would do anything to protect their "Jenny."

"Your sister seems great," I said, following the web my mind was spinning.

"She is."

"And your whole family—they've really been protective of you."

Her voice soft, she said, "They'd do anything for me."

Including murder? It was a thought I couldn't dismiss.

I pulled into Elena's driveway, cut the engine. I agreed to meet with Jennifer that night in town at a little Thai place in the South End. I wouldn't go alone and would stay just long enough to hear what she had to say—I owed as much to Michael.

After hanging up with her, I immediately dialed Sean, but his phone was off. I left a quick message about my suspicions.

51 times 3 is 153.

1089 divided by 11 is 99.

I knew I was in a high state of agitation when I started dividing. I hated division.

The one thing I couldn't quite figure out . . . If it had been Jennifer or her family behind Rachel's death, why was Elena still alive?

I pushed open the car door, squinted against the bright sunshine. Had it been because Elena moved away? Changed her life? Why give her, the main tormentor, a reprieve, but not Rachel?

It was a sticking point for sure. I wished Sean was here so I could talk it out.

I was headed up the walkway when I heard: "Back here!"

Elena stood at the side of the house, waving a trowel.

I followed a narrow path to the backyard. My feet protested mildly. The antibiotics had worked wonders, leaving me with only a few twinges and aches. It didn't help that I'd opted to wear heels with my trousers today. I should have chosen flat-heeled boots.

There was nothing to blame but vanity.

"Just doing a little gardening," she said, leading me around the back of the house to a small potting bench.

She wore tweed trousers, a deep purple blouse, a lovely floral silk scarf knotted around her throat, and gardening gloves. The bench was covered in gardening tools, plastic pots, and bits of soil.

She was tamping the edges of a planter brimming with mums. Slowly she pulled off the gloves. The trinket box sat on the corner of the bench. She picked it up and handed it over. "Is it true about you being psychic?"

"Good news travels fast," I said.

"I went online last night to read about Rachel. There was an article about you, too, and that little boy you found."

"It's true, but I can only find lost objects."

Her eyes widened. "Really?"

"Yes."

She glanced at my hands. "Is that how you knew I had the box?"

"Guilty."

"That's incredible."

"I'm still adjusting," I said. "Even though it's been fourteen years."

The backyard sloped upward toward the train tracks. Near the back door, a small fenced-in area held a swing set and a sandbox. Colorful plastic toys littered the ground.

Elena was watching me. "No matter how much I clean up . . ."

"Kids are like that."

"Oh, do you have any?"

For some reason an image of Sean and me in bed popped into my head. "No, but I worked for a day care once."

"And I thought I had it bad, trying to keep up with the messes!" She nodded to the mums. "I put this together for Marilyn and Ruth Ann. As I recall, mums are Ruth Ann's favorites."

Fluffy white clouds floated by overhead. Holding up the box, I said, "Thank you again for giving this back to Marilyn. I don't know if you've ever lost anything as sentimental as this, but I know she's going to be thrilled to get it back."

"I can imagine." She held out her hand. "It's been a pleasure meeting you, Ms. Valentine."

As my palm touched hers, images flew. I closed my eyes, fighting the dizziness. In a flash I saw a storage unit filled with boxes, with a beat-up sofa, a small dinette set with two chairs, a small jewelry box that held a gold locket, its clasp broken, with two photos in it.

Pictures of Rachel's parents.

Swaying, I opened my eyes, pulling my hand from hers. My heart pounded crazily.

"Are you all right?" she asked, setting the pot back on the bench.

There was only one way I could get a reading on that locket. If I touched the hand it belonged to . . .

Rachel.

I searched her face, looking for any trace of the young woman I'd seen in the grainy photo Sean had found.

As her gaze narrowed, I saw it in her eyes. The deep sadness.

"Rachel?" I said, not quite believing.

Her face paled. "H-how did you know?"

I clutched the trinket box so hard the jewels cut into my palms. "I saw your locket. I wouldn't have seen it unless it belonged to you."

She stifled a sob, leaned against the bench for support. "I didn't know I'd lost it during the fight. I never would have left it behind, but knew I couldn't go back for it."

"The fight with Elena?" I ventured. I forced myself to relax.

Tears fell from the corners of her eyes. "It continued at our apartment after the scene at work. She was mad I was talking to Michael. Mad I'd told him the truth about the pictures we'd taken. Then she showed me the engagement ring she'd stolen from his mail. Waved it in my face, saying she was going to be Mrs. Michael Lafferty. The ring was a family piece, an heirloom. I told her she couldn't keep it. I tried to get it off her hand."

Shadows spilled across the yard as a cloud covered part of the sun. Swallowing hard, I said, "What happened?"

"She . . . she hit me. And I don't know. Something snapped. I hit her over the head with a vase. She fell backward and smacked her head on the coffee table." Lifting her gaze, she added, "Elena didn't wake up."

With the sun blocked, a chill came over me. "Why not call the police?"

"I was scared," she said. "Terrified. I didn't think they'd believe me. I made a rash decision. I knew Great Esker well. Elena and I used to go there all the time to drink. And Elena always pointed out that there were lots of places to hide a body there, deep in the woods. She was right. But I didn't count on her being so heavy. I couldn't drag her very far, so I had to bury her close to the entrance. It was late fall, so there were lots of leaves. I hoped no one would see the fresh digging."

And they hadn't. No one had known about the grave until I came along.

I tried not to let my nerves get the better of me. This was Rachel—kindhearted Rachel, as Tess and Marilyn and Michael had pointed out. Elena was killed out of self-defense. Why then was I so ill at ease?

"I couldn't help but feel relief that she was gone," Rachel was saying. "Elena couldn't hurt anyone else. Yet . . ."

"What?" I prodded, wanting to know.

"All my life I knew how different we were. She was bad; I wasn't. Not really. What I told you yesterday was true. I did spend most of my time trying to get Elena to see the error of her ways."

"You were trying to convert her."

"I always felt that people could change. If they just tried hard enough."

It was a naïve outlook on the world, at best.

"But as I rolled Elena into the grave I dug, I suddenly realized that I wasn't who I thought I was, either. That in the blink of an eye, I'd become Elena. I didn't just hurt someone. I killed someone. You cannot imagine what that's like."

No, I couldn't.

"I made a snap decision to bury myself in that grave as well. I knew no one would really miss me. My grandmother was no longer lucid, and Marilyn . . . Well, I did feel badly about her. But I knew what I had to do."

"You took over Elena's identity to finally make her a decent person? The person you always thought she should be?" I wasn't by any means a psychologist, but that was a twisted way of thinking by anyone's standards.

"It was surprisingly easy. Elena had no family, so I had no one to answer to. All I had to do was dye my hair, move away, and start over. As Elena. I've accomplished everything I set out to do. And more. Along the way I found what I'd always wanted. A real family. I'm living the dream, Ms. Valentine."

"At Michael's expense, Rachel. You have to talk to the police."

Fingering a petal of the mum, she shook her head. "I can't do that. No one can know. It would ruin everything," she said, gesturing to the swing set, the toys.

In her eyes, I saw fear. And something else that had me suddenly very afraid.

"Well, that's understandable," I said brightly, backing up. I needed to go. Now. "But I hope you'll change your mind, and speak to the police. I should be going."

I spun around, but before I could even think to run, I was yanked backward, Rachel's silk scarf around my neck. Surprisingly strong, she easily cut off my airway. The trinket box crashed to the ground, smashing on the brick patio.

"You can't tell anyone!" she wailed.

Gasping for air, I jabbed an elbow into her rib cage. The scarf loosened enough for me to take a deep breath.

She bit out a cry as I stomped on her foot with the sharp heel of my shoe. I jabbed another elbow and reached behind me to get a fistful of hair. I yanked for all I was worth. The scarf fluttered to the ground as she screamed out.

I twisted sharply. Face-to-face with Rachel, I saw nothing in her face but pure raw terror. She would do anything to protect the life she was living. Even if it meant killing again.

I clawed, shoving her backward into the potting bench. The ceramic pot teetered, fell to the ground. It splintered on impact. Soil spilled out.

In the distance a crow cawed as Rachel grabbed a small pair of pruning shears from the bench.

My breaths came out in short puffs as I turned and ran.

I neared the corner of the house and suddenly lurched forward when my heel caught in the grass.

Rachel walked slowly forward, edging around me, the impossibly sharp shears at her side. She blocked the way to my car. To freedom.

Quickly I scrambled to my knees. "You're making this worse, Rachel. Elena died in self-defense. All you have to do is explain that to the police."

"As if it's that simple."

I shook so hard I could barely stand. Then I realized it wasn't just me shaking. It was the ground. The Providence commuter train was coming. I slowly stood, kicking off my heels.

She waved the shears at me. I lunged to my right. If I could just get to my car . . .

Jumping back and forth, she cut me off at every turn as if she were a fencer and the shears her foil. My arm burned where the shears pierced my jacket and sliced into my arm.

I backed away from her, looking for another way out.

She darted forward, and I spun away from her and took off running. I broke through the hedges at the back of the yard and scrambled up the hill toward the train tracks.

Rachel followed, panting as if she were hyper-ventilating. "I'm not going to let you ruin my life!"

She made guttural noises, a mix between a cry and a yell. I'd almost made it to the top of the incline when she stabbed my leg.

Crying out in pain, I heaved myself to the top of the incline, stood up, trying not to put weight on my left side. Blood seeped from the wound. Heat seared my calf.

Taking a deep breath, I hopped across the tracks, barely able to make it across. I fell down on the other side, too weak to stand.

Rachel finally made it up the hill, her trousers torn, blood covering her scratched hands. Blood-shot eyes wide with crazed fear sought me out.

The ground shook; the whistle on the train blew; brakes squealed.

The pain in my leg brought tears to my eyes. I tried to stand—I had to run. To get away. I dragged myself an inch, two. Stars shone behind my eyes.

Rachel's teary eyes narrowed on me. She took a step forward.

"You are not Elena!" I shouted. "You don't want to do this! You're better than this, Rachel!"

Sobs wracked her body. The train was 200 feet away, 150, 100.

Sparks flew from the rails; the whistle split the air. I covered my ears.

My thoughts swam, fog clouding my thoughts. My head swayed, the dizziness spinning my surroundings. Blood puddled under my leg. I struggled against giving in to the darkness creeping at the edges of my vision, against giving in to unconsciousness.

50 feet, 40, 30.

The world around me twirled and whirled. "Rachel!"

She bent double, a primal scream piercing the thundering noise, her gaze locked on mine.

20. 10.

"You're not Elena!" I shouted.

"No! I'm worse!" she cried as she dove forward.

The thick fog took over my thoughts, and I finally gave in to the blackness.

TWENTY-FIVE

I woke to arguing.

My father's voice, the one he saved for my most egregious errors, was being used on someone else.

I opened one eye, two.

A nurse backed away from the King of Love himself, saying, "This one time we'll make an exception. You have half an hour; then you all have to leave."

She hurried from the room.

All?

I looked around. Standing in a football-type huddle around my bed were my mother, my father, Dovie, Raphael, Marisol, and Em.

"Hello there," said a voice in my ear. A voice that set my heart thrumming happily.

I turned and smiled at Sean, who was leaning over my pillow. "Hi," I rasped.

My mother shoved him out of the way. Sunburn pinkened her already rosy nose, cheeks. "LucyD! My God what a scare you gave us!" She peppered my face with kisses, lovingly tucking my hair behind my ears, holding my head against her ample chest.

My father edged her out of the way. He kissed my forehead, then thumped his sternum. "Just about gave me another heart attack. Let's not let that happen again. Understand?"

I smiled. "Yes."

Raphael held my hand. Tears clouded his dark eyes. "Uva."

"I'm okay, Pasa," I whispered. "Really."

Oddly, I felt a little like Dorothy after she returned from Oz, though this hospital room was a far cry from no-place-like-home.

I lifted my arm, felt the ache in it and my leg. My whole body felt leaden, weighted to the bed. It took a lot of effort just to turn my head.

"War wounds," Em said. "You lost a lot of blood, and the doctors had to operate to fix the damage to your leg. With a little physical therapy, there won't be any permanent damage. In fact, you can probably head home tomorrow."

"Where am I?" I asked.

"Tufts Medical Center," Marisol answered. "Your father demanded you be airlifted here from Rhode Island Hospital."

"How long have I been asleep?"

"You've been drifting in and out of consciousness for about eight hours."

My heart clutched. "Rachel?" I asked.

"Rachel?" Sean said. Worried eyes took me in.

Obviously they all thought it had been Elena who died. I explained best I could, though my head was foggy. "What happened to her?"

Finally, Sean said, "The train . . . She jumped in front of it."

I closed my eyes. Raphael's hand squeezed mine, comforting me like he'd done all my life.

"I'm tired," I said, forcing my eyes open.

"That's probably our cue to go. We just wanted to be here when you woke up," Em said. She and Marisol gave me long hugs and kisses. "We'll be back tomorrow morning, first thing."

Dovie gave me a kiss, too. "I'll take care of the critters while you're here."

"Thanks, Dovie. I love you, you know."

"Enough of that sentimental crap," she said, her eyes welling. "I'll see you tomorrow. Get some rest."

"I'll take her home," Raphael said as he looked down at me, his eyes still moist. He leaned down and hugged me, whispering, "I don't know what I'd do without you."

"You won't have to find out."

He kissed my forehead.

Before he left, there was something I really wanted to know. "So, you and Maggie?"

At first he looked shocked that I knew, but he recovered well. "We're . . . friends, Uva."

"Mmm-hmm."

He laughed, shaking his head. "You're going to be just fine."

Sean and my mother were talking in low tones near the door. My father perched on the side of my bed. He caressed my arm. "I'll expect you'll be back at work soon enough."

"Work?"

"Of course. You have clients. And I've been thinking."

"But I can't—"

"Don't argue, Lucy Juliet. You cannot see auras,

but you most certainly can make matches." He reached over and grabbed a card from a nearby bouquet. The table next to my bed was filled with flowers. Thankfully they were roses, not mums. "Lola Fellows and Adam Atkinson wish you well and thank you for getting them together. That was all you."

"Not really. I just matched your swatches."

"I've dreaded finding a match for Lola. No one was bound to be good enough. I've dealt with types like her before, rather unsuccessfully. Like I said, that one was yours, one hundred percent. I don't know what you said to her that changed her ways, but you most certainly earned that match."

Suddenly I puffed with pride. "I will take credit for Raphael and Maggie."

"Oh no!" my father corrected. "That one is all mine."

"How can you say that? They got together this week. Thanks to me, kind of."

He laughed. "I suppose you may have played a role, but why do you think I leased the space to Maggie in the first place for a fraction of its worth? It was just a matter of time before she and Raphael realized what was meant to be."

My mouth dropped open. Huhn.

"Truth is, Lucy, it's obvious we make a good team. Have you enjoyed matchmaking?" he asked.

"More than I thought I would."

"Good. I've been thinking about your idea, letting it simmer."

"My idea?"

"This notion you have about reuniting lost loves. Sean told me all about it."

I shook my head. "That was specifically for Michael Lafferty and Jennifer Thompson. And that hasn't quite worked out the way I planned."

"Give it time. The idea is valid. You could re-unite first loves, lost loves, all kinds of loves."

I could? Then I realized . . . I could. "But . . . the auras. They might not match."

"Doesn't matter. We'll work with what we're given. I've seen through my long career that a first love is quite powerful and can often work, despite not having similar auras. When neces-sary we can use your ability to find objects to help in the reunions. It will be your own branch of the company, Lost Loves," he pro-claimed.

Lost Loves. I liked the sound of it.

And loved the idea of being able to work with my father. Suddenly I didn't feel like the black sheep of my matchmaking family.

"There are some kinks to work out," he said, "and you'll need help, of course. There is much investigative work with such a task." He looked over at Sean, still talking with my mother. "I suspect young Mr. Donahue will be a willing partner. If that is agreeable to you."

I looked into my father's deep brown eyes. "What color is he?" I asked, curious.

"A rare one. Charcoal gray with the vaguest hint of a steely blue undertone. I've never seen its exact shade before."

"Do you think that's my color?"

"I don't know, my love."

I chewed on my lip. "He doesn't know about you."

"You may as well tell him if he is to work with us. That is, if you trust him."

I looked over at Sean. He must have sensed me staring. He smiled with his eyes, without ever moving his lips. "I do," I said. "Trust him."

"Then we will all have a meeting at the end of the week. We will capitalize on this publicity surrounding you at the moment and launch the newest division of Valentine, Inc."

"New division?" my mother said, coming up behind my father.

"I'll discuss it with you later, Judie. Now I think we should leave and let Lucy get her rest."

"Leave! I can't leave her alone like this."

My father looked into her eyes. "I do not believe she will be alone."

My mother glanced between Sean and me, her cheeks coloring an even deeper shade of red beneath her sunburn. She gave me a big hug. "We'll talk tomorrow, LucyD. I love you."

"I love you, too."

"Come," my father insisted.

"So bossy," my mother said, tossing the edge of her shawl over her shoulder. She blew me a kiss before disappearing through the door. "It's a wonder I stay with you, Oscar." She laughed. "Oh, that's right. I don't!"

Sean stood next to the bed, running his fingers along the inside of my forearm. "What did your mother mean?"

"It's a long story. One you need to hear. Just not right now."

"Fair enough."

The nurse came in, smiling when she saw me awake. She checked my vitals, chatting about my family before leaving again.

Sean sat at the edge of my bed. He took a deep breath.

"Thanks for coming here. I know how you feel about hospitals."

"There's no other place I'd rather be. I just wish I'd gone with you this afternoon."

"Me, too. There was no way of knowing I was in danger." Softly I laughed. "I actually thought Elena, I mean Rachel," I shook my head—it was all so confusing—"was the one in danger."

"I spoke to Melissa about an hour ago. I wanted to follow up on your suspicions."

"And?"

"The big mystery is that she's pregnant again. She's been going to the doctor. She didn't want to announce it until she was sure."

"So it wasn't her or Jennifer at my house yesterday."

Sean smiled. "Melissa was there."

"What?"

"She was trying to work up the nerve to ask you if you could tell if her baby was a boy or a girl. She desperately wants a girl."

"I can't—"

"I know. And apparently someone in the crowd told her the same thing. So she went home."

I shook my head. What a crazy week it had been.

The nurse came back, checked my vitals once again. Before she left, she looked at Sean. "Will you be staying?"

"Yes."

"Would you like a cot?"

"That won't be necessary," I said. I inched over, patted the bed beside me.

The nurse smiled, pulled the curtain, and closed the door on her way out.

Sean kicked off his shoes, climbed onto the mattress. He slipped his arm around me, folding me into his chest. I heard his heart beating, and I smiled.

"As scared as I was, I knew I'd be all right," I said, yawning. My eyelids grew heavy.

"How?"

"Because of this. You and me, here in this bed. I saw it. I knew it had to happen. Maybe you're the one," I said, my words slurring. My eyes drifted closed.

"The one what?"

"The one to break Cupid's Curse, of course." I giggled. "Curse, course, that's funny."

"Curse?"

"The stupid curse," I said, drifting off. "Charcoal gray, steely blue, me and you, one plus one is two. . . ."

His chest rumbled with laughter, and I felt safer than I ever had in my whole life.

As I fell asleep, I refused to think about Cupid's Curse and its consequences. Just fill up my dance card, because I was dancing the dance, twirling and spinning to my heart's content. And for once, I wouldn't mind the dizziness.

Three days later I was at home, wrapped in a blanket, lying on the couch, Grendel and all his kitty weight stretched across my lap. Might be time to put him on a diet.

I'd had a lot of time to think about everything that had happened in the past week. And had talked it out with several law enforcement agencies. If I never saw a badge again, I'd be happy.

The police were still sorting out who was who, what was what. Their efforts to match dental records were futile, as both Rachel's and Elena's had mysteriously vanished from their dentist's storage. As of right now, the police were awaiting DNA compatibility results on Rachel and Ruth Ann.

My gaze wandered to the stacks of letters on my coffee table. Piles and piles of requests asking for my help in finding all things lost, from loved ones (which broke my heart) to sunken treasure.

"She's late," Michael Lafferty said, pacing in front of my fireplace. "Are you sure she's coming?"

Watching him made me dizzy. "No guarantees, remember?"

I'd received a surprise visitor in my hospital room. Jennifer Thompson. Once she learned Elena was dead, she felt it safe to come out of her self-imposed hiding. And much to my delight, she'd agreed to meet with Michael.

"I know," he said, wiping his hands down his jeans. He'd forgiven me immediately for involving him in a police investigation once he learned Jennifer was willing to meet with him. "Just a conversation. Right." He stopped pacing, looked at me. "I've missed her."

I stroked Grendel's fur. "I know."

A knock sounded. Michael looked at me, at the door.

"Go ahead," I said.

Slowly, he pulled it open. Jennifer Thompson stood on my porch, her dark hair swept into a ponytail, her eyes wide and curious.

Silently I watched as they stared at each other for a good long time. Finally, Jennifer rushed forward into Michael's arms.

I swiped at the tears in my eyes. Maybe I *was* a sap.

An hour later, the pair had decided to go into Cohasset Village for a cup of coffee. By all appearances, it looked as though they might be able to pick up the pieces. Maybe the Lost Loves division of Valentine, Inc., would have its first success story.

My phone rang. I'd recently gotten a new number and very few people had it. I checked the caller ID display and answered unhappily.

"I'm sorry to bother you again, Ms. Valentine."

"Detective Chapman, I've already answered all your questions. Hasn't this case been closed?"

He hesitated.

"Detective?"

"Actually, I'm calling about something else. . . ."

"What?"

"My ring. It went missing one day in my gym's locker room. My wife still hasn't forgiven me. Do you know the name of the pawnshop it's at?"

Well, well, well.

Good thing for him I was in a forgiving mood. I told him the name of the shop I'd seen.

"Thanks, and uh, well, thanks."

Shaking my head, I hung up, thinking back to the crazy week I'd had. It certainly had been life-altering.

My father had been by yesterday with a business plan for the new division of Valentine, Inc., and it was nice to see him happy.

He wasn't perfect, not by a long shot. But life wasn't perfect, either.

I'd learned that the hard way.

The phone rang again. I was beginning to question my judgment on having it reconnected.

"Hello?" I said.

"Funny thing just happened," Marisol said.

"What's that?"

"Our director just announced that an anonymous fifty-thousand-dollar donation had come in. The animal hospital is going to stay open."

"Imagine that."

I peeked in on Odysseus, who was asleep under his water bottle, fluff stuck to his flyaway fur. Grendel paid him no attention. He rarely paid me any attention anymore, especially when Thoreau was around, which, happily, was often.

"Yeah, imagine that," Marisol said, her voice thick. "Tell me again what you did with your reward money?"

There was a knock on the door. "I've got to go, Marisol, someone's knocking."

There was a sniffle, followed by a long pause. "Thank you, Lucy."

"You're welcome."

Smiling, I dislodged a put-out Grendel and reached for my crutches. Taking a deep breath, I looked at the file sitting on the table, that of Jamie Gallagher. She'd been missing almost eight months. Her mother was coming over, and I was going to try to get a reading on earrings that had been given to Jamie for her birthday.

Yesterday I had met with Aiden, who was now officially my contact for the Massachusetts State Police. I had agreed to work on missing person cases, new and cold.

Finally. Finally my gift could be used to really help people. It did my heart good and made me feel for once that my life had purpose, meaning. I was done with floundering through different careers.

Slowly, I made my way to the door and pulled it open.

To my surprise, Preston Bailey stood on my doorstep, looking eager to see me. She wore a long belted trench coat, jeans, and leather boots. Her hands were empty—no offerings for forgiveness.

My first inclination was to slam the door.

So was my second.

I slammed it.

Preston stuck her booted foot in between the door and the jamb. I was pleased by her yelp of pain.

"Lucy, please!"

Reluctantly, I opened the door. "I have nothing to say to you."

Serious eyes peered at me under fringed bangs. "I know you're mad."

"Mad? You don't know mad!"

"All right. Pissed. I understand. I do." Crazy blonde hair stuck out every which way.

"No, you don't."

"Well, okay. But that's why I'm here."

"What are you talking about?"

"Your father contacted me about the new division of Valentine, Inc."

"He did?" The backstabbing traitor.

"It's a great idea. And I'd like to be your first client."

"What?"

"We'll document it. Prove to every naysayer that you really are psychic. I'll write an article that documents our journey and sets everything right. One written with your full consent and approval. What do you say?"

"I don't know."

"What can it hurt? And won't it be nice to stop all the speculation? Plus, it will drum up clients for you, which must appeal to your business sense."

A car appeared at the top of the drive, pausing in front of Dovie's house.

I wanted to get rid of Preston Bailey before Jamie's mom arrived. So, I did the last thing I ever expected.

I agreed.

But as Preston walked triumphantly toward her car, I couldn't help but feel I'd just made a deal with the devil.

Read on for an excerpt from
Heather Webber's next book

Deeply, Desperately

A Lucy Valentine Novel

Coming soon from St. Martin's Paperbacks

My brand new GPS unit glowed in the darkness of the car as I carefully navigated the narrow side roads leading to Aerie, Dovie's cliffside estate in Cohasset, south of the city. I foresaw a lot of traveling with Lost Loves. Or so I hoped once I acquired a few more clients.

Bare branches hovered over two copper mailboxes standing side by side along a small half-moon dirt turnoff just before Aerie's drive. I checked my rearview mirror to make sure I hadn't been followed (all clear), pulled up to the second box, reached in, and scooped out a stack of mail.

Setting the stack on the passenger seat, I cut the wheel sharply, turning between two stacked stone columns. To my right, a wooden sign that read "Aerie" in elegant script was lit from a hidden up-light. Graceful garden lanterns lined the sides of the drive, guiding me up the sloped, twisting gravel driveway. Around a bend, Dovie's house suddenly appeared as if by magic, a sprawling, classic, century-old, New England estate, complete with weathered shingles, gorgeous slate roof, juts, jogs, angles, and utter elegance. It was decked out in sedate white Christmas lights, twinkling happily.

Forgoing her three-car garage, I veered to the right, off the main drive. A crushed-shell lane led down to home sweet home. Dovie generously let me stay in the estate's cottage-style guest house.

The one-bedroom cottage, shingle-style in design, was almost all windows, mostly arched. A narrow wraparound front porch with wooden archways curved around the foundation. Throw in the antique front door, stone steps, and attic dormer, and charm oozed from its rafters.

Colorful Christmas lights dripped from the edges of the eaves, wrapped the columns on the front porch, and adorned the dormers, doorframe, and windows.

A brisk breeze blew off the ocean, climbing the bluffs and sweeping across the yard. A fieldstone path led to the porch, flanked on each side by a short boxwood hedge. In the warmer months, flowering annuals would color the way to my door. I turned up my collar, slipped in the key in the lock, and turned the deadbolt.

The circles on the alarm keypad blinked a bright red, blending well with the whole Christmas theme. I turned off the alarm. My cautious gaze swept the open layout, bouncing like a racquetball from the small Christmas tree near the fireplace, into the kitchen, over the breakfast bar, into the dining room, and beyond into my bedroom. Other than the fact that I'd forgotten to make my bed that morning, everything seemed just right.

No intruders. No stalkers. No fanatic looking to snuff out the "Devil's Handmaiden."

I set the stack of mail on the table next to the door, reluctant to go through it. The first letter addressed to the "Devil's Handmaiden" had arrived two weeks ago. It had spewed about my sins, harping on the First Commandment, and how being psychic was akin to being evil. A new letter arrived every couple of days, each one more intense than the last. And more threatening. I stopped opening them after the fifth—I simply passed the envelopes on to Aiden.

I dumped the rest of my things on the floor next to the door, slipped off my boots. Grendel, a Maine Coon cat, sauntered out of my bedroom on his three legs, meowing pathetically, pawing the hem of my trousers. He hated being left alone. And he hardly counted Odysseus, my one-eyed hamster, as company. Both had come to me via Marisol and the animal hospital where she worked. The consequences of having a best friend who was a veterinarian.

I drew in a deep breath, inhaling the scent of the Charlie Brown tree in the corner. The live Balsam fir was the runt of the litter on the lot this year with its four-and-a-half-foot height, sparse branches, tilting stance. After Christmas, the sad little tree would have a chance to grow into a strong mature fir, mixed in with those from Christmases past on Dovie's acreage.

It was a lovely little tree. Really. Just . . . a bit . . . crooked.

From the fridge, I pulled a slice of white American. As soon as Grendel heard the crinkling of the cellophane wrapper, he hopped down, circled excitedly. I broke the cheese into quarters, dropping one on the floor for him. He pounced, dragging it around the corner into the dining area to feast in privacy under the rickety plastic table. I'd yet to save enough to buy my dream table, so the folding card table had to suffice for now. Thankfully, a tablecloth hid its many flaws.

I tossed another quarter of cheese over the breakfast bar into the dining room. Grendel attacked with a loud thump.

Trying my best, I fought to rid my thoughts of my father's voice and the anxiety I'd heard in his tone. What was going on with him lately? I needed to talk to him, look him in the eye to get some answers. Tomorrow at the office, I'd sit down with him, have a heart to heart, and get to the bottom of his bad mood.

For now, I didn't want to think about it anymore. I picked up the phone, dialed Sean.

Cupid's Curse was one of the reasons I wanted to take things slowly with sexy Sean Donahue, the former firefighter turned private investigator I worked with. Tall, dark hair, milky gray eyes, superhero chin, hockey player's nose. Lips to die for, kisses that melted, and a heart in need of healing. Literally.

A defibrillator had been implanted last year after he almost died from undiagnosed cardiomyopathy. He quit the fire department and took his brother Sam's offer to join his PI firm. Sean was working under the umbrella of his brother's license until he accrued enough experience to get his own.

These days we worked almost solely together, investigating not only Lost Love cases but the missing person cases for the state police as well.

Our chemistry was pure magic, but I knew

the outcome of any potential serious relationship we'd have. Doom. Crushing dark doom.

And that would simply break my heart. Further, I should say. Because I'd already fallen for
him. And not having him in a serious committed
relationship with me was almost as painful as
not having him at all. Dating him casually was a
wonderful torture, one I loved *and* hated.

Sometimes being a Valentine just plain sucked.

After four rings a woman picked up. Stunned, I
leaned against the counter. "May I speak to Sean,
please?"

"You have the wrong number," she said sharply
and hung up on me.

I hit the redial button, watched the numbers
fill in on the caller ID screen.

It had *not* been the wrong number.

My call went immediately to voice mail. I left
a quick message for Sean to call me back.

Absently, I nibbled one of Grendel's remain-
ing cheese squares, trying not to get worked up
and jealous.

So what, a woman answered Sean's cell phone,
claiming it wasn't his.

Big deal.

No problem.

We weren't in a committed relationship.

I looked down. Grendel's last corner of cheese
had been squished into the tiniest cheese ball
known to man.

I dropped it in the garbage disposal and poured
a cup of veterinarian-approved kitty kibble into
his bowl as he looked on.

His tail shot into the air as he prowled around
my feet, staring at me accusingly. I'd veered from

our norm. He was missing two cheese squares and wasn't happy about it.

And I had to admit I wasn't happy about a woman answering Sean's damn phone.

"You're supposed to be on a diet anyway," I said to him. "Take it up with Marisol."

He gave me a look that promised revenge.

I ignored it (probably a mistake) and grabbed a grape from the bunch on the granite countertop. I dropped it in Odysseus's cage on the bureau in my bedroom. He was nowhere to be seen, but I heard scratching from beneath his shavings. I made kissy noises, but he didn't surface. I gave up.

Who was she?

Stop thinking about it!

81 − 11 is 70.

5 + 3 is 8.

In the living room I turned on the gas-burning fireplace, gathered up the mail, and sank into the coziest chair ever made. It was a deep club chair that rocked *and* swiveled. Using the hearth as my footstool, I put my feet up. Crackling orange flames danced, warming my toes.

The stack of mail was larger than usual, with an assortment of Christmas cards mixed into the usual delivery. I put the cards aside, leaving me with a pile of mail from strangers, most wanting my help, some wanting me to know what happens to sinners.

Inevitably, I separated my fan mail (as I'd come to call it for lack of a better term) into four piles: Crackpot, Consider, Can't Help You, and Copy. I was continuously torn between wanting to help everyone and wanting to protect my sanity. Some of the letters were simply heartbreaking. If I worked every case, I'd need anti-depressants. The flip side of that was the guilt. What if I could help these families find their loved one, find closure?

It was wrenching.

Grendel pouted near his food dish as I opened the first letter. It went into the "Can't Help" pile, as it was a request for me to connect a woman with her dead husband. Sorry. I didn't do séances.

There were three missing children requests in a row. Desperate parents who had heard about the little boy I'd found. Unfortunately most cases of missing children didn't turn out with happy endings, but I knew after working with the Massachusetts State Police that most people, though hopeful to have their loved ones returned home, were searching for closure. The first case I worked on with the MSP was to help locate teenager Jamie Gallagher. She'd been missing for months. When I was able to find her remains, her mother told me that it was the first time she'd slept the whole night through.

I set the letters in the Consider pile.

The next letter had familiar handwriting. My heart froze in fear. Carefully, I put the envelope in a plastic baggie. Tomorrow, I'd give it to Aiden.

The handle on my front door rattled, and I nearly jumped clear out of my skin.

"It's me, LucyD!" Dovie called out.

I dumped the rest of the mail onto the coffee table and opened the door for my grandmother.

"I can't get used to you locking that thing," she said, rushing past me waving a binder, a whirl of energy.

I dropped back into my chair.

Seeing Dovie this late at night wasn't the least bit surprising. She tended to spend more time here than at her own home. I put up with her intrusions into my life because I loved my cottage, its view of the ocean, and her—most of the time. More now that she'd let up on trying to match-make me. She was convinced Sean and I would be walking down the aisle any minute now. A notion we played into for my sake. It was nice not coming home to strange men invited to dinner by Dovie in hopes I'd fall madly in love and promptly produce a dozen babies.

I eyed the Handmaiden letter. The envelope itself looked innocuous enough. It was the message inside that had me locking my doors and windows for the first time in my life. No one other than Aiden knew of the threats I'd been receiving. There was no need to worry anyone else. The only thing that would come out of that was a stifling over-protectiveness. No. It was better they didn't know. And that included Sean. He'd probably want to move in.

And while that didn't sound like a horrible idea to me, I wanted him to move in for the right reasons, not to be my private bodyguard.

Hmm. I let that idea sit for a minute before I shook myself out of the fantasy. Dovie sat on the sofa, her long legs stretched out. She wore a silk pajama-and-robe set complete with a fancy marabou-feathered heel. She'd been a burlesque dancer when she met my grandfather and still had a dancer's physique over sixty years later. Her eyes glowed.

I eyed the binder. "What brings you down here?"

Her long white hair had been pulled into a beautiful knot at the base of her neck. "Party stuff. Guest list, food. Thought I'd have you take a look, a second pair of eyes. RSVPs are rolling in."

Dovie's famous Five Days before Christmas Bash was next Sunday night.

With my toe I nudged the Handmaiden letter under the stack of mail. "Tea?" I asked, heading for the kitchen.

"Lovely!"

Grendel leapt onto the couch, blatantly bathing Dovie with his affection, trying to make me jealous. Too late—that particular sentiment had already been claimed for the night.

Who was she?

Stop!

I glanced at my grandmother over the curved granite breakfast bar separating the kitchen from the open living and dining rooms. "Preston mentioned she was invited to the party." Maybe Dovie could shed some light as to *why*.

"Your father insisted," she said, pointing to her guest list as if to confirm Preston was indeed was on the list.

I came around the counter. "Did he say why?"

"No."

A few weeks ago, I had reunited Preston with a long-lost boyfriend . . . only to find out it had been an act, a publicity stunt for a newspaper article she was writing on me. There had been no love lost between the two. It had been a waste of my time, but the article had been so popular that Preston had talked my father into more articles, a full series. A year-in-the-life kind of thing. Which was all well and good—phone calls from potential clients were coming faster than we could keep up—but it also meant Preston was around. A lot.

Dovie never partied lightly. My gaze slid over the list of over two hundred names, skidding to a stop on Sean's.

Who was she? A date? Would he bring her to the party?

She rose. "Keep the list overnight for a looksee. I should be going; it's getting late and maybe you have company coming?"

"Sean and I don't have that kind of relationship." Much to my dismay.

"I know. And it's getting old. I'm getting old. Too old to enjoy my great-grandbabies should you *ever* have any."

"You're forgetting the Curse . . ."

"I've been thinking."

"Dangerous."

She shook her finger at me. "Sass! I'm wondering if you're crying Curse every time you get close to someone out of fear."

"Of course I am. I've seen what happens to the relationships in this family!"

"But LucyD, you've never been a victim of the curse. Perhaps you wouldn't even be afflicted. Maybe that lightning strike zapped it out of you? Have you ever thought of that? Hmm? Hmm?"

I hadn't.

"I didn't think so," she went on. "It's time you gave commitment a chance. Maybe there's hope for you yet."

The possibility excited and frightened me at the same time. It was something to think about.